INTO
XINJIANG

INTO
XINJIANG

BEN COLBRIDGE

Matador
Unit E2 Airfield Business Park,
Harrison Road, Market Harborough,
Leicestershire. LE16 7UL
Tel: 0116 2792299
Email: books@troubador.co.uk
Web: www.troubador.co.uk/matador
Twitter: @matadorbooks

ISBN 978 1803136 554

British Library Cataloguing in Publication Data.
A catalogue record for this book is available from the British Library.

Printed and bound in Great Britain by 4edge Limited
Typeset in 11pt Adobe Garamond Pro by Troubador Publishing Ltd, Leicester, UK

Matador is an imprint of Troubador Publishing Ltd

For Aliya & Seiya

Map of China and surrounding countries

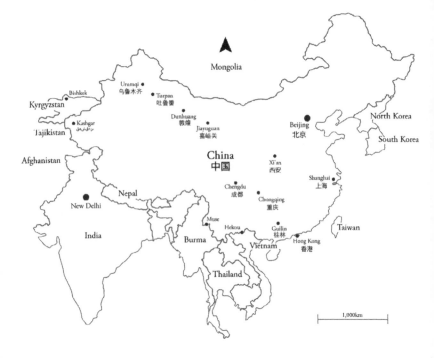

INTRODUCTION

With a population of 1.4 billion people, China is the world's most populous country. It covers an area of over 9.6 million square kilometres and borders fourteen countries, from Mongolia in the north to Tajikistan in the west and Vietnam in the south.

China is a beautiful country steeped in history, culture and natural beauty. For the traveller, it offers adventure and intrigue and can be altogether captivating for those who get under its skin.

But, for all its beauty, the country is tightly controlled by the Chinese Communist Party – an authoritarian leadership that restricts access to information, the freedom of assembly, the freedom to have children and freedom of religion. Internal security is enforced by the People's Armed Police – a paramilitary organisation reporting into the Central Military Commission. With an estimated 1.5 million members, the People's Armed Police can be seen implementing the rule of law on the streets of China, identifiable in their olive-green fatigues.

1

THE PHOTO

April 2003

From the moment Daniel Weaver stepped off the overnight plane from London, alone, into the thick grey air of Beijing, China felt edgy. Thousands upon thousands of dishevelled travellers swarmed across the brilliant white floors of the arrivals lounge, their clothes a drab palette of navy-blues and browns. Members of the People's Armed Police stood watch, their dark olive-green uniforms impeccably pressed, guns primed and ready should they be required. A cacophony of noise and loudspeaker announcements conspired to deliver a dizzying experience.

But Dan, as he was known to the friends he'd left behind at university, was glad to finally be here after the events of the last few weeks. It was his turn now. Time to strike out alone, see the world, feel it all for himself. Dazed from the lack of sleep but excited by what lay ahead, he walked quickly through the airport hallways, overtaking many of his fellow passengers as he went.

At that very moment, on the other side of the city in a small apartment close to the fourth ring road, an eighteen-year-old woman was getting ready to go out. Today she would go by the name of Margaret, but tomorrow, she decided, working her way through the alphabet again, she would call herself Nancy. She tore the page from her notebook containing the instructions she had just written down. To be on the safe side, she also tore out the two pages from under it, as she always did in these situations. Folding the pieces of paper and putting them safely inside the zipped pocket of her red jacket, she left her apartment. Avoiding the CCTV in the lift, the young woman took the seven flights of stairs to the ground floor and headed towards the metro that would carry her into the centre of Beijing. Thirty minutes later she emerged among the hustle and bustle of Tiananmen Square and without a moment of hesitation was on her way to the Forbidden City.

At the airport, Dan was in the queue for passport control. He didn't know it then, as he waited in line, that he was about to enter the most terrifying two weeks of his life. He had no idea that in just twenty-four hours' time he would be the most wanted man in China or just how far from Beijing he would have to run. He had no idea of the fear and turmoil that were waiting for him, nor the frantic game of wits that was about to play out as he fought to survive. He had no idea of the people he was about to encounter: those who were to help him in his flight and those who would seek to stop him. And he had no idea that Nancy was to become the first of those.

But, then, neither did she.

Once through immigration, Dan was free at last. When his long-term girlfriend had been caught in bed with one of her lecturers a little over a month ago, Dan's world had shattered and he dropped out of university just weeks away from graduation. Using the last few hundred pounds of his student loan, he'd bought a ticket to Beijing, keen to forget everything and eager for a new start. He stood there now, face crumpled with the imprints of the overnight flight and his nose blocked from the long-haul airlessness of economy class. Yet his spine tingled with anticipation for the adventure that lay ahead: the places he would go, the things he would see, the people he would meet.

Collecting his backpack from carousel number six, Dan made his way through the crowds of people towards the exit, optimistically scanning the name cards being held aloft by the waiting drivers and chauffeurs as he went. That was obviously pointless because at that very moment nobody in China had ever heard of this young backpacker from England. That would all soon change, of course.

At just over six feet tall and with shoulder-length brown hair tied in a ponytail, Dan stood out among the crowds. He couldn't help but notice the curious stares of young children looking up at him as he picked his way through the throngs of people filling the arrivals area.

Outside, the air was damp with a distinct metallic taste. The sun was a faintly glowing disc in a sky largely obscured by a thick, cloudy haze. Dan found the bus that would take him to towards the city centre, bought a ticket from the driver and climbed on board. Weary from his journey, he collapsed into two empty seats on the left-hand side about halfway down the quietly idling vehicle. With his head pressed against the gently vibrating window, he allowed his mind to wander.

He was here to explore China – a country he'd always wanted to visit, fascinated by its thousands of years of history, by its culture and by its architecture. He'd heard that in places China was impossibly beautiful – small villages of colourful minority communities clinging to verdant valley sides, rugged snow-capped mountains towering over rushing rivers and rice terraces snaking their way through steep-sided gorges. From Beijing, his plan was to head to Xi'an to see the Terracotta Warriors, Guilin to set eyes upon the famous karst landscape of the Li River and then to make his way over to Yunnan province in search of traditional, minority cultures and the mountains of the eastern Himalayas before ending with a few days in bustling Hong Kong. His ticket home was booked from there in eighteen days' time, but the promise of adventure lay between now and then. The hair on the back of his neck tingled with excitement as he thought about the places he was about to travel to. He couldn't wait.

The bus picked its way through the traffic on the busy outskirts of the city. Industrial parks and the dried-out grasses of the interstitial wastelands began to yield to endless urban sprawl. Vast developments of carbon-copy apartment blocks, each home to thousands of people, stretched as far as one could see into the smog. Factory chimneys belched clouds of smoke and steam into the thick atmosphere and horns blared all around as frustrated drivers vented their annoyances. A motorbike carrying three people picked its way between two lanes of traffic, steadily weaving through the gauntlet of protruding wing mirrors. Beside Dan's bus a battered old truck piled precariously high with scrap metal lurched slowly forward spewing clouds of black diesel fumes on to the windows of the cars beside it. Another motorbike picked its way through the traffic, its rider inhaling the exhaust of a thousand idling cars as he went.

The twenty-five-kilometre journey took just under an hour. As the bus approached the city centre, the chaotic suburbs gave way to attractive streets lined with trees that were just coming into leaf. Those that weren't, were dead. In the distance the skyline was filled with bright, modern buildings – office blocks, apartments, hotels and restaurants – but here in the suburbs old buildings of grey brick construction lined either side of the road. The cars tussled with an increasing number of bicycles, while overhead a puzzle of telegraph wires and electricity cables obscured the view of the hazy blue spring sky. Dan struggled to take it all in as the bus made its way towards downtown Beijing.

The small hotel he had chosen was in the city's traditional *hutong*s – a labyrinth of single-storey buildings connected by a warren of narrow alleyways. This was the traditional heart of Beijing – once a thriving, pulsating muscle of life. Now these streets clung on to life itself – a relic of a time so backwards in the eyes of Beijing's eager town planners as to be almost embarrassing. This was prime real estate in the centre of one of the world's fastest growing cities. Imagine the tower blocks one could construct.

Confident he was in approximately the right area, Dan got off the bus to find himself standing outside a school. It was mid-afternoon and before long a stream of students in smart grey uniforms began to file out past him. As the line of students dwindled, a young man of around seventeen, with a pockmarked face, thin-framed glasses, shaggy black hair and a light blue raincoat stopped in front of him.

"Are you lost?" he asked in almost perfect English.

Truthfully, Dan *was* lost and quickly became self-conscious that it was so obvious.

"Yes," he replied cautiously. "I'm trying to find this place." Dan pointed to a small advert in one corner of his tourist map of the city.

"It's near. I take you," said the student, who began to introduce himself as they walked.

"My name is Zhang, but please call me Michael. I study engineering at college. Where are you from?"

"I'm from England," Dan replied.

"Wow, fantastic! One day, I want to go to Europe and maybe live in Berlin or London," responded Michael. "I like your hair!" he continued. "In China, men don't have long hair!"

A few moments later they left the main road and entered the *hutong* of Banchang Lane – a narrow street with high grey walls broken up by ornate gateways behind which stood the courtyards of private homes. Thin, underfed dogs, dusty from a life on the street, sat nonchalantly watching *hutong* life go on around them.

Around a hundred metres from the main road the two young men came to the broad red door of the hotel above which two small round red lanterns swung gently in the afternoon breeze.

"OK, here you are. Have a nice stay in Beijing. See you."

With that, the young man left Dan gazing up at the ornate doorway and by the time he turned back to thank him the student was already some distance away.

"Thank you!" Dan called after him. He glanced over his shoulder, smiled, waved, then disappeared down another alleyway to the right. Dan pushed open the door to the small Lu Yuan hotel. Inside, a young woman in her early twenties with long straight black hair and a red full-length silk dress smiled and greeted him from behind the reception desk as he gently closed the door.

"Hello," she said. "Please come in. Do you have reservation?"

Dan walked up to the desk, relieved to find himself in the right place. He heaved his backpack off his tired shoulders and laid it on the polished tile floor at his feet.

"No," he replied. "But I would like to stay for four nights. Do you have space? I would like a room just for me, please."

"Yes, we have standard room for four night. Is three hundred seventy Chinese yuan for one night. Is OK?"

"Perfect," Dan replied. "That's fantastic."

He found his room at the end of a long corridor. It was almost perfectly square, with brilliant white walls, a large dark wooden bed with immaculate white sheets in the centre and an ornate, antique-style side table under the window. On the table sat a leather-bound folder of information including escape routes and useful phone numbers. Next to the table was a dark wooden chair onto which he dropped his bag. He turned, sat on the edge of the bed and fell backwards onto the clean white sheets, exhausted.

Several miles away, the young woman in the red coat hurried out of the Forbidden City and into the backstreets of

Beijing. Her work for the day was almost done, save for one last, important task. She twisted and turned her way through the warren of alleyways until she arrived at an old wooden doorway, identifiable by the peeling red paint. Checking that she wasn't being followed, she pulled a small wooden thimble from her pocket and threw it quickly over the high grey wall. It bounced twice on the flagstone floor beyond with a shrill, hollow, whistle-like sound, and came to a rest. A moment later the door creaked open and with one last quick glance down the street the young woman stepped over the threshold.

A man of around thirty greeted her with a nod, gave her back the thimble and showed her into the small house. She found herself in a dark, cramped, multifunctional room that simultaneously served as kitchen, living room and workshop. A pillow and blanket on the Ottoman-style bed suggested it was also where the man slept. Along one wall a workbench sat strewn with tools lit by an improvised Anglepoise-style lamp. A thin wisp of smoke rose from a hot soldering iron while the room smelled unmistakably of melted plastic. The young woman stood quietly in the doorway as the man eased past her to his workbench. The two said nothing for risk of being overheard. As the man sat down, he opened a drawer in the bench and produced a small round disc no more than two inches across and an inch thick. It was wrapped tightly in black heat-shrink plastic. His eyes sparkled with pride as he gave it proudly to the woman. She smiled in return as she admired his handiwork, turning the device over and over in her hand like a large coin. With a nod, she clutched the disc firmly and turned to let herself out into the street again. Closing the old wooden door quietly behind her, she disappeared back into the maze of alleyways once more.

It was early April and, although the air was still cool, Dan's T-shirt clung to his body, sticky with sweat, but he had been too distracted by the chaos that had greeted his arrival into China to notice. His sinuses were blocked from the overnight flight and his hands and feet felt filthy.

After a warm and much-needed shower, Dan headed out into the *hutongs* in search of an evening meal. It had begun to drizzle and with the sun beginning to set, the sky was a pale grey. Turning into an adjacent *hutong*, he passed two old men playing cards under a large, fading Coca-Cola parasol, their faces tanned and wrinkled. They shelled sunflower seeds with their teeth and spat the husks onto the road as they played. A large brown rat ran along the ankle of the *hutong* wall behind them, collected a mouthful of the discarded husks and disappeared into a drain in the kerb.

Almost twenty minutes later and attracted by the mouth-watering cooking aromas lingering in the close confines of the narrow street, Dan came upon a small restaurant. The drizzle had stopped and the restaurant was busy as he sat down at a table in one corner.

A few moments later a man appeared, a cigarette hanging from the corner of his mouth as he spoke to Dan in Mandarin. Dan shrugged his shoulders and shook his head, pointing to the menu. The man laughed, took it out of Dan's hand and said, "OK." Leaving Dan to people-watch, the man disappeared into the kitchen.

Before long the man reappeared, carrying a tray of food that he set down on the table: a bowl of steaming hot white rice, a dish of what Dan took to be strips of pork on toasted peanuts and a plate of long, wilted green leaves. He placed a cold beer in front of Dan and, indicating that this was a good combination, smiled and gestured for him to eat. Dan was ravenous and soon finished, washing it down with several large swigs of the local beer. Full and replenished, Dan slumped back in his chair, revelling in the success of his first meal out in China. He vowed he would come back here before he left Beijing. He didn't know it then, of course, but that chance would never come. This time tomorrow he would be running for his life.

As far down the *hutong*s as Dan could see, small lanterns provided the only light – a faint but sufficient glow in the evening light. In the shade of the narrow streets, several trees were just starting to come into leaf, and Dan could see that in a few weeks' time the alleyways would take on a beautiful avenue-like feel. On either side, ornate eves hung down from the grey-tiled roofs.

He unlocked the door to his room and slumped on to the plump sheets of the bed. Tomorrow he would explore Beijing.

He was asleep before he knew it.

The next morning he woke with a start to the clattering sound of tables being set in the courtyard outside his window. It was seven o'clock and he'd slept soundly all night. His whole body felt heavy as he lay there listening to the sounds of the hotel waking up. The sun was still below the rooftops but bright enough to illuminate his room through the curtainless window. He showered and left his room, yawning his way out to the courtyard. As he sat down, a young woman approached his table holding a dark ceramic teapot in both hands and poured a hot, pale-green liquid into a white porcelain cup on his table from which rose the invigorating smell of jasmine tea.

His sinuses had cleared overnight and the aroma seeped deep into his jetlagged body. Inhaling the perfume, he closed his eyes and reminded himself of where he was. He smiled contentedly.

As he did so, across town, Nancy – as she was known today – had descended the seven flights of stairs and was walking towards the metro station. It was a route she knew well and had timed to perfection.

After breakfast Dan left the hotel and walked to a bicycle hire shop at the end of the *hutong*. Handing over sixteen yuan from the grubby notes that he received at last night's restaurant, he took one of the bikes off the stand and pushed it to the edge of the road. In full flow of the morning traffic, a dizzying stampede of cars and heavy trucks churning sooty fumes onto the pavement surged past him. Primary school-aged children, women in their eighties and men in suits all swept by, three abreast. Spotting a gap in the traffic, Dan got on his bike and joined the chaos of Beijing's rush hour roads.

Heading south, he wove his way through the column of bikes that stretched as far into the distance as he could see. There appeared to be few road rules; trucks turned left across his path, apparently oblivious to every bike and car they carved up in doing so. Bikes pulled out in front of him, causing him to swerve into the lanes of cars.

Meanwhile, bang on schedule, Nancy had arrived in Tiananmen Square and was making her way to the Forbidden City.

Just under half an hour after setting off, Dan arrived at the gates of the Temple of Heaven and, locking his bike to railings outside, made his way in. Inside, the grass was a monochromatic shade of brown as if it hadn't seen water since it was planted.

He watched three elderly Chinese men flying kites that danced in the hazy blue skies, adding a splash of colour to an otherwise largely colourless scene. The men were in their eighties, but they moved with the ease and agility of children, their deeply furrowed faces beaming with youthful delight.

The temple itself had been designed as a place to connect the mortal human world with the celestial one. It was an attempt to reach the heavens, to replicate the proximity to the gods that the Celestial Mountains over four thousand kilometres from here in the far-flung west of China offered. The same Celestial Mountains that were about to define the terrifying next few days of Dan's time in China.

Nancy had had a busy morning striking up conversations with young backpackers visiting the Forbidden City as Dan returned to his bike and made his way back through the traffic towards Tiananmen Square. Parking his bike close to the billboard-size portrait of Chairman Mao, he stood watching the endless stream of couples and tour groups taking photos of each other in front of it. He didn't know a lot about Chairman Mao, but he was still very much celebrated in China as a hero. He'd read that Mao had brought stability and unity to an unruly country and had given China a much-needed sense of identity. The rights of women improved under his rule, yet millions of people died and many invaluable cultural treasures were lost. China became a one-party state and famine ravaged the country, yet he was still held dear by the older generations who lived through his rule. But none of that turbulence of little more than a generation ago was particularly evident today.

Ahead was the Meridian Gate and beyond that lay the grounds of the Forbidden City, for centuries unseen by the eyes of commoners but now besieged by tour groups. Dan paid the sixty-yuan entrance fee and slipped inside. A gasp of awe involuntarily left his mouth: ahead of him was the imposing Hall of Supreme Harmony sitting atop a sweeping flight of steps, its tiled roof glinting gold-like in the early afternoon sunshine.

There was irony in the name as he sat alone watching what must have been thousands of people pushing and shoving their way past each other on the steps up to the hall. As he walked around the edge of the courtyard he gazed up at it and wondered what ceremonies must have gone on here in centuries past. It was a vast, rectangular room with a polished black floor. Save for a golden altar-like throne in the middle, the room was empty.

On either side of the steps, people were burning incense sticks in two large cauldrons filled with sand. The smoke took their prayers up to the heavens in the belief they would be answered by the gods who reside there. The air in the courtyard was filled with the unmistakable sickly smell. Dan turned around to look back across Tianhedian Square. From here he could see over the steady stream of people still flooding into the Palace. The noise of the crowds around him somehow quietened as he gazed across the orange-tiled rooftops and into the haze of Beijing beyond. In the distance the skyline was dotted with cranes swinging construction materials onto gleaming new buildings that were emerging all around. China was industrious, that was for sure.

As he turned back towards the Hall of Supreme Harmony, there right in front of him, looking straight at him, was a young woman in a red jacket. Startled, Dan could say nothing.

She broke the silence.

"Hello. My name is Nancy," she said confidently, her head cocked to one side in an effort to seduce him with her radiant amiability. Before Dan had chance to reply, she continued as she had unsuccessfully done several times that morning. "I am a student of art and English. We have a show of our work over there. Please come and see. I would be very happy if you see my art."

Her eyes sparkled in expectation as she awaited his response. She didn't flinch as Dan stood there somewhat bemused, weighing up his options. After a moment or two, he decided to embrace the encounter and the young woman's eagerness to engage him.

"OK, please show me. Where are we going?" he replied, half laughing.

Nancy pointed to a small squat building in a corner of the square, where Dan could see a group of five young people milling around outside.

"Over there. Please come with me."

She put her hand on his shoulder to usher him forwards, making him jump in the process. Again, she didn't flinch, continuing straight ahead. She was a professional, after all. As Dan and Nancy approached, two of the group disappeared inside the building, while the other three formed a welcome party. They clasped their hands in front of themselves and bowed their heads gently in acknowledgement as Dan reached them. He felt an uneasy weight of expectation growing as it dawned on him where this was heading.

Inside, the small room was decorated with scroll paintings, most in a classical Chinese style depicting well-fed men and slender women sitting under weeping willows or on riverbanks watching koi that swam in clear, rippling waters. The cynic in him wondered that, if ancient China really was this laid-back and idyllic, how the millions of ordinary workers become enslaved to the furnace of modern productivity that it now was.

The scrolls were brightly painted in a limited palette of pastel pinks, reds and greens. Dan spent around ten minutes or so looking around. One of the male students who had been outside now stood in the entrance, leaning against the doorframe as Dan looked around. He knew he wasn't going to get out of here empty-handed, but thought he would at least try. As he headed towards the door, Nancy spoke. "Where are you going in China?"

"Oh, I'm hoping to make my way south to Hong Kong. That's the plan, anyway!" he replied.

"Which picture do you like?"

"I like all of them," Dan responded without thinking.

"One painting, one hundred yuan," she replied. "Or you can buy two for one hundred and fifty yuan."

There was a pause, the golden silence of an artful saleswoman, as he considered his next move. A hundred yuan was around ten UK pounds. It wasn't really very much and he was actually quite taken by the pictures.

"OK, I'll take this one," he said, naively believing he was back in control of proceedings. He pointed to a scroll that hung in the middle of one wall. It was around two feet top to bottom and ten inches wide. On it an overweight man sat cross-legged while a slim woman poured steaming tea from a pot into the cup sat on a small table. All of this was taking place beneath a weeping willow tree on the banks of a stream as koi frolicked at their feet. It was the one scroll that summed up all the others and to him was the obvious choice.

Barely had the words left his mouth when one of the male students quickly took the scroll from the wall and rolled it up in front of him. He slid it into a brown cardboard tube and put it on the small counter in front of Dan.

Nancy spoke again. "If you like, I can give you one more for twenty yuan. It is a present from me because I like you very much. I hope you will have a wonderful travel in China."

"Actually, I have a long way to go and I'm only just starting. This one picture is perfect. It will look good on my wall back home in England," Dan replied and took out a hundred-yuan note, passing it to the young man.

Gratefully the man took the money and offered, "Thank you, safe time in China," in return.

Dan smiled, not realising then how many times those words would resonate in his head in the days to come. He put the scroll in his small rucksack and left the shop. Nancy followed, pausing briefly to say something to her colleagues before catching up to speak to him.

"I like you. You are nice man. I want to show you our Forbidden City. Sometimes I am guide here," Nancy lied.

Nancy's English was good enough to maintain a decent conversation and Dan was impressed by her apparent knowledge of the Forbidden City. She guided him through the various courtyards and buildings, each with its overtly ostentatious-sounding name – the Garden of Benevolent Peace, the Palace of Gathering Essence and the Hall of Earthly Tranquility. Dan found Nancy engaging as she regaled stories about emperors and their concubines and the strange, exotic world they lived in behind these high stone walls, shielded from the struggles of life on the outside.

As they came to the exit, Dan found himself back on the streets of Beijing.

"Are you hungry?" Nancy asked him as they cleared the crowds.

It was now almost four o'clock in the afternoon and Dan hadn't eaten anything since breakfast.

"Yes, actually I am. I forgot to have lunch – I was too busy exploring Beijing!" he replied.

"OK, there is nice restaurant near here. I make a call to my friend, then I take you. It's nice, small Chinese place. I know you will like it. Wait here."

With that and before he could protest, Nancy disappeared into the crowd, leaving Dan standing on the path looking up at Jingshan Park.

As he turned back to look at the Forbidden City, he noticed two young Chinese women walking towards him. Arm in arm they strode, both strikingly attractive. In an instantaneous moment of dread, Dan realised they were coming straight towards him. As they approached, he spotted their brightly manicured fingernails, clutching expensive-looking Gucci handbags. They walked up to him, and one produced a camera. Although neither spoke English, they gestured that they wanted a photo. Taken aback at their confidence, Dan laughed, nodded his head and shrugged his shoulders in surrender. The two young women called to a man who was standing nearby and beckoned him over. Standing either side of Dan, their arms pushed hard into his, forcing him to put his arms around their shoulders. As he did, the young women leaned in even closer, as if they were all school friends taking photos on the last day of term. The man nodded and pressed the button.

Dan didn't know it then, but in the fractions of a second that the shutter was open his fate in China was sealed. It was the detonator in a chain of events that would push his survival instincts to the limits, an explosion that would send ripples throughout this vast country and change his life forever.

As quickly as it had begun the whole incident was over. The two young women giggled a polite "*Xie xie*" and disappeared back into the crowd. They had exactly what they needed. The wheels were in motion and there was nothing Dan could do to stop them. Out of sight, the two women climbed into a waiting car and were driven back to the leafy, wealthy suburb of the city from where they had arrived just twenty minutes earlier.

Nancy, who had been watching from a distance, reappeared, laughing.

"You are handsome western man. I think Chinese girls like you very much. Often Chinese men do not have long hair. You look like Brad Pitt!"

Embarrassed, Dan laughed and quickly changed the subject.

"Are we going to eat?" he enquired.

"Yes," Nancy replied. "Come with me. It is close."

Nancy and Dan walked around the edge of the Forbidden City towards Beihai Park, turning left into Beichang Jie – a narrow one-lane street. On one side of the road were the perimeter walls of the Forbidden City and a footpath lined with trees. On the other, a single-storey terrace of dirty, white-walled buildings with dusty, faded red doors.

Around halfway down the road, Nancy pointed to one such doorway.

"This one," she said and they crossed the street.

Pushing the door open revealed a small courtyard restaurant filled with hungry diners. Waitresses in traditional dress scurried between tables fulfilling orders that were coming at them from all directions. A man appeared from the back of the restaurant as they arrived, waving and smiling to Nancy as he picked his way through the courtyard. He greeted Nancy like a friend and she nodded at him with an enthusiastic "*Nihao*!" The man pointed to a table that Nancy had reserved for them.

As they sat down, Dan reflected that, if it hadn't been for Nancy he would never have found this little place, completely hidden behind the dusty red door. As he sat among the wondrous aromas that hung in the still air of the courtyard, he smiled to himself and the decision he had made to trust this young woman who now sat in front of him.

Nancy ordered food for both of them and it arrived a few moments later. The sun was beginning to set as they finished, and the temperature was dropping rapidly. Dan shivered and Nancy spotted it.

"Shall we go?" she asked. "I get the check."

She gave the bill to Dan and he laughed to himself, incorrectly assuming Nancy earned most meals this way. He paid and left a small tip on the table for the waitress.

"I hope you liked the food. That man is old friend of mine," Nancy said as they crossed the street outside and made their way back to where Dan had left his bike.

"Nancy, I've had a really good time," he said, reflecting on the day's events. "I need to go back to my hotel now, so we have to say goodbye. Thank you for showing me around this afternoon. I had a lot of fun. The food was delicious as well – I would never have found it without you."

"Today I had good day too. I met an angel today," she replied, surprising him.

"Ha ha! I'm not sure I saw any angels today," he replied, before realising that his rushed attempt at humility could be misinterpreted as rude.

"OK. I hope you have great adventure in China. I had fun today too," she replied.

Dan said goodbye to Nancy and suggested she should visit England one day. Standing up to make himself more visible among the evening traffic, Dan cycled back to the *hutong*s, arriving at his hotel some fifteen minutes later.

He threw his bag into the corner of his room, sat on the edge of the bed, tired from a full day of exploration, and put the television on, flicking channels until he arrived at an English-language channel. He watched the adverts before they segued into the national news.

In an instant his heart stopped and he froze on the edge of the bed. His entire body turned cold and rigid. He felt queasy and nauseous as his throat tightened like he was being strangled. The room seemed to melt and warp around him as if he were caught in a drug-induced hallucination. The newsreader's voice slowed to a crawl and began to churn like an old tape caught in the spindles of its player.

In Beijing today, the eighteen-year-old daughter of Zhou Jun, the former Minister for Housing and Urban-Rural Development, and her nineteen year old friend, were sexually assaulted by a tourist in a hotel room. Police do not know his name or whereabouts, but he is seen in this photo taken shortly before the attack happened in a downtown hotel, leaving both young women needing hospital treatment. Anyone with information on the man's location is asked to contact police immediately.

It should be remembered that Zhou Jun himself is in the midst of an investigation into claims of corruption and nepotism, so this incident heaps trauma on a family already under immense pressure. That investigation has been put on hold while Zhou's daughter recovers from this vicious assault.

In the meantime, in Beijing, a manhunt is under way.

Dan recoiled in revulsion at what he was seeing. He had to steady himself on the end of the bed to stop himself collapsing on to the floor. He felt lightheaded and dizzy. This could not *possibly* be real. He stared at the television, where the photo of him taken outside the Forbidden City was now burning itself into the screen. He could no longer hear the words that were being said.

His thoughts spun uncontrollably for several minutes before he began running through his possible options. The first and obvious choice was to hand himself in to the police. He was obviously completely innocent so, other than the photo, there would be not a shred of evidence to connect him to any alleged attack. This could all be over within a few hours and he could continue his travels with his name cleared. But then he panicked. What if it went wrong? What if he was falsely convicted? What was the Chinese judicial process like? Did he even stand a chance of a fair trial? If found guilty, he could probably expect to spend years decaying in the atrocious conditions of a Chinese prison. Or do they just send you to the firing squad for this sort of thing over here? What if this was a professional extortion and the police were involved? If that were true, he wouldn't stand a hope in hell. His mind was racing. He needed to avoid the police at all costs.

The questions surged around his head like a thousand tsunamis crashing into one another as they did so. He was coming up with the next question quicker than he could finish the last. Giving himself up was too big a gamble. There was too much at stake, too much to lose. His entire freedom, his entire life was now at risk of being wiped out in an alien and bemusing country thousands of miles from home. It was a sickening series of thoughts. What purgatory would he have to endure just to clear his name?

It was then that the most repulsive thought in this dizzying few minutes hit him: what if... No. Not possible.

What if *Nancy* was involved?

She couldn't be. That would be one unbelievable twist too far. Dan began to retrace his steps through the afternoon. The art shop, the photo, the restaurant. Where had she disappeared to while the photo was being taken? Where had she gone for those critical few seconds? He understood she had gone to arrange the table at the restaurant, and he hadn't questioned it until now. How much of his day had actually been what he thought it had been? And why him? And what about the corruption investigation? How could that possibly involve him?

Anger began to creep in. He had believed that today had been a good day; he had trusted Nancy. He had enjoyed her company. He had allowed those two girls to take his photo. He had bought Nancy dinner. He now felt like an angry, naïve little schoolboy. How could he have been so stupid?

"You fucking idiot." He chastised himself out loud as his head fell into his hands.

His mind racing, every sound from the hotel making him jump as he searched frantically for answers. He had never travelled alone before and felt utterly lost. The situation seemed hopeless and he was fighting for his life.

Panicking and with his heart pounding, it began to dawn on him: there was really only one option.

It was at that moment, with his head in his hands, that he made his decision.

Run.

2

THE TRAIN TO XI'AN

Dan sat straight back up. The anger turned to gritted determination. He clenched his fist; he would get the hell out of China. He would escape the hellishness of this situation first and clear his name once he got out. He could *not* go to prison here. With his mind made up, it was time to get out of the hotel.

He jumped to his feet, expecting the police to burst through that door at any second. Scrambling around, he threw everything he owned into his backpack. There was no time to pack in any sort of order so he stuffed his clothes, camera and passport in as quickly as he could, tightening the drawstrings and fastening the clips. He gave the room a quick once-over to make sure he hadn't forgotten anything, grabbed the room key from the table beside the wall and opened the door. The corridor was empty and the hotel was quiet. He looked down at the room key in his hand. He didn't need it so threw it back onto the bed. Leaving the room locked from the inside might slow the police down for a moment or two. The lock clicked shut as he closed the door quietly behind him.

Creeping along the corridor towards reception, he could see that ahead of him the desk was unmanned and, beyond it, the front door that he had to aim for. His heart was pounding and his palms were sweaty as he half ran, half walked through the lobby. His feet barely made a sound as he passed the office where the young woman was playing solitaire on her computer. If that front door opened now it would all be over.

It didn't, and Dan pushed the heavy door open slowly. It creaked slightly but not enough to be heard. A gust of fresh, damp air hit him as he stepped over the raised threshold. He glanced over his shoulder. There was not another person in the hotel that had seen him leave. He closed the door quietly and stood in the darkened street. To the left the lane led deeper into the dim light of the *hutong*s. To the right was the main road where the bike shop stood.

Looking back to his left he paused for a second before running into the inky blackness. His backpack bounced and swung on his shoulders as he sped deeper into the labyrinth of alleyways. He skipped over drainage gullies at the sides of the road, fearful of twisting an ankle in the darkness. Just as he turned right into another narrow alleyway, flashing red and blue lights suddenly illuminated the far end of the *hutong* behind him. The lights bounced off the grey brick walls all the way down to where he was now standing just out of sight, frozen in fear. The police car pulled up at the door to the Lu Yuan as he crouched around two hundred metres away. A second car joined it, followed by a third. He didn't stop to watch what happened next; he turned and ran deeper into the *hutong*s.

He ran for almost ten minutes, weaving his way through lanes that became narrower and darker. He didn't pass a single other person as he sped through the flickering light that spilled from the small lamps hanging above the intermittent doorways. Eventually he saw a main road ahead of him glowing a bright yellow from the streetlights that illuminated it. He slowed to a walk before hunkering down in a darkened old doorway to consider his next move. His heart was pounding as he heaved deep breaths and tried to focus his thoughts on a strategy.

The sight of the police cars arriving at the hotel had shaken him to his core. This was real. As he sat crouched in the semi-darkness of the quiet Beijing *hutong* it dawned on him that it would be suicidal to try to leave China by air, no matter which airport he ran to. This realisation changed everything.

He began to consider alternatives. He could still turn himself in but given that he had run from the Lu Yuan would only serve to imply that he was guilty. He was already in too deep to give up.

That left him the options of leaving China by land or by sea. But he didn't know how international ferries or cargo ships worked. Presumably they were just as vigilant at seaports as they were at airports, so the chances of stowing aboard were impractically slim. That left the option of leaving by land, but to cross a border into another country threw up a whole new set of questions. Questions that he didn't have time to work out hiding there in the damp alleyways of the *hutong*s. He needed to get out of Beijing so made the decision to board the overnight train to Xi'an that he had been planning to take in a few days' time.

As he reached the end of the lane a taxi swept down the road towards him. He flagged it down and pointed to the word "station" he had written on a list of useful words he kept in his wallet and said, "Xi'an." The driver nodded and sped off. Dan slumped back in the seat, keeping a low profile as they weaved through the evening traffic towards the station.

They arrived quicker than Dan had hoped. The confines of the taxi had felt relatively safe but he felt exposed again as he stood on the imposing front concourse of Beijing West Station. By day the gargantuan arch of the station could well have been mistaken for the mouth of hell, but by night it was illuminated in seductive gold and yellow lighting. Beijingers flocked to it like moths to a streetlamp in the chilly April air.

Inside, the station was heaving with people. As with all stations there was little to distinguish between arrivals and departures but this felt particularly chaotic. It was exactly what he had been hoping for; it would be difficult to find him in here. Not impossible, but difficult. Ahead was a set of eight vast escalators taking people up to a second floor, on either side of which were walls of ticket offices. Dan joined what turned out to be a very slow-moving queue to the left of the escalators. Checking the electronic departure board on the wall above the ticket windows, he noticed the next train to Xi'an was the 20:43 departure, number Z19. That was about thirty minutes from now – perfect.

Eventually it was his turn and he stepped forward to the window at the far left-hand end of the row and wrote "Z19 20:43" and said "Xi'an". The woman on the other side of the Plexiglas nodded. Dan's palms were sweaty, worried that she would ask to see his passport.

She turned to him and asked, "You want soft sleep?"

He nodded in reply.

The digital display changed to show "CNY415.50" and Dan handed over five one-hundred-yuan notes. In return the woman passed him a bundle of tatty browned notes that looked like they had passed through the hands of every person in Beijing before arriving into his. She printed his ticket and pointed to the platform number. He said thank you, picked his backpack up from the floor beside him and left the queue. She hadn't asked him for his name or passport. Could he really pull this off?

It was as he stepped away from the ticket window that he realised the whole transaction was most likely to have been captured on CCTV. It dawned on him that even if he did make it out of Beijing it wouldn't be too hard to work out that he was en route to Xi'an. He needed to throw the police off his scent and to make them think he was heading somewhere else.

As Dan stood in the middle of the bustling concourse surrounded by departure boards and train times, an idea began to form. He ran over to another ticket office at the other side of the hall and joined the shortest queue he could find. Reaching the window, he wrote "K507 Chongqing" on another page of his notebook. This train was leaving at 21:35 – just forty minutes or so after his train to Xi'an. The woman at the window smiled at him.

"You are going to Chongqing. It is big city near Yangtze River. I have never been to there, but one day, I want to go with my family."

"Yes," Dan replied. "I want to see the Yangtze, so I am going to Chongqing. I have heard it is a very big city!" he lied. In truth, he knew only that Chongqing was roughly in the middle of the country, a long way south of where he was now.

The woman continued to smile as she worked out the price for a soft sleeper – CNY416. He handed over another five one-hundred-yuan notes. At this rate he would need to withdraw some more money before long – a potentially dangerous practice that could reveal his location. Dan had arrived in China with three thousand yuan in his wallet – the equivalent of around three hundred pounds. It was fast running out and he still had another ticket to buy. The woman passed him his change, again in grubby notes, before speaking to him one last time. "I hope you have wonderful time in China."

"I hope so too," he said hurriedly but politely, trying desperately hard to remain calm as his heart pounded. He had work to do and the clock was ticking.

Dan took his ticket, returned to the first ticket office and rejoined the queue, hoping he could avoid the lady who had given him the ticket to Xi'an. He shuffled slowly forward, resisting the constant urge to look over his shoulder. At last he arrived at the front of the queue. An elderly Chinese couple at the far left-hand window collected their tickets and left. Shit.

He hesitated briefly before the man behind him tapped him on the shoulder and pointed to the empty window. Just as Dan was about to step forward the elderly couple stopped and returned to the kiosk. Dan heaved a sigh of relief. That was too close. A window to his right became available and he walked up to it. Again he took out his notepad, opened a blank page and scribbled "22:15 – K1363 Chengdu".

"Soft sleeper," he requested.

The price appeared on the screen in front of him – CNY416. Dan passed the man four one-hundred-yuan notes and a handful of the grubby notes he had just been given, making four hundred and sixteen yuan exactly. The man printed off the ticket and slid it through the slot under the window.

Grabbing his bag, Dan headed into the middle of the concourse, where it was busiest. He joined the hundreds of other people standing looking up at the departures and arrivals boards, waiting for his platform to be called. There were twenty minutes to go until the train was due to leave. The minute hand on the large central clock barely seemed to move as he waited, running down the minutes. Eventually the platform number appeared on the departures board and, picking his bag up, Dan headed to the train. As the crowds of people thinned out he felt increasingly exposed. Hunching over, he lifted his backpack high onto his shoulders and lowered his face towards the floor, looking up only occasionally as he made his way towards platform nine. There had been no sign of the apparent manhunt since the three police cars had turned up at the Lu Yuan. Had they not even considered that he might flee to the station?

Dan got all the way to his carriage without being stopped. He paused, looking up and down the platform for signs of police or that he had been followed. He didn't appear to have been. He took another deep breath and climbed the steep, ladder-like steps into the train. As he climbed aboard he found himself staring straight at a pair of polished black shoes and a well-ironed uniform. A female conductor looked back down at him. She took a step back to let him on board and said something in Chinese as she held her hand out. Dan passed her his ticket and looked anxiously down the carriage to see if there were police waiting for him. There weren't.

The carriage was like sleeper trains the world over: a long corridor with curtained windows on the outside and individual compartments with narrow, plasticky faux-wood doors on the other. At each end of the carriage was a small washroom with a pair of sinks set in a cream Formica unit, and a dirty full-width mirror mounted on the wall. Adjacent to the basic washroom was a Chinese-style squat toilet to be shared by half the carriage. The conductor took Dan to his compartment, three doors down on the left. It was a four-berth cabin with two bunk beds on either side. There was a large picture window at the far end beneath which stood a small table that nestled neatly between the two lower bunks. A hot-water urn and an ashtray sat on the table. The female conductor tucked Dan's ticket into a leather-bound photo album-like book and left him to himself.

Dan dropped his backpack on the lower bunk on the right that was to be his bed for the night. Closing the door, he sat down beside his bag in disbelief that he had made it this far. The train was still to leave Beijing, and Xi'an was unlikely to be much safer but he had managed to escape the hotel, make it through the darkened *hutong*s, and get himself to the station and on board a train out of the city. He had also booked himself onto three different trains and could, as far as the police were aware, be heading anywhere in this expansive country. What difference those two extra tickets made he didn't know, but he felt slightly more secure at the thought that he might be one step ahead.

Then, without warning, there was a loud bang on the door and Dan jumped to his feet. There was a fumbling sound outside the compartment before the door swung open. Filling the narrow doorway was a heavily overweight businessman in a navy-blue suit. He wore a white shirt that was open to the midpoint on his chest, a tie hanging loosely around his neck. Judging by the colour of his face, the man was suffering with a chronic blood pressure problem. His eyes were bloodshot and he struggled to stay upright, drunk almost to the point of semi-consciousness. Grabbing the doorframe with both hands, the man launched himself into the cabin and in one sweeping movement stumbled onto the lower bunk opposite Dan. He ended up face down on the bed, face buried in the thin white pillow and his right arm hanging down to the floor. In his wake came the foul smell of a cocktail of cigarettes and alcohol. It was all over in ten seconds or so but it was to be another fifteen minutes before Dan's heartrate returned to normal.

The door to the cabin was wide open so Dan checked the corridor once more and closed it quietly.

As he shut the door, the train began to lurch forwards with the distinctive sound of metal couplings clanking and straining as the carriages reluctantly moved off their standing. Dan watched cautiously through the window as the train pulled out of Beijing station, being careful not to be seen. As they gathered pace, Dan looked back at the place where the taxi had dropped him off, his head in a spin from the events of the last couple of hours.

Suddenly, his delirious gaze was shattered by the sight of four police cars sweeping into the station concourse. A number of policemen jumped out and ran into the station, leaving flashing lights to illuminate the front of the building. His heartrate intensifying, Dan waited for the train to grind to a halt. But it didn't. If the police knew he was on a train they would surely be waiting for him in Xi'an and there was nothing he could do about it now, he thought. The train was en route and he was captive aboard it.

As he sat there, heart pounding, an idea for the next leg of his journey began to form in his mind. This train was an express service. There were no scheduled stops between Beijing and Xi'an, but that certainly wasn't the case for the majority of other train journeys in China. He would buy a ticket to one destination but get off the train at an earlier station, allowing him to completely disappear. The more remote the place he got off, the less chance they would be looking for him. But that begged the questions – where to go from Xi'an and when?

Despite the stench emanating from his uninvited travelling companion, Dan was grateful that the man was unconscious and would likely have no recollection of having seen him. Dan sat on the edge of the bed, trying to ignore the stale smell, and began to run through his options.

Perhaps the most obvious option was to continue south, somehow cross into Hong Kong unnoticed and seek refuge at the British consulate. But that was not without significant risk. He would have to travel through some of the most densely populated cities in the world and crossing the border into Hong Kong without detection would be virtually impossible.

As his heartrate began to settle and clarity of thought began to return, a horrifying thought struck him: the British embassy! Why hadn't he just headed straight to the British embassy in Beijing? He could have taken the taxi straight there, explained what had happened and been on a plane out of China that evening.

Dan was in over his head and a long way out of his depth. He had panicked, run from the Lu Yuan and had seen the police sweep into the station as the train left – it was highly likely they knew he was on the run. Even though he wasn't guilty, anyone fleeing a hotel or any tourist just vanishing into thin air in China was bound to only intensify the suspicion. He couldn't get back to Beijing and the safety of the embassy now. If he had stopped to think for just five minutes he might have thought about the embassy option. This thought would haunt him for the rest of his journey.

He took out his guidebook and turned to the full-page map of China. He saw that it had borders with fourteen other countries. Many of them were pretty dysfunctional: North Korea, Tajikistan, Afghanistan, Pakistan. Mongolia would get him nowhere. The border with Russia would take him into Siberia and the thought of ending up in a gulag in the frozen middle of Russia made him shudder. They probably had an extradition agreement with China anyway and he'd end up back in Beijing before he knew it. Just the thought of crossing that border scared him.

He scanned his way clockwise around the map: South East Asia, Tibet, Nepal, Central Asia. None of the options really appealed. There was no way he could cross the Himalayas into Tibet, Nepal or northern India: the terrain alone ruled them out. Afghanistan and Pakistan had been mostly off limits for a westerner since 9/11. He'd heard Tajikistan was unstable too – a trading corridor from the opium fields of Afghanistan into the lucrative markets of Europe. Besides, it looked mountainous, rugged and probably impassable.

This left South East Asia, into which the largest border was that with Burma. He studied his map. There appeared to be one crossing point at a place called Muse. He would have to travel through the industrial heartland of China, probably via Chengdu, then onto Dali, Baoshan, Dehong and ultimately the border at Muse. Dali was a tourist town; it was one of the places he had been planning to visit. It would be crawling with foreigners, making it easier to blend in than in other places. But, would they be looking for him there *because* of the number of foreigners? The hostels were likely to be on the lookout for him. He pictured his face photocopied in black and white ten thousand times and taped to hostel reception walls everywhere. He wouldn't understand the "He's here! He's just checked in!" phone calls even if they made them right in front of him. It was too risky. Burma was also an unknown – what would he find when he got there? Would it be any safer? Could it be worse? Burma was still very much opening up to the outside world and it was far from utopic. He ruled it out.

To the north of Burma was the Indian state of Arunachal Pradesh. The land between it and China was mountainous. The Himalayas again. As he read on, he learned that the state was also claimed by the Chinese, who referred to it as South Tibet. The Chinese were everywhere! They were crawling all over Tibet and now they were heading south into India. It would be suicidal to venture into disputed territories, no matter how welcoming India felt to him right now. He longed for a gentle Indian greeting, a soft, warm handshake, a big smile and sparkling, friendly eyes.

The final border crossing he could make out was into Vietnam. There was a crossing close to the Chinese town of Hekou. This would take him into the north of the country, where he could travel straight to Hanoi and fly home. Vietnam was backpacker heaven so it would be little effort to blend in, disappear and escape unnoticed.

Almost instantly he got cold feet. It was the Dali scenario all over again. It was probably an obvious choice and, Christ, there was a lot of ground to cover between Xi'an and Hekou. Was it humanly possible to traverse the very heart of China, under the gaze of a billion people, without being spotted? Doubts began to flood his mind. It was too obvious. They would be all over the Vietnam border just as they would the airports.

His escape strategy had to be cleverer. The route he chose could not be allowed to become his fatal mistake. He had to outsmart the people looking for him. He had to be at least two steps ahead if he was to make it out of China.

It was at that point that a path began to present itself on the map in front of him. A line through the western deserts of the Gobi and Taklamakan began to appear, one that took him away from major cities and airports. This was remote China. There was a possibility that it was so remote that news of his escape hadn't reached this far. Dan part-hoped, part-imagined the authorities here to be less well equipped than those in the cities of central China. Surely no fugitive would head west. He traced the train lines through Gansu province, up into Xinjiang and to the city of Urumqi. From there, the train line continued south-west into the furthest corner of the country and a small city called Kashgar. It was not far from the border with Pakistan and the easternmost tip of the Afghan Wakhan Corridor. The more he studied the map, the more this route began to make sense. Just north of Kashgar was Kyrgyzstan.

He imagined it to be a small, undeveloped country with little infrastructure and therefore probably very little up-to-date contact with China. If he could get across that border and make it to the capital, Bishkek, he might just endure. This was as rugged and remote as travelling in China could get and, for reasons he didn't really understand, it sat comfortably in his mind: he would find passage to safety via the Torugart Pass, a high mountain road into Kyrgyzstan.

Dan fell back on his bed, his head spinning with the thought of everything that lay ahead as he stared up at the metal slats on the underside of the bunk above. He had to get to Kyrgyzstan. As this thought enveloped him, he felt the energy draining from his limbs, his body relaxed and a few moments later he drifted into an exhausted sleep.

He would head deep into Xinjiang.

3

TURNING WEST

Dan was woken with a start by a loud clattering sound. Instantly he remembered where he was and his heart was already racing as he blinked the sleep out of his eyes. In the middle of the cabin stood the businessman, face and eyes still as red as they had been the evening before. His open shirt now revealed the flabby, blotched skin of his torso. As Dan lay watching through half-open eyes, the man tore open a large pot of dried instant noodles and began to fill it with hot water from the urn. He ripped a pair of disposable bamboo chopsticks out of their paper packet and pulled them apart with his fat fingers.

As the man began fiercely stirring the noodles, the compartment filled with the sickly smell of the spicy soup. The man let it rest for a few minutes before sitting down on the edge of his bed to slurp the noodles down his throat. They were gone in a matter of minutes and Dan felt queasy from the whole episode. This man was disgusting. Neanderthal, almost.

Outside, the sky was turning a bluish-grey as the sun began to rise. It was ten past six in the morning and the train was due to arrive into Xi'an just before eight o'clock. Dan was hungry. He hadn't eaten since that meal with Nancy the afternoon before and had nothing with him. Realising that the businessman hadn't been carrying anything when he stumbled through the door, Dan set off in search of food.

From the corridor Dan could hear conversations going on behind the closed doors as people began to wake. A man emerged from his cabin cleaning his teeth and disappeared into the washroom. As the train swayed gently from side to side, Dan staggered down the corridor to where the female conductor stood beside a shelf piled with instant noodles and clear plastic bags of a sticky dark fruit. She nodded and greeted Dan in Mandarin as he appeared.

There were three types of noodle on the shelves with different coloured labels – brown, red and green – but there was nothing to distinguish between the pictures on the front and he couldn't read the descriptions. Dan paid the conductor for one of the green pots, leaving her a tip of ten yuan as he did. She smiled gratefully at him and Dan returned to his cabin. The businessman was lying on his back, fast asleep again, his large, rotund belly now visible where his shirt had come untucked from his trousers. A dark wisp of wiry hair curled around his belly button as he lay with his mouth hanging open, snoring loudly. Dan could see the dark fillings in his yellowing teeth.

Just as the man had done, Dan opened the pot noodle, filled it with hot water and stirred it. It steamed furiously as he mixed the dry powder through the concoction. Outside, the sky was growing lighter and Dan could see more of the dry, arid landscape. A brown dust filled the morning air, coating buildings and cars. It looked like it hadn't rained for weeks. The train continued past towns of low-rise buildings dwarfed by factories and industrial plants on their outskirts. Tractors and trucks began to fill the roads as the time approached seven o'clock. Dan caught glimpses of toddlers playing in the streets as vehicles coursed past them. Chickens and dogs could be seen running through alleyways and, although the sun was up, the sky was a hazy light grey. Everywhere he looked the infrastructure was crumbling: dilapidated concrete bridges carried trucks burdened with scrap metal and farm animals over churning brown rivers. Millions of Chinese were waking up to similar scenes all over the country. And millions of Chinese were about to turn on the news.

Eventually the factories and chimneys became larger and uninterrupted. The train was approaching the outskirts of Xi'an. The industrial buildings gave way to vast rows of tower blocks that housed the workers from the factories. As the landscape turned to city, Dan heaved a deep breath realising that in a few moments' time he would be out on the streets again, running for his life.

The train slowed to a crawl and pulled into a crowded platform. Scanning the station from the safety of the corner of the compartment a sense of doom loomed large over him. The station was full of police. His game was up.

But as the train continued into the station Dan noticed that they were all waiting at the end of the platform – the one that they had just passed. There must have been thirty or forty of them, spread out along the platform but only to about two carriage-lengths in. Surely not. If they were waiting for him, did they really think he was in one of the carriages at the back of the train?

As the train ground to a halt Dan quickly grabbed his bag, left the cabin and joined the queue of people waiting to get off the train. He pulled his black woollen hat low over his head so it covered everything just above his eyes.

Climbing down the steps from the train, Dan soon spotted the exit signs. Waiting on the platform as he alighted the train, the conductor smiled at Dan and gave him the quickest of winks that took Dan a few seconds to register. He glanced back, but she didn't return the look, continuing to bow to the remaining disembarking passengers.

Dan turned back to where he was heading, confused by what had just happened. The exit was only about sixty metres away at the other side of the concourse. To his left the train extended back towards the entrance to the station. The police were checking everyone who got off. Dan kept his head low, aware that he was taller than most people around him. His backpack felt conspicuous as he weaved his way through the crowds, but he didn't look back. Keeping his head down, he walked briskly towards the exit and wondered to himself what was going on in Chongqing and Chengdu at the moment. Had the conductor just aided his escape? Why would she do that? It would be almost two weeks before he learned the truth.

Dan glanced up at the departures board that had just flickered into English as he passed by. It was 07:53. There was no security at the exit and Dan passed through the doors unimpeded. Outside, the sky was now a smoggy brown colour and filled with the sounds of traffic. Dan glanced back up at the station building. It was a long grey box with large vertical windows and red banners that hung down from the roof. He had slipped out unnoticed and kept walking towards a line of taxis he could see waiting at the end of the piazza.

As he got within a few metres of the taxis Dan heard a commotion behind him. Ten or so policeman ran out of the station doors shouting. They fanned out desperately looking all around them. Dan quickened his pace and jumped into the nearest taxi a few seconds later. On the back seat he fumbled around frantically in his bag for his guidebook. His hands shaking, he flicked to the Xi'an accommodation page and pointed to first one on the list. The Bell Tower Hotel. The driver took off. As Dan looked back through the rear window at the piazza, he could see the police still running from person to person. He watched as they stopped two other backpackers walking out of the station. Dan didn't see what happened but the last he saw of them they were being surrounded by three or four policemen. That was the third lucky escape he had had. It was all far too close for comfort.

The driver took Dan to the Bell Tower Hotel and dropped him off in a car park to the rear. Dan paid the driver but didn't go into the hotel immediately; he decided to walk around to the front of the building to make sure it was safe to go in. Stopping at a Bank of China ATM en route, he withdrew three thousand yuan to tide him over. He would withdraw more before he left Xi'an.

The six-storey facia of the hotel was vast, with limestone-coloured blocks and windows that shone yellowy-gold in the morning light. There was a large foyer and Dan peered cautiously through the doors that lead to the lobby. To the left of the front door a man lay begging. A quadruple amputee, he shuffled around, face down on a skateboard-like contraption, his entire life spent just inches off the ground. On a normal day Dan would have offered the man money, but he was too focused to really register. There didn't yet appear to be any police at the hotel but the lobby was filled with tour groups waiting to leave for the day. As he stood outside, a coach appeared and one of the groups filed out of the hotel and on to it. In the commotion, Dan made his way into the hotel and up to the front desk. One of the young men at reception greeted him in English. "Hello. May I help you?"

"Yes, I would like a room for two nights please. Just for myself," Dan replied.

The man looked down at his computer and tapped a few keys. He looked up at him and said, "Yes, sir, we have room available for two night. It is five hundred and sixty yuan for one night. Is that OK?"

"Can I pay when I check out?" Dan asked. It was more money than he wanted to pay, given that he had no intention of staying here.

"Yes, sir. But I take card for your room now."

Dan paid the man in cash for one night and said he would pay for the second night tomorrow if he was happy with it. The man gave him his room key and pointed to the lifts to the left of the lobby. As he walked, legs weak with nerves, Dan noticed a short hallway leading to a restaurant at the rear of the hotel. Another tour group was just finishing breakfast and they were filing out of a door straight into the car park, where their coach was waiting for them.

Dan stood in the lift, frantically pressing the close button. On the third floor, his palms sweaty again, he found his room, number 326, and opened the door to a bland room of cream and beige décor. The television was on. He hadn't seen the news since yesterday evening, when he had first seen his own image etched into the screen. The television now made him feel sick but he changed channels until he found CCTV news again. Within thirty seconds his face was back on the screen. Fuck, this was really happening. The police were still looking for him. Dan tried to work out where the images were. It looked like Beijing, but he hadn't spent enough time in the city to be sure. The coverage showed two women apparently lying in adjacent beds, tubes in their noses and ventilators helping them breathe. Teams of worried-looking doctors attended to their every need. The footage then quickly changed and Dan recognised it instantly: the Lu Yuan.

Jesus! They showed his room! They showed the towels he had discarded on the edge of the bed and the key still lying in the middle of it. Then they showed a roll of 35mm film strewn across the bed. What the fuck? That wasn't *his*! His camera was a brand-new digital one! He was clearly being well and truly framed for this. A policeman in pristine navy-blue uniform was showing the camera crew around the room, pointing out the roll of film as Dan watched on from nearly seven hundred miles away. The officer then pointed to marks on the wall next to the bed and Dan could tell from the man's body language that he was suggesting they were the result of a struggle. Fuming, Dan turned the television off and threw the remote onto a chair in the corner of the room. He felt the anger rising inside him. Game on. He was going to get out of China.

It was time to implement his change of direction. Dan picked up his backpack and took the lift back to the ground floor. He propped his bag against the wall under the stairs before walking over to the front desk again to speak to the same man who had checked him in a few moments earlier.

"I want to go to Guilin in two days' time. Can you recommend a hotel for me?" Dan asked.

"Yes, sir," the man replied, "I know a good hotel in Guilin City. It is the Sheraton Hotel."

"If I want you to, can you book a room for me there?" Dan enquired.

"Yes. I will make phone call to that hotel when you say me to," the man answered.

"If I book now, can I pay when I get there? If so, can you book it for me now please?" Dan continued.

The man nodded, confirming that it was possible, and picked up the phone to book Dan the Sheraton in Guilin for two nights' time. For anyone looking for him, he was en route to Guilin. That also confirmed he was intending to stay in Xi'an for the next two nights. Dan told the man he would take the train to Guilin in two days' time and thanked him for his help.

Making his way back towards the lift, Dan picked his backpack up from under the stairs, headed down the hallway he had seen when he first arrived and walked straight out of the back door. Crossing the road behind the hotel, Dan pulled his hat down low again and made his way past the old Drum Tower, noting the McDonald's at its base, and continued to the Muslim Quarter. It was almost 09:30 and he needed to move fast. The streets were already busy and vibrant, filled with the steam and cooking smells of dozens of small eateries. He sat down at one small café about a third of the way down the road where simple tables and chairs had been set out on the pavement. He ordered breakfast – mutton soup with a bowl of fried rice and a plate of steamed bread buns. Ravenous and nervous, he wolfed it down.

Just two shops further along the road, Dan found a small barber's shop. The proprietor was an old man with a long beard and shaved head. He wore an embroidered *doppa* and long brown gown. Dan gestured that he wanted to shave his head, just like another man who stood nearby. He gave Dan a large, toothless smile and gestured for him to sit in the torn brown leather chair that stood out on the street. Dan watched carts and tricycles pass him as the barber began to shave his head with a long cut-throat razor. Within no more than ten minutes, Dan's long hair was gone and his head was completely shaved. The man held up a cracked mirror for Dan to inspect his work. It was perfect – he didn't even recognise himself.

It had just gone quarter past ten. Dan paid the man, tipping the same amount again, and pulled his black hat over his head. The gratitude in the man's eyes was clear, and the feeling was mutual – Dan felt the same for his radical change of image.

At the same time, in a leafy suburb of Beijing, Zhou Jun and his family were preparing to leave for Singapore. Their bags had been packed and were being carried to a fleet of three waiting cars by a team of smartly dressed young men who hurried between the house and the vehicles. At a small airfield just outside the city a private jet was being prepared for take-off. Zhou Jun couldn't be happier with how things were progressing.

Returning to the Drum Tower, Dan flagged down the first taxi that passed. He pointed to the word "station" in his book and sat back, running his hands over his newly shaven head.

He hoped to God that the station was free of police by now given that they knew they had lost him. At that very moment, a patrol car came screaming past them in the other direction. Dan ducked down in the seat trying to hide himself. His heart was racing again, partly from this game of chase, partly in the knowledge that the train he was heading for was due to depart in just twenty-five minutes' time and he still had to buy a ticket.

They arrived at the station in good time. Dan paid the driver and walked confidently across the piazza again, his throat dry and tight as he entered the station building, clenching his fist tightly around the strap of his backpack. The large entrance hall was teeming with people waiting for their trains to be called. It took a moment or two but he spotted the ticket counter and began picking his way through the crowds to reach it. He had just over twenty minutes until the train was due to leave and there was a lengthy queue for tickets. His heart was pounding; if he missed this train he would be stuck in Xi'an.

It took around ten minutes to reach the front of the queue. He moved quickly up to the window and produced his notebook on which he had written "K591 – Dunhuang. 10:53. Soft Sleeper". The man on the other side of the window barely made eye contact but turned to look at the wall clock behind him. 10:44. Dan paid the fee of five hundred and eighty-eight yuan and the man circled "Platform 12" for him in black biro. Dan thanked him and turned around. As he did, he found himself staring straight at two uniformed members of the People's Armed Police who had appeared beside him. They asked to see his ticket. His hands were visible shaking as he passed them his boarding pass. They looked at the ticket, at each other, shook their heads and passed the ticket back to him, waving him on his way. He stood motionless for a second, hardly daring to breathe as he tried to gather his composure.

Dan picked up his bag, made an overly deliberate gesture of looking at his watch and began to run, darting through the crowds of Chinese passengers, taking care not to crash into anyone as he searched for platform twelve. His head was fuzzy and the sounds of the busy concourse began to fade as he made his way through the crowds. With just two minutes to spare he found platform twelve and clambered aboard the train at the first door he could find. The female conductor who greeted him indicated that he was in the wrong carriage so he walked through three or four other cars, just as the train began to pull out of the station. Dan made his way to his cabin door unsure what he was going to find on the other side of it.

Inside, two young Chinese women sat on the lower bunk on the right-hand side of the cabin. His bed was on the left. Both women wore black faux leather jackets and black jeans, their lips painted with bright red lipstick. Between the two women was a young boy of around eight dressed in blue tracksuit trousers and a grubby white T-shirt. The three turned to look at Dan as he entered the cabin and smiled politely at him. He returned the smile before remembering that it was two young Chinese women who got him into this situation in the first place. The boy stared at him transfixed.

Ten minutes later, the train was trundling through the suburbs of Xi'an. Dan's brief stay in the city had been frantic; he had only narrowly escaped from the police at the station on arrival, and he still had no idea what role the conductor on the train had played in that. He had checked into a hotel for two nights, booked false onward arrangements to Guilin, eaten breakfast and fundamentally changed his appearance. All of this had happened in the space of just two hours or so. As he lay there, his mind spinning and heart pounding, Dan felt delirious. He closed his eyes and fell into a deep sleep, exhausted.

He woke sometime later as the conductor entered the cabin, asking for tickets. She tucked Dan's into her book under a tab that said "Dunhuang", smiled and left. It was her job to come and wake the passengers when the time arose. Dan sat on his bed looking out of the window. They had left the urban sprawl behind and the countryside had opened up into dusty villages of red-brick shacks. Dusty asphalt roads lined with dusty trees dissected dusty farmlands. Much as he had seen earlier this morning, rusting metal bridges crossed convulsing brown rivers. He got up and left the compartment, walking to the end of the carriage where the windows in the doors opened. Dan pushed the window down and cautiously put his head outside. Despite being early afternoon the air was cool as they travelled north-west. Before long they would be in the Hexi Corridor. To the south of him would be the high and inhospitable Tibetan Plateau and beyond that the highest mountains in the world. To the north, separated by the shifting sands of the Gobi, would lie the vast steppe grasslands and big skies of Mongolia. He felt the history of the Silk Route weigh heavy on his shoulders as he pictured the caravans that once travelled through here in both directions, laden with not only silk from Xi'an and goods from Europe but language, knowledge and culture. This was one of the most significant vascular systems of interaction in the history of mankind and he felt humbled to be travelling through it. It was responsible for the mixing of east and west, but he was here as a fugitive from the east, desperately trying to make his way west. Pangs of sadness kicked in as it dawned on him that he was ever unlikely to return to explore it properly. He stood for an hour watching the landscape go by from the window. It rarely changed, but the scale of the factories that appeared from nowhere, dwarfing the villages they towered over, never failed to both surprise and appal him. Great white clouds of smoke and steam spewed skywards while all around farmlands produced crops for the factory workers. It was a vicious ecosystem of ill health that would, he suspected, ultimately lead to the factory's own demise.

Dan returned to his cabin to find the two young women lying on their bunks. The boy was asleep on the lower bed curled up next to one of them. The weight of the situation slowly began to sink in and Dan started to imagine what it would be like if the police ever caught him. Where and how violent would his capture be? Would he even be caught alive? If they didn't shoot him during his arrest where would he be imprisoned? What horrors would he find behind the high walls of Chinese incarceration? Would he be mistreated? Would he become one of those prisoners you hear about, decaying in far off countries beyond the reach of British diplomatic intervention? Would it make the news back home?

Every single one of these questions scared him, so he resolved to stop thinking about all the "*what ifs*". He had eluded capture thus far and the only thing to tie him to this train was the one ticket he had purchased. There was more to suggest that he was heading south to Guilin and Hong Kong, or even still in Xi'an. It struck him then that he had forgotten to withdraw any more money before he left. The next time he used his card, they would see exactly where he was. This was a big oversight and he berated himself for it in his head. He only managed to calm down when he remembered how close he had been to missing this train as it was, but he needed cash without accessing his bank account. He had a little over two thousand yuan left on him and it was going fast.

Every centimetre this train moved, the closer he was to freedom. He started to imagine what it would be like to walk across that border into Kyrgyzstan, picturing a mountain pass, rugged and barren on the Chinese side, falling away to the freedom of vast meadows and snow-capped peaks on the Kyrgyz side. He imagined walking through waist-high grasses, allowing alpine flowers to flow through his hands as he wandered. He pictured horses grazing and crystal clear streams trickling along pebble-strewn riverbeds. This whole image motivated him intensely; it was the very freedom he was fighting for with every breath in his body. Despite his total exhaustion, he felt reinvigorated to succeed.

Gradually, Dan became aware that the sky outside the train was darkening. His watch showed that it was approaching seven o'clock. It was too early to be getting this dark. Sunset wasn't due for another hour or so. This was a different kind of ambience; there was something more sinister about the colour of the sky. Within minutes, the train burst into urban sprawl again. Vast factories now filled the view from the window, gargantuan and numerous. Dan could see the fumes that were spilling from the forest of chimneys becoming mixed into the low cloud that hung over the approaching city. They were approaching Lanzhou – one of the most polluted cities in the world. The train began to slow and there was a knock at the door. The conductor walked in and told the two young women that they were about to arrive. As the women collected their things together, Dan remembered that he still had the room key from the Bell Tower Hotel in his backpack. He needed to dispose of it.

Around ten minutes after they had arrived in Lanzhou the train started pulling away again. Dan breathed a sigh of relief; another major city passed and as far as he was aware there were still no police on board. He was alone in his cabin – just the way he liked it. As he peered out of the window the train began to cross a deep gorge. Below them a vast, swirling brown river coursed its way through the outskirts of the city. Dan grabbed the room key and ran to the end of the carriage. He pushed the window down again and threw the key out, watching as it tumbled away until it was out of sight, heading for a watery end in the Yellow River.

Dan was free of the industrial heartland of China and making progress westwards. There were thousands of miles still to cover and the reality that he could be captured at any second was a constant weight on his mind.

In contrast, and unbeknownst to Dan or all but a very small handful of people in China, the Zhou family was approaching Singapore and would touch down within the hour. A discreet convoy of cars was waiting airside to whisk the family away to a villa on the exclusive Nassim Road and into obscurity.

Before long, darkness was falling over Dan's train. He watched as they passed through remote station after remote station, lit only by dim fluorescent bulbs and largely abandoned, save for the occasional cleaner sweeping sand from the platforms and a few moths fluttering fruitlessly at the station lights. Hunger pains began to set in as Dan hadn't eaten since breakfast in the Muslim Quarter. He couldn't stomach another pot of instant noodles even though he suspected it was the only food on board. He lay on his bed and set his alarm for 04:00.

He had no intention of going as far as Dunhuang.

4

INTO THE DESERT

At 04:00 the alarm on his phone went off. It felt brutally early and his cabin was cold. Outside the sky was pitch black, hostile and uninviting. Dan couldn't make out a single thing in the darkness. The gentle rocking motion of the train and the sound of the tracks beneath were the only confirmation that they were actually moving. Before long the train began to slow and Dan left his cabin. The conductor always stood at the end of the carriage to his right, so Dan turned left and headed down the hallway away from her. As the train pulled into the station, a sign in English floated past the window. "Jia Yu Guan" it read. This was it.

The train ground to a halt and Dan opened the doors on the opposite side of the carriage to the platform. This side of the station was dark and deserted as Dan dropped his backpack down onto the tracks and clambered backwards down the ladder, jumping the last two feet onto the stone ballast between the rails. He quickly closed the door behind him, the latch conspicuously clicking back into place. He momentarily crouched close to the carriage to ensure no-one had heard him. The air was freezing and he could hardly see where he was going as he picked up his bag, skipped quickly across the adjacent tracks and climbed on to the opposing platform. A clock hanging in the empty waiting room read 04:38. There was only a low railing between the platform and the road outside so Dan climbed over it and, leaving the station behind, began walking towards the town he could see ahead of him. Behind him the train began to pull out of the station and he turned to watch it leave, wondering what fallout there would be in Dunhuang when the conductor would knock on his cabin door only to find he wasn't there.

Dan had no idea where he was going or what he was going to do for the next few hours. He hadn't even really thought through the next part of his plan. The only thing he knew was that he wanted the authorities to know that he wasn't in Dunhuang, if they even thought he was heading in that direction.

He needed to rest and he needed to eat, so the priority was to find a cheap hotel where he could catch up on sleep and get breakfast later that morning. The sun was just starting to rise and the sky was turning from black to dark blue. He yawned a deep yawn, inhaling the cold desert air.

As he approached the town he found a hotel on the left-hand side of the road – the Huatian Hotel. It was a large white building with dark floor-to-ceiling windows. As he pushed open the door and walked into the lobby, a woman emerged from a side room, half asleep with a blanket wrapped around her shoulders. His arrival had clearly woken her, but she stopped as soon as she saw he was neither someone she knew nor Chinese. Dan kept walking towards the front desk. The woman stood still and started talking to him in Mandarin, puzzled by the early-morning visitor. He gestured that he needed to sleep and for one night only. She continued talking at him, starting to look annoyed by the interruption. He continued gesturing "one night".

Eventually and with an audible sigh the woman sat down at the front desk. She turned the monitor of the computer on and waited for it to light up. Picking up a pair of reading glasses, she shuffled them around with her cheeks, her contorted face reflective of her mood. Eventually the computer woke up and she turned to Dan, her head cocked to one side in annoyance, and muttered what sounded like numbers. Dan shrugged his shoulders; all he wanted was one bed for the night.

The woman picked up her calculator, pushed numbers into it with her chubby pink fingers and held it up. Three hundred and fifty-six yuan. Dan shrugged his shoulders again and nodded in agreement. Taking out his rapidly depleting wad of cash, he paid for the night. It was early in the day and he assumed he had paid for the following night as well as the rest of this morning, but he wasn't going to be able to ask. The woman took the room key off a hook on the wall behind her and pointed to the stairs. His room was number 223. She hadn't asked for his passport. Dan offered an uncertain "*xie xie*", which was met with a meagre smile, before he picked up his dusty backpack. The woman turned the monitor off and walked back to her room at the side of the lobby, the blanket still wrapped around her shoulders. Outside, the sky was now a dark blue and only a few delivery lorries roamed the streets. It had just gone quarter past five in the morning as he climbed the stairs of the hotel to his room, opened the door and flicked on the light.

Inside, the room was like every other cheap hotel he had stayed in; small, with cheap tan-coloured wooden furniture. The walls were papered an off-white colour, dirtied by the scuffmarks of the hundreds of suitcases to have collided with them over the years. The small sofa that ran along the wall near the bed was beige and unforgivingly hard. The headboard and lampshades were the same colour as the sofa. On one wall hung a faded A4-size print of Van Gogh's *Sunflowers* in a cheap plastic frame. In the corner of the room on a dark wood table stood a large CRT television that was as deep as it was wide. Above it hung an air conditioning unit from out of which ran a large hose that disappeared through a hole in the wall next to the window. The white plastic from the unit had turned yellow with age, and the room smelled of tobacco. There was a large dark ring on the ceiling around the light – the grime of ten thousand cigarettes smoked beneath it. On the bedside table stood a glass ashtray, dirtied by the ten thousand cigarettes stubbed out on it. But at least the room was dark, and it was significantly warmer than frigid desert air outside. Dan was tired from a poor night's sleep on the train, broken at four o'clock that morning. He kept his clothes on as a climbed under the sheets of the bed and curled into the foetal position to catch a few more hours' sleep. He turned the light off and was out within seconds.

It was noisy outside the hotel when he woke up several hours later. He could hear traffic in the street beyond the window and the sound of rooms being cleaned further down the corridor. Yawning and aching, Dan craned his neck towards the clock on the bedside table. As he watched, it flashed from 13:14 to 13:15. His body clock was all over the place – a combination of jet lag, exhaustion and the broken night on the train earlier that day. He rolled onto his back and stared at the smoke-stained ceiling. His stomach was painfully empty and he needed to eat. He lay there half considering his situation, half slipping back into sleep. His head was heavy with anxiety as he was yet to work out where he was going to go from here. It all seemed too much to think about in that moment and his stomach was talking louder than his head.

With a guttural groan he hauled himself to his feet. He felt disgusting: tired, hungry and unwashed. Rubbing his eyes, which bore the strain of his erratic and opportunistic sleep patterns over the last few days, he undressed and showered, washing the aches from his muscles in the warm water. Although the bathroom was grubby, with dirty grouting, cracked tiles and black mildew around the showerhead, the shower itself was pleasantly revitalising. Dan sat on the side of the bed, the rough white hotel towel wrapped around his waist. As he did, he shook his head slowly as he ran through the events of the last couple of days. The whole situation still felt unreal.

Before long he got dressed, picked up his key and left the room to make his way down the stairs to the lobby. A blast of cool air rushed in through the main door that stood propped open to the street outside. He pulled his hat low over his head again and wrapped a thin grey and white *shemagh* around his neck. Behind the front desk now stood a man and woman, much younger than the miserable old woman who had checked him in. They wore pale pink uniforms that matched the fake marble tiling on the lobby floor and nodded politely as he walked past them towards the front door. In the far corner of the lobby a young woman wearing a New York Yankees baseball cap sat on a wooden bench and read what looked like a map. She didn't look up as Dan crossed the lobby, her shoulder-length blonde hair forming almost perfect curtains around her face.

Outside the hotel the air was cold and the sand-strewn wind bit at his face, but the sky was clear and brilliant blue. Dan scanned the street for signs of trouble. With his hands in his pockets and his head covered as best he could manage, he walked in search of food, sticking close the walls wherever possible. The road outside the hotel was busy and he felt exposed, so he headed down a side street into a series of backstreets of small shops and run-down houses. Old women squatted on their haunches washing vegetables in buckets in the street. There was stagnant grey water in the gullies at the side of the road and dogs chased each other, oblivious to the motorbikes and cars that picked their way through the narrow alleyways. Few people even looked at Dan as he walked past. He was either inconspicuous or they just didn't care. He hoped it was the former.

Eventually Dan found a small convenience store that seemed to sell everything from chocolate bars to plastic coat hangers. Inside, a boy of around three played with toy cars on the white-tiled floor while a woman who Dan guessed to be the boy's mother arranged saucepans into crooked stacks on the shelves. Dan picked up a large packet of crisps, a bottle of 7up and a bag of doughnut-like bread rolls. It wasn't particularly nutritious but it would fill him up until later when he could venture out under the cover of darkness and find something proper to eat. Right now he just needed food in his stomach.

Dan paid for the food and left the shop. In case anyone had followed him, he tried to find a different route back to the hotel and wandered deeper into the side streets before eventually resurfacing at a main road. He felt vulnerable again as he tried to work out where he was and where the sanctuary of his hotel lay. It was diagonally opposite him, across the main road.

It was then that he saw it. His heart stopped and his throat ran dry in an instant. His stomach wretched as he saw his face filing a poster outside a small shop. The grainy image of him had obviously been cropped from the photo taken outside the Forbidden City – the only photo they had of him. The faces of the two girls on either side had been blurred so as to render them anonymous. Dan recoiled in horror. The poster was taken from a newspaper that sat in bundles on the pavement outside the shop. He recognised the characters for "Beijing" and "Xi'an" in the headlines, but he felt sick as the image of his face, blown up and printed in black and white, stared back at him. His eyes, which had been smiling at the time of the photo, now pierced his heart with an emotion that for the first time felt like guilt. How could he have done that? He heaved a weary sigh and turned his head away in disgust. He was innocent and this was a set-up. He needed to get out of China – a vast country that seemed to be getting smaller and smaller around him.

Dan walked briskly across the four lanes of the road, into the hotel lobby and straight up the stairs to his room. He closed and locked the door behind him and fell onto his bed. For the first time since this all started, he wept. He sobbed into the bed sheets, exhausted and scared. This was real. The news had made it to the far reaches of remote Gansu province, hundreds of miles from either Beijing or Xi'an. His resolve had carried him this far and his wit and courage hadn't failed him. But now, as images of his face on both the newspaper and the television burned themselves into his mind, he felt like giving up. This was all too much for one person to handle.

Dan decided that he needed to find out what was going on, why his face was in the paper and what the references to Beijing and Xi'an were. It didn't take long to find out. He found a Chinese news channel that showed images of rioting in both cities. In Beijing a car had been overturned and set on fire outside the British embassy. Rioters were throwing stones over the walls and a number of windows had been smashed. Police were arresting people and forming barricades across the street. Dan flicked through the channels until he found an English translation and watched transfixed as the story unfurled in front of him. The riots were taking place in the two cities where it was apparent that the police had let him slip through their fingers. The people were demanding justice. This was turning into a nationwide witch-hunt and he was becoming the object of intense hatred. This was serious and scary. In Xi'an, the unrest was centred on the station, where the piazza was crowded with people chanting and burning Union Jack flags. These were angry, angry people. Was this the notorious "*renrou sousuo*" – the "human flesh search engine" – the online vigilantism responsible for ousting criminals and exposing corrupt officials? If so and if they caught him, he would be torn to shreds like a fox in the teeth of rabid dogs. Dan inhaled the tasteless bread buns he had bought and soothed the burning dryness in his throat with the 7up as he sat in stunned silence and watched the news.

After about twenty minutes he'd seen enough but as he got up to turn the television off the picture shifted to Guilin. A massive army of police was shown scouring the streets, some carrying batons, others clearly armed with guns. They were seen pouring into the Sheraton Hotel and crawling all over the modern white concourse of Guilin train station. The effort to find him was ramping up, but it appeared they believed he was heading south towards Hong Kong. Dan drew encouragement that perhaps the heat was off him for the time being, although he realised that before long all border crossings would be subject to intense scrutiny. Time was running out and he had to make progress.

Dan turned the television off and crashed out on his bed, his head spinning. Tonight, he would eat a good meal, get a good night's sleep and tomorrow he would continue his run towards the westernmost reaches of China with added urgency; a billion people were now looking for him.

He didn't know it then, but he had already met one of those people earlier in the day and her motivations were quite different.

5

LISA

Without realising it he had fallen asleep again and by the time he woke up it was dark outside. The clock read 20:24. He stood up, straightened himself out in the small mirror in the bathroom and grabbed his hat, scarf and jacket. His renewed determination required a good meal to get him back on track. Outside, the temperature had dropped significantly and between the streetlights Dan could see stars in the clear night's sky. The desert was cold again.

Dan clung to the shadows as he made his way down the street in the opposite direction to the one he had taken earlier. As he passed one small alleyway he noticed light spilling into the narrow lane and could hear the distinctive hustle and bustle of food being served. Smoke and steam spilled from a grilled window and the clattering of pots and pans from inside made his stomach rumble in anticipation. Outside the front door two people stood smoking cigarettes in the yellow glow of an exposed light bulb. Dan watched cautiously from the main road before deciding they posed little threat. As he approached, a young woman with shoulder-length blonde hair stopped smoking and turned to at him.

"Hey. You're the guy from the hotel, right?" she said in a thick American accent. "You looking for somewhere to eat?"

Startled and scared that he had been recognised, Dan replied, "Yes. This place any good?" being careful not to confirm where he was staying.

"Sure," she replied. "It's one of the most popular in Jiayuguan. If the locals rate it, I'll take it! Mind if I join you? I could do with some English-speaking company, and I don't see you with anyone else."

Resisting the temptation to run, Dan was instantly wary. This woman had no idea who he was and had no obvious reason to be this friendly. She hadn't even known that he spoke English. Was this a trap? Dan shrugged his shoulders in reluctant acceptance. A westerner in China wouldn't pose a danger to another westerner, would they?

"Sure," he said hesitantly.

The woman stubbed her cigarette out on the wall of the restaurant and slipped the crumpled butt back into the packet. She muttered something to the man who stood with her. He nodded and continued smoking.

"Come on," she said to Dan as she made her way into the restaurant.

Dan followed behind her, glancing over his shoulder to make sure he wasn't being watched. The man turned away as Dan walked past him into the restaurant. What had she said to him, Dan wondered. He hoped to God she hadn't just told him to phone the police.

Inside, the restaurant was far bigger than the facia had suggested. The room stretched back for most of the depth of the block and accommodated well over a hundred people. The clientele was distinctly Uighur and the food smelled incredible. The restaurant was grubby, with sticky plastic tablecloths and rickety wooden furniture. The air was thick with a heady combination of cigarette smoke and cooking smells. In one corner of the open kitchen stood a huge shashlik barbecue from which rose billowing clouds of smoke that disappeared up a vast extractor hood, stained a sticky dark brown from the years of use it had endured.

Dan and his unexpected dining companion found a table on the far side of the restaurant and sat down. This woman seemed at home here and, despite his caution, Dan was starting to find her quite captivating. Her sun-bleached hair gave way to darker roots and she wore only minimal make-up: a little mascara and a touch of eye shadow. Her eyebrows were so pale as to be almost invisible in the semi-light of the restaurant. She had a broad and attractive smile that gave rise to a small dimple on the right-hand side of her face as he looked at her. Dan guessed her to be around twenty-four or twenty-five. Her self-confidence was obvious, but she was in control and Dan admired that, particularly given how far from control he felt. She nodded to a few people she recognised and they returned the gesture.

"This is a nice place," she said. "They do great food."

She waved her hand, signalling to a young waiter who was dashing between tables carrying trays of food to the diners around them. She called something out in Mandarin and the young man hurried over with two menus, setting them down on their table. He returned a moment or two later with a small teapot of steaming hot water and two round handleless cups. The faint smell of tea rose from the pot, masked by the aromas of grilling meat.

The woman studied the menu while Dan sat bemused. Bemused that she hadn't introduced herself yet or asked him who he was. Bemused by the menu. Bemused by the frenetic restaurant. He stared blankly at the menu, which he held propped up on the table in front of him.

"Can you not read the menu?" she asked with a teasing tone in her voice. He said nothing but he couldn't hide his body language.

"How would you have ordered if I hadn't come to your rescue? They don't speak English in here!" she continued.

It was a good question and Dan could do nothing but shrug his shoulders and start to gesticulate with his hands. He felt like a child being scolded by a teacher or bullied by an older sibling. He had no answer so gave up trying to respond.

"Shall I order for us?" she said sympathetically, sparing him the agony of coming up with a response to the first question. "I'll just choose a few things and we can share them."

"That's fine. I'm happy to take your suggestions," Dan replied gratefully.

The woman waved the young waiter over again, reeled off a list of about ten items, took Dan's menu off him and passed them both back to the waiter. She then clasped her teacup with both hands and inhaled the steam, sighing with satisfaction.

"So, I'm Lisa," she said at last, thrusting a hand forward to shake Dan's. "I'm a tour guide here in China. At the moment I'm leading a group of American oil executives who've just been at a conference in Urumqi. We got here from Dunhuang yesterday and they're flying back to Urumqi tomorrow morning. I've lived here for three years taking groups to all corners of China. It's a pretty cool job, but it ain't forever. We're driving back to Urumqi via Dunhuang tomorrow then I'm off for a few days before the next group gets here. That was my driver, Feng, you saw outside. So, what's with you? What the hell are you doing in Jiayuguan by yourself?"

Dan's mind was working overtime as he tried to concoct a watertight story.

"I'm Sam," he lied. "I'm just backpacking along the Silk Route. I've always wanted to see the Gobi, so here I am. I'm hoping to leave for Dunhuang sometime soon too," he continued, realising that once he'd sussed Lisa out there might be an opportunity developing.

"That's cool. Not many people backpack out here," she replied.

The food arrived in the form of several small white plates, piled high with skewered meat, rice and vegetables. Another man followed, carrying two glasses of ice-cold beer.

"No need for manners here. Dive in," Lisa said as she picked up a lamb skewer and began to tear into it.

Dan was starting to relax. Lisa didn't appear to know who he was and she hadn't yet mentioned the news. She seemed trustworthy and he assumed she posed very little threat. But he had to remain cautious. He had to keep his guard up.

"How come you're not flying back to Urumqi as well?" he

asked, pulling a large chunk of the succulent barbecued lamb off the metal skewer with his teeth.

"Money, I guess," she replied without looking up from her food. "Guess that as the car was going back anyway there was no need to buy me a plane ticket. They'll be met at the other end, so they'll be fine. I just have to get them onto the plane." She paused momentarily and then carried on eating.

"Hey. When did you say you're going to Dunhuang?" she asked at last.

"Ah, I don't know. Tomorrow, maybe. Maybe the day after. I just need to work out how best to get there, really," Dan replied nonchalantly, avoiding eye contact.

"You wanna ride with us? We're leaving early tomorrow morning. There's plenty of room in the van. Will save you a few bucks on the train. I'll just speak to Feng, but he'll be fine."

"Wow, you sure? That would be amazing," Dan replied, stifling a smirk of satisfaction. "Perhaps you could teach me a thing or two about this part of the world," he continued, trying to steer the conversation away from the free ride.

"Ha! Yeah, maybe. There are only a few watchtowers between here and Dunhuang, but they're pretty cool. You'll see the end of the Great Wall as well as it peters out into the Gobi. That's pretty cool as well. You seen the fort here yet?"

Dan had no desire to visit the town's biggest tourist attraction so was careful to avoid being taken; those places were always crawling with police at the best of times so he lied that he had, with only the paragraph he had read in his guide book from which to construct his story. He'd seen a photo of it once too, so was vaguely familiar with Jiayuguan Fort.

"Yeah, I was there this morning. It's pretty impressive, but it feels a little reconstructed to me. It's a little too perfect in places," he blagged.

"Yeah, but there are some more authentic parts to it," Lisa replied. "But I know what you mean. The views of the Wall from there are cool, though, aren't they? I love the clear skies we get out here in the desert. It's not like Urumqi, where it's grey and smoggy most of the time. Funny, we were at the fort this morning too, but we didn't see you. I guess you were either just ahead of us or somewhere behind us."

"You live in Urumqi?" Dan asked, changing the subject and sensing that, with a bit of luck, this new acquaintance might get him further than Dunhuang. "You're American, right? Three years, huh?"

"Yeah – three years now. Yeah, my folks live in the States. My dad is American and my mom spent a lot of time in Guangzhou, near Hong Kong. I grew up speaking Cantonese and Mandarin, came to Beijing University for a year. I wrote my thesis on the Uighur people of Xinjiang. Now I'm here trying to learn the language. It's not going too well, to be honest with you. Too much time working, leading these business groups around the desert, not enough time studying."

"What time are you leaving in the morning?" Dan enquired, trying to guarantee the ride. "I'll take you up on the offer."

"We're leaving at eight o'clock tomorrow morning. We're taking the group out to the airport and then heading straight off to Dunhuang. See you in the lobby then." She looked at her watch. "You had enough? You ready to go? I gotta write up today's trip report when I get back to my room."

Dan agreed. Lisa called the waiter over and asked him for the bill. When it arrived, they split the total, paid and left. Outside, it was cold and dark, and the only light came from a few yellow streetlights that lit the pavement in circular pools. The air was so cold that Dan's breath billowed out in clouds in front of him as they walked. After a few minutes' brisk walk with his head hung low, they arrived back at the hotel. Dan reconfirmed the time with Lisa for the following morning and headed back to his room. The next phase of his plan was in place and he was pretty sure he could now get at least as far as Urumqi. From there he would just have to get to Kashgar and then over the border into Kyrgyzstan. His confidence was buoyed by having met Lisa; he had a savvy Chinese-speaker on his side. An ally outnumbered a billion times over but one that could be the difference between his freedom and a life behind bars, the fear of which had fuelled his flight since day one.

He slept well that evening, his belly full of barbecued meat. The alarm went off at 07:00 and he was in the shower a few seconds later knowing that today was going to be a productive day, travelling as close to incognito as he could imagine. No risking exposure on public transport, no train stations, bus stations or crowded areas. He could keep his head down and this time tomorrow he would be waking up four hundred kilometres closer to freedom. He was still full with the food from the evening before and thought it wise to avoid what was likely to be a busy breakfast room.

Dan packed his belongings, moving his last remaining clean clothes to the top of his backpack. He had no idea when he would get to do any laundry, but that was the least of his worries. At five to eight he pulled his black hat low over his head, closed the door to his room and headed downstairs.

As expected, the lobby was a hive of activity, unnerving at first, before he realised the safety the numbers presented. Lisa was sat on the bench in the corner, wearing a New York Yankees baseball cap. He realised then that she was the girl he had seen in the same place yesterday. Around her, the group of American oil executives had begun to gather. The men wore black or navy polo shirts and pale chinos, their wives pastel-coloured shirts and cream trousers.

Dan walked over to Lisa, who looked up as he approached, smiled and greeted him with a friendly "Good morning!". She got up as he arrived.

"Morning," Dan said. "Did you get your report written last night?"

"Yeah, wasn't too bad. Got it all done eventually. I was out like a light after that. That was good food, huh?"

Dan was just about to reply when Lisa began calling out to the group: "OK, folks. The bus is just outside and your bags have all be loaded on board. If you'd like to make your way outside, we can get this show on the road."

Dan saw the driver, Mr Feng, outside the front doors enjoying a cigarette as he chatted to a man who Dan assumed to be the hotel manager. As the group moved out of the lobby Mr Feng threw his cigarette to the ground and smothered it with the sole of his shoe, leaving a black smudge on the pavement. Turning his head, he blew the remaining smoke from his lungs and opened the door to the minibus. He was a ratty-looking man with tanned leathery skin and a thin moustache that stretched to either edge of his mouth. He had scruffy black hair that blew around in the desert breeze. Wearing a light blue shirt, untucked but with the sleeves rolled up to the elbow and black formal trousers with a crease down the front of each leg, he had clearly made an effort to look professional. Lisa was busy marking everyone off the list. There were fourteen people in total. Seven couples. As the last of the group climbed into the back of the minibus, Lisa did a final headcount. Everyone accounted for.

"Come on, you can ride up front with Feng and me. Saves having to explain who you are," she said as she opened the passenger door, climbing into the middle seat. Dan climbed in after her, putting his backpack between his feet in the foot well before slamming the door. They were off.

They headed east out of the city before turning north towards the airport, the boundary between the city and the desert almost unnoticeable. As the buildings disappeared the desert unfolded into undulating waves of sand and scrub. It wasn't particularly attractive, but the brilliant blue sky more than compensated for the relative ugliness of the desert around them. As they approached the airport Dan felt his heart begin racing and his palms begin to sweat. The security stop was manned by two young male soldiers, who spoke to Mr Feng as the van slowed to a halt. They peered into window, checking out the passengers who sat quietly in the back. After a moment or two of verbal exchange, the soldiers opened the gate and waved the tourists on their way. Dan's hands were still shaking as they pulled up to the departures entrance. Lisa pretended not to notice. This was the closest he had been to an airport since he'd arrived in Beijing a few crazy days earlier. As they stopped, Dan opened the door and got out to let Lisa out behind him.

Mr Feng began loading the bags and suitcases onto trolleys for their guests.

Lisa followed the group inside the terminal building as Mr Feng moved the van to a large bay in the car park nearby and got out for a cigarette. Dan slid low into the seat, rested his head on his hand and closed his eyes, pretending to sleep. Around thirty minutes later Lisa reappeared and called out to Mr Feng, who was talking to another minibus driver, still smoking. Lisa opened the door of the cab and spoke to Dan. "Why don't we sit in the back? There's more space to spread out. It's a good four-hour drive to Dunhuang from here."

"That makes sense," Dan replied and got into the back of the bus, throwing his backpack down at the front before climbing into a row of seats around halfway down. He sat with his back against the window, legs stretched out across the seats. Lisa sat on the row in front of him and removed her baseball cap as she settled in for the journey ahead. As Mr Feng got back in, he leaned over and spoke to Lisa in Mandarin. She agreed with him, and they set off once again.

Dan realised at that point that he still had no idea who he was really travelling with or whether they were trustworthy at all. He had let himself become too comfortable in Lisa's presence and he needed to raise his game again. He was no longer in control of the situation. Lisa was. His fate rested with this stranger and he began to feel nauseous as the gravity of his situation once again came flooding back.

Trying to distract himself from his thoughts, Dan took his guidebook out of his bag. From the left-hand window he watched as the Qilian Mountains began to fade behind them into the desert. Beyond lay the Qaidam Basin and the vast

Tibetan Plateau. The mountains he gazed at were the outermost ripples of the ancient collision between the Indian tectonic plate and the Eurasian plate, the coming together of two vast continents that gave rise to the highest mountains on earth. Everest itself was somewhere out of that window. His mind wandered over the Qilian range, across the Kunlun Mountains and into the wilds of the Himalayas. He felt small again.

Eventually, the Qilian Mountains disappeared and Dan and Lisa found themselves surrounded by sand and scrub once more; small wispy bushes here and there broke up the monotony of the dunes. The road was well maintained given the remoteness of their location, and progress was relatively quick. The sun rose higher overhead and Dan gazed at the vastness of his surroundings. Again, the pangs of sadness hit him, knowing that he would never get to return to this part of the world. It would be the first and last time he would set eyes upon these parts and each second that passed was to be remembered. These would be his only memories of the Chinese Silk Route, of the Gobi and of the Qilian Mountains. If he ever wanted to get close to this part of the world again he would have to be on the other side of the Himalayas, a world away and only "close" in the loosest sense of the word.

An hour or so passed as Dan lost himself in his geographical wanderings. Lisa had fallen asleep some time earlier, her head hanging low as she sat upright with her back against the window. Mr Feng was driving at a good speed, every kilometre a thousand metres closer to freedom. Dan hadn't done so to date but he now wondered what would have happened if he *had* just gone to Beijing Airport that night. If he hadn't run, but had caught a flight instead. Would he even have made it out or would he now be festering in custody somewhere? He realised then, at that very moment, he was actually free: free to be travelling between Jiayuguan and Dunhuang. Free to choose who to trust. To an extent it had been forced upon him but he breathed the desert air and gazed upon wild mountain ranges a free man. He clenched his jaw, renewing his resolve to escape.

Before long Mr Feng pulled the minibus into a roadside café and Lisa woke as they began to slow. She blinked her eyes in the brightness of the desert sun.

"Hey," she said as she came to. "Sorry, I'm tired."

"Hey, no worries whatsoever," Dan replied. "You've been asleep for a good hour or so. You haven't missed much."

Mr Feng stopped the van and they got out. It was midday and the sun was hot overhead. Dan felt the heat burning into his arms almost as soon as they left the vehicle. In front of them stood a dilapidated shack-like building made of rusting corrugated metal with broken garden furniture scattered about the dusty desert clearing. Two other men, both in black leather jackets and sunglasses were walking around smoking and kicking stones into the scrub that surrounded the car park.

Lisa, Mr Feng and Dan sat down at a table of three white plastic chairs, all of which were splintered in one way or another. After a few minutes Mr Feng disappeared into the building before emerging with two bottles of Tsingtao beer and an opener. He said something to Lisa and flipped the tops off the two beers, giving one each to Dan and Lisa. The caps spun in the dusty sand for a moment before coming to a stop.

"He's ordered some chicken and noodles for us," Lisa said. "I hope that's alright."

Mr Feng didn't wait for an answer and disappeared back inside again. He returned a few minutes later with a bottle of Coke, which he began to drink as he sat down. Taking out a cigarette, he lit up and sat back, staring at the clear blue sky above them. An elderly man with badly hunched shoulders soon appeared, carrying a tray with five bowls of steaming chicken and noodle soup. He gave two to the men in leather jackets and one to each of Lisa, Dan and Mr Feng. Trying to avoid looking at the twisted pile of chickens' feet that sat in a contorted heap in the centre of the bowl, Dan began to slurp the noodles. As he finished he saw Lisa wrestling a meagre piece of meat from one of the feet, tugging at it with her teeth while pulling it away with her chopsticks. It wasn't attractive.

Despite rapidly running out of cash, Dan paid for all three of them so as to maintain the air of normalcy. Back in the minibus, they continued their journey westwards. There were less than two hours to go before they would reach the desert city of Dunhuang. The road was straight and the scenery monotonous but every so often large stone towers appeared, crumbling back into the desert from where they once came.

"What *are* those?" Dan asked as they passed particularly close to one.

"Watchtowers," Lisa replied. "Most of them are from the Han dynasty – *hundreds* of years old. They're pretty cool, huh? Crazy to think that they were once manned. I mean, what the hell those people did with their time and how they survived out here in the desert, I have no clue."

"Yeah, that's nuts," Dan replied. "A different time entirely."

Buoyed by the start of a new conversation, Lisa changed the subject. She chose one that Dan had been dreading. One that made him squirm for answers as he tried to reply to her calmly.

"So, where you from in England, Sam? It *is* England, right? I mean, I'm just guessing from your accent."

"Yeah, it's England. Just a small town in the south of the country. You won't have heard of it. You ever been to England?" he replied, trying to skirt the question and change the subject at the same time.

"No, but I've been to Europe. I took a road-trip when I left college. I like it a lot, man. I travelled through France, Belgium, Germany, Italy and Switzerland by myself. I bought a cheap car from some guy at a hostel outside Paris and drove it around Europe for two months. I guess I was born to travel. I get bored pretty quick. That was a good trip. So what do you do, back in England?"

"I was made redundant a few weeks ago," Dan lied. "I'm travelling on the money I got from that. I'd always wanted to come to western China. I read a book about it a few years ago and it caught my imagination. So here I am. I'll look for a new job when he get back, but I have money to tide me over for a while, so I'm enjoying the freedom!"

"Damn, sorry to hear you lost your job," Lisa replied. "But I guess the silver lining is that you are here now, doing exactly what you want to do, seeing the world."

Dan let the conversation go quiet and stared out of the window. This was far from where he wanted to be. He wanted to be exploring Guilin and the small town of Yangshuo on the banks of the Li River, before heading over to Yunnan province. That is what he really wanted to be doing. Instead, he found himself running for his life through the inhospitable sands of the Gobi desert. He was living a lie. At that very moment, he was deceiving two people who were helping him. Helping him slip through the fingers of the law of the land they lived in. As far as Dan knew, they were unwittingly aiding a wanted criminal. They were his mules and he believed they were entirely ignorant of the fact they were being played. This thought made him both queasy with guilt but equally satisfied with his ability to survive the impossible adversity he found himself in.

It was almost two o'clock in the afternoon when they pulled into Dunhuang, which for the most part was like every other Chinese town he had seen so far; colourless, square buildings, dusty bushes full of litter, dogs running in the streets and trucks and tractors spewing fumes into the desert air. Windblown sand collected in the kerbs along roadsides and against buildings, giving everything in the town a yellowy tinge. Previously names for Dunhuang had included "City of Sands" and he could see why immediately.

Donkey-drawn carts laden with goods made their way along the main street, as coachloads of tourists headed out to the famous Buddhist caves at Mogao, a short journey from here into the desert. Eventually Dan's driver pulled into the driveway of a large hotel.

"This is the Silk Road Hotel. It's the best hotel in town, so I hope it'll do for you!" Lisa joked.

It looked good but the thought of walking into such grandiose surroundings as a wanted man filled him with fear once again.

"Have you already booked this place?" Dan asked. "I would be happy to stay somewhere much more low key. I hope you're not just here because of me!" he continued.

"Ha! Of course not. My company always books this place for us. It's the best on the entire Silk Route, in my mind, and we get a really good rate. Feng knows the manager too. I'll have to book you a room but I'm sure it won't be a problem."

It dawned on him at that point that if he had to produce a passport to register at the hotel his game would probably be up. He hadn't thought about this at all. What scene would develop as they realised the name on the passport matched the name on the wanted posters that were surely being circulated? He'd made it to Dunhuang. He was almost exactly halfway between Beijing and Kashgar and this would be as far as he would get. Half way.

His palms started to sweat as Mr Feng drew the car to a stop outside the front door. Dan wiped them nervously on his jeans as Lisa slid the door open and got out.

"Wait here," she said. "I'll go and make sure they've got a room first."

She left the door open, letting the warm Gobi air fill the minibus. Dan could feel the heat bouncing off the road, rapidly raising the temperature inside the van. He reached forward and closed the door. Mr Feng got out and lit a cigarette.

Lisa was inside the hotel for around five minutes before she reappeared and called out them. Mr Feng opened his door and said, "OK." Dan realised it was the first word his driver had spoken to him. He got out and walked into the hotel, his backpack hanging over one shoulder.

"How many nights do you want?" she asked.

He remembered then that Lisa thought he was here on holiday! She thought he'd want to explore Dunhuang, see the caves at Mogao, ride a camel on the Singing Sand Dunes, perhaps head out to the rock formations at Yadan. Do what everyone else visiting Dunhuang did. She had no idea, because they hadn't even discussed it, that he intended to join her all the way to Urumqi tomorrow. It made no sense to pass straight through Dunhuang – it was one of the most famous places on the Chinese Silk Route. It would have been one of the highlights of the book he told her he'd read when he was younger. His mind was racing as he struggled to think.

"Err, three for now, I... I guess," he stammered.

Lisa then asked the question he had been dreading: "Have you got your passport? They'll need it to check you in."

"It's in my bag somewhere. Probably right at the bottom, where I keep it for safety when I'm travelling on the trains. Can I bring it down later?" he asked optimistically.

Lisa turned and spoke to the man and woman behind the front desk. She appeared to know them well. They smiled and she turned back to him.

"That's fine. You can bring it down any time before you check out," she said to his relief. "They just need your name then."

"Sam. Sam Cook," Dan replied without hesitation. None of it was true of course. His passport was in his pocket and he'd made the name up as he'd walked through the front door moments earlier. Lisa checked him in for three nights.

"You can pay when you check out too. I got you a special price, so it's a good deal. They'll put the bill under your door later." She thanked her two friends and picked up their room keys. Lisa knew where she was going and led the way. Climbing the stairs to the first floor, they found Lisa's room. She gave Dan his key and pointed down the corridor.

"Yours is about four doors down on the left," she said. "I'm going to crash out for a bit. If you want to go out you can get to the sand dunes in about thirty minutes. Just go out the front door and head round the back of the hotel. You'll see them right ahead of you."

"Cool, thanks. I might take a wander," Dan said, with every intention of staying well out of sight in his room; he had things to think about.

Inside, the room was spacious and sparsely furnished, with wooden framed beds that were covered with colourful woollen blankets. At the far end of the room was a window that was open and from it he had an uninterrupted view of the famous Singing Sand Dunes. They were truly massive and filled the horizon left to right. Dan dropped his bag on the first of the two single beds and took a closer look. Apart from the courtyard of the hotel in front of him, Dan could see nothing from the window but the vast sand mountains of the Kumtag desert. Crisp ridges snaked their way down the otherwise perfect faces of the dunes like the curving spines of dragons. The sky around them was hazy, quite unlike the blue skies they'd had on the drive here from Jiayuguan. Dan desperately wanted to get out and see the dunes but knew that doing so could be suicide.

He lay on the bed nearest the window and gazed at the ceiling. His throat was dry with sadness. He no longer wanted to be in China but longed to be back in the safety of home where things made sense, where he wasn't the subject of a manhunt, where people were not baying for his blood. Dan thought about the girls who had set him up and wondered whether they were able to stick by their story, despite the scenes in Xi'an and Beijing. He wondered why on earth they had made those claims against him in the first place and whether they regretted any of what they had started. He wondered whether they had actually already retracted their stories. Was there any chance that this was all over? These thoughts plagued him but Dan couldn't face watching the news again.

As he lay there, he tried to work out where the authorities most likely thought he was. If they had worked out that he was on the train to Dunhuang two days ago, then they may well be looking for him here. If they had realised that he had jumped off the train somewhere else, then they would be looking for him back down the track. If they were unaware that he was ever on that train, then he really could be anywhere in China. He'd seen the footage of the police raiding the Sheraton in Guilin so as far as he knew that is the last place they thought he had been. His whereabouts was beginning to confuse even him.

His head spinning again, he drifted to sleep.

But it wouldn't last long.

6

EXPOSED

The banging on the door woke Dan with a start. It was still light outside and he was groggy from the broken sleep. He stared at the door and did nothing. The banging came again.

"Sam! It's Lisa. We fucking need to talk. I know you're in there. They told me at the front desk you hadn't gone out. Open the fucking door."

Shit.

She knew.

Dan got up and opened the door carefully, making sure she was alone. Lisa pushed the door open in his face and barged past him into the room. Heading straight to the bed Dan had been sleeping on, Lisa sat down and faced him. Her face was pale and her whole body was shaking.

"What the fuck? What the fuck is going on? And who the fuck are you really?"

Her tone was more of panic than of anger, underpinned by

an unmistakable element of distress. Dan tried to pretend he had no idea what she was talking about, as he closed the door behind him.

"Huh?" he said pathetically. "What do you mean? What have I done? What's going on?"

"You fucking know what's going on. Your name's not even Sam, is it? You're the guy on the TV. The guy the whole fucking country is looking for. You're the guy they say attacked two girls in Beijing last week. I've seen everything. I'm such a fucking idiot, picking up a hitchhiker in the middle of fucking nowhere. No wonder you didn't want to get your passport out. You wanna tell me what's going on? I should fucking call the police. You know that?"

Dan's throat ran dry as he struggled to work out where to start. He swallowed hard.

"I didn't do it. You *must* know that. It's a complete set-up. I think there's a professional gang, a criminal gang behind all this. That photo on the news was taken outside the Forbidden City in Beijing. I don't even know who those girls are. They just came up to me, took the photo and boom! I find myself running for my life."

"Why the hell did you run?" Lisa replied, her tone softening slightly. "You know you totally incriminated yourself by running?"

"I couldn't risk it. I just couldn't. I ran everything over and over in my mind but made the decision that it was too dangerous to let myself get arrested here. I don't speak a word of the language; I have no idea how anything works. So I ran. They were all over me in a matter of minutes. I saw the police cars turn up at the hotel as I ran from them. The whole thing is a trap. I've been framed and I'm fucking scared," Dan continued desperately.

Lisa's head slumped. She understood, but realised the gravity of the situation she found herself in. She'd assisted the most wanted man in the country and was an integral part of the maelstrom. There were now serious consequences for her too. She was quiet as Dan fidgeted uncomfortably like a boy in trouble, waiting for the next torrent of abuse from his berating father. Eventually Lisa spoke up. Her voice sounded sympathetic.

"What's your plan? Where are you going? How the hell are you going to get out of this place? You know pretty much the whole country is looking for you, right?"

Dan sat down on the second bed, staring straight into Lisa's eyes so the sincerity of what he was about to say was not lost.

"I need to get to Kashgar. I figure that the further from Beijing I can get, the better my chances of getting away. I'm going over the border into Kyrgyzstan. Once I get out, I can prove my innocence. I just can't do that whilst I'm stuck in China. This place is fucked up. I've read too many horror stories about the hopelessness of Chinese prisons and the way they treat prisoners over here to even consider turning myself in."

Lisa was silent as she computed what he'd just said. She shook her head as she realised the sense in what he was saying. She realised the route he'd taken made sense. She understood what he was trying to achieve but at the same time made sure Dan believed she was struggling with the morality of the situation. He decided to continue talking. "Can you help me get to Kashgar? I need you to help me get there somehow.

You're my only friend in this whole fucked-up situation. I can't believe it's real. But it is. This is my freedom, my life we're talking about here. Everything I am is at stake."

Dan stopped short of saying he couldn't do it without her or that he needed her now. But he sure as hell felt it. He'd been able to rely on her; for over a day he'd relied on her to order food for him, to drive him from Jiayuguan to Dunhuang, to check him into this hotel without having to produce his passport. He had been prepared to get himself out of this and he could probably continue alone, but having Lisa brought obvious advantages. The thought of continuing without her was daunting and he was struggling to find the mental energy to do so.

Lisa sat in silence. She stared through him as he sat just a metre or so from her. Dan breathed in deeply through his nose, exhaling loudly through his mouth. His cover had finally been blown and he felt shattered. Questions began racing through his mind again, just as they had every other time he hadn't physically been running from something or someone. Lisa began shaking her head with slow, deliberate movements. Just as she intended, Dan could see that she was struggling to comprehend the predicament.

The way he saw it, as he looked over at her, she had three choices. She could turn him in and insist that she had had no idea who he was, that he had lied to her and used her to get what he wanted. She could let him go, let him fend for himself and pretend she had never met him. Or the third choice was to help him escape.

If she turned him in she'd have to live with the knowledge that she had subjected an innocent man to the hell of a Chinese prison, the almost certain lack of a fair trial and whatever punishment he would have to endure for a crime he believed she knew he hadn't committed. If she helped him escape she would be risking her own freedom, her own safety and exposing herself to as much trouble as he was in.

In his mind he willed her to turn her back on him, let him walk out of here and continue his run to the border as if the two of them had never met. This time yesterday, Lisa had been instrumental to his successful escape. She had been facilitating his flight through the heart of China. Now, his freedom hung precariously in the balance. He had no idea which way Lisa was going to tip.

The silence began banging in his ears. There was no clock in the room but Dan could hear the slow tick, tick, tick of time passing as Lisa grappled with her situation. He stared out of the window behind her, gazing longingly at the sand dunes that filled the skyline. He longed to be climbing them like any other tourist passing through Dunhuang. He longed to be free to float aimlessly from one sand mountain to the next like the grains being carried on the wind. Instead he was trapped. He already felt like a prisoner.

Lisa slowly lifted her head from her hands. Her eyes were red and glossy from where they had been pressed into her palms. She looked straight into his eyes.

"I'll help you," she said defiantly. "I'll help you escape. I hate this fucking country. You're right – it's fucked up. I'm only here because I'm supposed to be studying, but I haven't studied a thing for almost two years. It's just fucking work, that's all. But," she continued "I can only get you as far as Urumqi. After that, you're on your own again."

Dan collapsed backwards on to the bed in disbelief. His arms fell stretched out above his head. What Lisa had just said left him speechless. He covered his face with his hands and exhaled loudly into them. He didn't move or say anything for a few minutes until eventually he slowly sat back up to face her. Lisa's eyes were teary. She was doing a good job.

"Thank you," he said.

It was possibly the most genuine and grateful "thank you" he had ever uttered in his life. He sighed deeply and his shoulders dropped with the intense relief that washed over his weary body. Lisa spoke again.

"We need to leave tonight. They're setting up roadblocks between here and Urumqi. They said so on the news earlier. That's when I realised who you are. They have no idea where you are. Truth be told, you've done well hiding yourself – they think you're en route to Hong Kong or Yunnan province. They know you were in Xi'an. They thought you went to Guilin, but they know now that was a wild goose chase. The head of Beijing police was fucking mad about that! He was on the news earlier – his face was bright red with rage!" Lisa laughed, choking back a few tears at the same time. She wiped her eyes with her sleeve.

"Ha!" Dan said with satisfaction.

"The border crossing with Hong Kong has been closed to all but Chinese passport holders. The main focus is now on Chengdu." Lisa continued. "Damn. Heading out this way was inspired. Whatever made you think of it?"

"What are these roadblocks? Where are they?" Dan asked, ignoring the question.

"There are two or three. I'm not sure where. They're looking for you, man. They're checking passports. That's why we need to travel by night."

"They're closed at night?" he asked, surprised at what seemed an obvious oversight.

"No, but things are easier. Even the most dedicated soldier is groggy in the middle of the night. Mr Feng will get us through – he knows everyone out here and they all know him. It'll help. If this goes wrong, I'm sorry, man."

"But if they're checking passports, how do I get through? It's pretty much guaranteed to fail, isn't it? I don't stand a chance."

Lisa paused for a moment. Dan could see her mind working overtime. She searched for ideas as he sat and waited, clueless as to how the next chapter was going to play out without him falling into the hands of those looking for him. It seemed the whole country was on lock-down. The noose was tightening around his neck, slowly suffocating his chances of escape. Dan felt increasingly desperate.

"I've got it," Lisa cried out, shattering his train of thought. She stood up and walked briskly over to the door. With her hand firmly on the door handle, she turned to look at him.

"One of the oil execs left a bag in the van. I have to return it to their hotel in Urumqi when we get there. I bet there's something in it we can use. His passport's not there – he used it to get on the flight – but there must be something. Wait here. Get your shit together; we need to leave soon. I'll tell Feng that we're leaving and to get provisions."

Lisa opened the door and left, leaving it to swing shut behind her. The latch clicked into place and Dan was alone again surrounded by the empty silence. His throat tightened with anxiety as he sat daunted by what lay ahead. Realising he was about to embark on the riskiest part of his journey so far, Dan sat for a few minutes and breathed deeply. He didn't fancy an encounter with the chief of Beijing police or anyone similar after Lisa's account of the trail of destruction he was leaving behind him. Several moments passed but just as he began to question his decision to run again there was a loud knock at the door that made his heart thump hard inside his chest.

"It's me. Open up."

Dan opened the door and Lisa threw a sports bag onto the bed. She ripped open the zip and pulled out a black polo shirt that lay crumpled on top of a messy pile of clothes inside the bag.

"Here, put this on," she instructed as she continued to rummage through the bag. As Dan changed into the polo shirt, Lisa passed him an ID badge that was written in both English and Chinese – "David Shapiro, Exco Oil".

Dan pinned the badge on and tried to rub some of the creases out of the polo shirt. He looked at his watch. It was five past six and it felt like the sun was a couple of hours from setting.

"We have to make it to Turpan before sunrise. It's gonna take us about ten hours straight. We'll be there early morning, which means we have to lie low until tomorrow night, when we set off again for Urumqi. Feng's been asleep this afternoon. He's good to go. You ready?"

"Yeah, let's get outta here," Dan replied with false confidence. "Does Mr Feng know who I am?" he asked cautiously gathering the T-shirt he had been wearing.

"Sort of," Lisa replied without looking at him. "I had to explain the sudden change in plan. I told him a drug gang in Xi'an had been tailing you, trying to set you up to cash in on reward money they're offering in Shaanxi at the moment. He's not happy, but he'll do it. You might want to think about paying him when we get to Urumqi."

It was something Dan hadn't thought about for a while. He was desperately short of money of his own.

"I need some cash, Lisa," he said. "Is there any where I can get some money without having to use my card? I don't want them to trace it. I have a few hundred yuan left."

"OK. I'll get you some money. I'll use my own card. How much do you want – a couple of thousand? Will that do you?"

"You don't have to do that," Dan said. "How can I get the money back to you?"

"We'll talk about that later," Lisa said confidently. She seemed keen to leave. "I've paid the hotel for three nights for you so they think you're still here. There's a worker's entrance to the side of the hotel that I've used before. Feng is waiting there for us. We need to leave now."

"Damn. Thanks," Dan replied, humbled by Lisa's grasp of the situation. He hadn't given much thought to paying for the hotel.

Lisa turned and clutched the door handle as Dan swung his backpack over his shoulder. She paused and looked him in the eye briefly.

"Good luck," she said with a gentle nod as she inhaled deeply.

With that, Lisa pulled the door open and checked the corridor. She looked both ways, whispered a decisive "come on" to Dan and headed towards the stairs. He followed closely behind her, leaving the door to close behind him. As they reached the end of the corridor, the door closed with a quiet "clunk" that was loud enough to make him jump. His heart was pounding and his palms were sweaty once more as he clutched his backpack tightly again.

At the bottom of the stairs, Lisa swerved to the right and headed into a darkened passageway with scuffed walls and only dim emergency lighting for illumination. Ahead, Dan could hear the sounds of a large washing machine and the clattering of pots and pans. The air was thick with a giddying mix of cooking smells and fabric softener. They passed a small room where a young woman in a white lab coat was folding towels and sheets before putting them on great racks piled high with identical white laundry. She glanced up as Lisa and Dan sped past her, confused as to what two foreigners were doing in this part of the hotel.

In front of them Dan could see a door with a frosted glass window through which shone the bright white sunlight of the outside. Lisa pushed the door open and a blaze of light streamed into the dingy hallway. Dan squinted and held his arm in front of his face to protect his eyes from the intense glare of the desert sun. Immediately outside stood Mr Feng beside his minivan. He was wearing sunglasses and smoking a cigarette. He took one last deep draw and flicked the butt into the dust. Lisa opened the side door and climbed in, her bag already on one of the back seats. Dan threw his onto the floor by the front row and climbed in, closing the door behind him.

Mr Feng wasted no time and they sped off, kicking sand up off the road that left a cloud of dust hanging in the air in their wake. Speeding through the streets of Dunhuang, Dan felt as conspicuous as he had done walking across the piazza in Xi'an a few days earlier, diving into the taxi at the last minute as the police fanned out behind him. He felt certain they would be pulled over any minute for Mr Feng's reckless driving alone. He didn't blame him, of course – he'd be in serious trouble too if they got caught. Lisa also appeared to be on edge.

They made their way through the streets of Dunhuang, passing a small but bustling local market and white-tiled building after white-tiled building. In every corner, sand lay piled, clinging to every surface while more blew in on the wind. It whipped at people as they tried to make their way down the streets, forcing them to cover their faces from the biting wind. A police car approached from behind and overtook their minivan as Dan slunk deeper into his seat and hid his face.

After a while, Lisa started talking. "We'll get you there, you know that?" she said.

The sudden sound of her voice made Dan jump and he turned to her.

"What do you mean?" he replied.

"Out. You're going to get out. You're going to make it across the border."

Her sentiment caught him off guard and he was lost for words. He smiled an almost sympathetic smile. Sympathetic perhaps that she really believed he could do this. Sympathetic that she believed he would actually be able to walk across the border into Kyrgyzstan in a few days' time. He almost felt sorry for her naivety. But it was a shared naivety. They both believed it. If they didn't they wouldn't be here. And that meant Mr Feng believed it too. Dan felt a strange sense of power – power that he had been able to convince two people to do this for him, to drive him to freedom in the face of utmost adversity. He felt like he was winning this war, one battle at a time. Little did he know, of course.

Then, without warning, Mr Feng slammed on the brakes and Dan hit the back of the seat in front of him. Lisa's face slammed into the back of his seat. The van skidded and came to a halt in the middle of the road. After a moment or two, Mr Feng got out of the car while Lisa and Dan winced from the injuries they'd just received. A stabbing pain ran the length of Dan's neck as he cushioned it with his palm, his face contorted and teeth clenched. His neck was so stiff he had to turn his entire body round to see Lisa behind him. She was slumped up against the window, having fallen across two seats. Her mouth hung open and her teeth were stained red with blood flowing from her upper gums. The right side of her face was grazed red from the impact with the plastic covering on the seat she'd hit. Her eyes rolled in their sockets as she tried to understand what had just happened.

"You OK?" Dan asked groggily.

Lisa groaned in response and slowly began to sit up. Her neck was stiff and she winced as she hauled herself upright. She touched her mouth immediately turning her fingers red with blood. Realising the state she was in, she grimaced again.

"Wait here," she mumbled as she shuffled to the end of the seat and climbed forward to the front of the van. She slid the door open and clambered out, holding her neck as she went. Dan slowly pushed his way forward towards the door, taking care not to move his neck too much. He stumbled out and made his way to the front of the minivan, where Lisa and Mr

Feng were standing. Feng had lit a cigarette and was inspecting the van for damage.

They'd hit a dog that now lay in a crumpled heap in the road behind them. While Lisa and Mr Feng discussed what had happened, Dan walked over to the buckled corpse of the animal. It was bloodied and clearly dead, its head skewed backwards looking along its own spine as it lay flat on the road. One of its rear legs was obviously broken splayed perpendicular to the rest of its body. The scrawny, malnourished dog was some sort of mongrel – the progeny of several generations of mongrels before it. This one was the colour of a golden Labrador, although its coat was dirty from a life on the streets. Dan noted that sadly it was the same colour as the dusty road surface in which it lay. Already, sand had begun to stick to the dark crimson pools that stained the tarmac. It wouldn't be long before any traces of blood would be completely covered by the windblown desert, dried out and carried off by the wind again. The desert had already begun the clean-up job. Life in this part of the world was harsh and unforgiving.

Mr Feng walked over and looked at Dan with a stare that was half apologetic, half accusatory, as if to say, "If you weren't on the fucking run, this wouldn't have happened." Mr Feng looked down at the dog, realising it was dead. For a couple of minutes he stood staring down at the animal while he finished his cigarette. He threw the butt into the sand in front of them before taking hold the dog by the one rear leg that remained intact, and dragged it to the side of the road. Dan felt sick as he watched Mr Feng haul the body of the dog across the road surface in one final undignified journey. There was no pavement here, just a bank of sand a few inches deep piled against a line of coarse desert grass. Mr Feng dumped the dog a short distance into the desert where it was clear of the road and left it to decompose in the warm evening sun. The corpse would be flyblown within minutes of them leaving.

Mr Feng gestured to Dan that they should be leaving, so he took one last look at the dog, sympathising that this animal's life had been snuffed out in a split-second, free to roam no longer. Dan realised that the dog was a metaphor and stark reminder that his own freedom was just as precarious and that his own game could be up at any moment. His own body would then similarly be left to rot in some forgotten corner of China while the world carried on speeding past. Again, his throat tightened and he felt queasy at the prospect of not making it out of China.

Back at the car Lisa had found some medicine in her bag and passed some to Dan, along with a bottle of water.

"Here. Ibuprofen," she said. "It'll help take the pain away and reduce any inflammation."

"Thanks," Dan replied humbly taking the medicine from her, slightly surprised but relieved to see the packet written in English. He swallowed the two tablets with one gulp of water. The sense of power he had been feeling moments earlier now switched back into Lisa's hands. She had moved into *Guide Mode* and was treating him like any other client she'd ever looked after. He realised that actually Lisa was now vital to his survival out here. Vital in the dictionary definition of the word.

They got back in the car and Mr Feng started the engine. Save for a mark or two on the front bumper the minivan was undamaged by the impact, and they were able to continue on their way towards Turpan. It wasn't a great start to the long journey that lay ahead and both Lisa and Dan nursed their injuries for most of the night.

As they left Dunhuang the vegetation of the oasis town began to peter out. The road opened up into vast desert that stretched to the horizon in all directions. As they drove, the sand changed colour from yellows through orange and red into almost black. The desert surface was hard, baked solid by thousands of years of relentless sun. On top it was speckled with fragments of rocks that had been shattered by the heat of the sun over time. The landscape was strange and alien.

A couple of hours later, with the sun now well below the horizon, total darkness enveloped the car. Only the road ahead, illuminated by the headlights, was visible. Staring out into the inky blackness, Dan searched for any sign of life or geological feature but it was impossible. Although still warm, he could feel the temperature starting to drop. As Dan gazed hopelessly out of the window, his eyes glazed over and he began to feel sleepy. Eventually he nodded off sitting upright in his seat, the pain in his neck preventing any other option.

He woke up a short time later, being dazzled back into consciousness by orange streetlights that flashed past the car every few seconds. He was confused and the lights hurt his eyes as he adjusted to the new surroundings. Lisa was awake on the seats next to him and smiled as Dan came to. He blinked a few more times and rubbed the sleep out of his eyes, heaving himself back on to the seat from which he had slumped. His neck was less painful now although he suspected that was just the pain killers working.

"Where are we?" Dan asked as they entered a small town. "We can't be in Turpan yet, can we?"

"No, This is Liuyuan," Lisa replied. "You've only been asleep for an hour or so. Turpan is another seven hours from here."

Liuyuan was a strange place, clearly dominated by the railway station, sitting on the main Urumqi to Xi'an line. It was the most brightly lit part of the whole town, glowing like a beacon in the desert night. As they approached, Dan could see freight wagons sitting in sidings waiting to be heaved through this inhospitable terrain. A train engine was being moved into position, shunting into a line of flatbed carriages while two men ensured the couplings. A few insects gathered around each of the lights on the dimly lit platform, darting backwards and forwards, careering into the bulbs every few seconds. The rest of the town was deserted such that Dan felt like he was on an empty movie set. They didn't see another person or vehicle as they drove through the centre of town before pulling into a petrol station. A tired old man appeared from a shed-like building behind the forecourt as Mr Feng filled the van with fuel for the journey ahead. He paid the man in cash and climbed back in.

It had just gone ten o'clock when they joined the main road, turning left towards Turpan. The next few hours flew past considering the distances they were covering. The road was good and there were no interruptions en route as Mr Feng drove effortlessly through the night. They saw barely another vehicle save for a truck or two ferrying goods from Xinjiang east into Gansu and beyond, but even they were gone in an instant.

For the most part, it was just the thick, black darkness of the cold desert night and, for Lisa, everything was going to plan.

7

THE OTHER BACKPACKER

At around one-thirty a.m., Dan woke with a start. The minivan had slowed and the pain in Dan's neck had returned as he looked around for Lisa. She had also just woken up and made her way forward to sit immediately behind her driver. They chatted briefly before she turned to Dan and said the two words he did not want to hear. Two words that almost made his heart stop.

"Check point."

Ahead, on the right-hand side of the road, what initially looked like a shipping container turned out to be a small hut made of breezeblocks with a corrugated tin roof and decrepit wooden door. There were no windows in the building but a couple of upper bricks at the end had been removed for ventilation. In front of it, four painted oil drums had been placed on alternate sides of the road, reducing traffic to one snaking lane. Between the middle two drums a rudimentary gate had been constructed across the road. As they got close, Dan could see in the glare of their headlights that it was a bamboo pole crudely painted red and white.

As the van approached, a young soldier emerged from the building rubbing his eyes. He had a rifle slung over his shoulder and was in military fatigues. He waved to Mr Feng, signalling him to stop while shielding his eyes from the glare of the headlights with his other arm. Dan's heart was pounding as Lisa told him to be as calm as he could. They were going to talk their way through but even Lisa looked nervous.

Mr Feng stopped at the flimsy barrier and the soldier walked around the minivan, inspecting it with his torch. He flashed the light into the window and Dan turned his head quickly out of its glare. Mr Feng had wound his window down by the time the soldier got back to him. The conversation between the two men started calmly but Mr Feng soon became agitated. The soldier was firing questions at him and Dan could see it was starting to irritate. Lisa whispered, "He just asked who you and me are. Mr Feng just said you were the oil exec on your way to a conference in Urumqi and that I'm your translator."

Lisa paused for a moment as the conversation continued.

"The guy wants to know why we're driving at night and if we know what the roadblocks are for. Mr Feng just said you have a fear of flying and it would be too hot to make this journey during the day! He also said he doesn't care what the roadblocks are for!"

Mr Feng's courage in the face of this bombardment of questions was commendable and Dan admired the conviction with which he was answering them. Eventually, Mr Feng turned to Lisa and said something to her. Lisa leaned forward and whispered to Dan, "Look pissed off," before shouting back at the young solider in perfect Mandarin. Her tirade lasted a good thirty seconds before she returned to her seat. Even Mr Feng, whose face Dan now caught reflected in the rear-view mirror, looked taken aback. The startled young solider took a step back, sheepishly muttered something to Mr Feng and went to open the barrier. He lifted the bamboo pole into the night's sky as the car weaved its way through the oil drums and back onto open road. The young soldier trudged wearily back to his hut. Dan's heart was racing and he wiped his sweaty palms on his polo shirt.

"What the hell did you say to him?" Dan asked Lisa, as the van got up to speed again.

"He wanted to see your passport," Lisa replied. "I told him that my client shows his passport to no-one and that you are a very important and influential businessman, here by invitation of the governor of Xinjiang, with whom you would be meeting in two days' time in Urumqi. I told him that we had noted his name and would report him for harassment if he didn't let you through immediately! The poor kid is only about nineteen, posted out here in the middle of nowhere. There's an army barracks near here hence the roadblock, but I'm guessing he drew the short straw. Sent out here in the desert to do this shitty job. You're lucky it wasn't anyone more experienced," she continued. "That might not have been so easy."

Dan exhaled a long, deep breath of relief but said nothing. This had proven in the cold reality of the night that the hunt for him was well and truly on. This was now a full-on fight for survival against increasingly impossible odds and the border with Kyrgyzstan was still hundreds of miles away. He had days of travelling ahead of him and as yet had no idea how he was going to get beyond Urumqi, from where the journey to Kashgar was just shy of a thousand miles and would take almost twenty-four hours of driving in itself.

They sped into the night, racing the sunrise. By the time they arrived in Turpan several hours later the sun was already up and the sky was a hazy pale blue. Dan had dozed off several times throughout the night but never for more than an hour at a time such that it felt like he hadn't really slept at all. The approach to the city looked much like that of Dunhuang, but Turpan was much greener. It was busier too. There were motorbikes, trucks and donkey-drawn carts everywhere. Again there appeared to be few traffic rules.

As they reached the suburbs, Dan noticed fields of grape vines stretching away on either side of the road. It was a strange sight following almost twelve hours of desert.

"They're irrigated with water from the Tian Shan Mountains to the north of here," Lisa proclaimed, sensing Dan's confusion. "It's quite clever actually – there are over a thousand tunnels dug from the base of the mountains to these fields, which sit in the Turpan Depression – the second deepest geographical depression on the planet."

Lisa was in *Guide Mode* again.

"The tunnels are known as *karez* in the Uighur language," she continued. "It just means 'well', but I think there are something like five thousand kilometres of *karez* around here. It makes Turpan an oasis in the desert. Actually, it's not just the Tian Shan. There is a cool mountain range not too far north of Turpan called the Flaming Mountains – they glow orangey-red in the desert sun. I normally take groups there when we stay in Turpan overnight."

Dan was impressed and longed to see the mountains she was talking about. He sighed knowing that again this would be something he could only ever drive past and wonder about.

"That's pretty cool," Dan replied, trying to conceal his despondence. The Turpan Depression seemed a pretty apt place to be right then.

Dan slunk deeper into his seat as they made their way through the early-morning traffic. Peering out of the window, his face half hidden by the curtain that hung down in front of him, Dan began to grow concerned again about where they were going to stay, about stepping out into public again. His heart began to race and he felt sick.

"What's the plan from here, Lisa?" he asked somewhat tentatively.

"We're going to Feng's brother's house. He lives in a suburb of Turpan. We can lie low there while we plan the next bit. Feng's brother is in Urumqi for a few days on a job – Feng spoke to him while you were sleeping."

This was an incredible development. Dan hadn't seen this coming but yet again he felt humbled by the effort that Lisa and Mr Feng were going to. He wondered if Mr Feng's brother knew who would be sleeping in his house that evening.

Dan didn't know it then, but Mr Feng's brother was well aware of who was heading to his house.

Turpan appeared to be laid out on a rough grid structure. They approached from the east, passing green fields that eventually gave way to more white-tiled buildings. Again dust and desert sand lay piled in the corners of every kerb, building and window. The trees that lined the streets were covered in the same pale brown coating of the desert.

They turned left off the main road into the centre of town. There were few obvious landmarks to identify it as such save for a couple of large hotels that dwarfed everything around them. Turpan wasn't unattractive. The streets were lined with trees and there seemed to be serious money tied up in some of the buildings and cars they passed. Despite its remote location in the middle of this unforgiving desert, it appeared to be a relatively prosperous and bustling town. With Dan lying low, the car zig-zagged through the streets before arriving in a run-down part of town where children played in the dusty alleyways, old men sat on doorsteps smoking unfiltered cigarettes and women beat sand from carpets that hung in the gentle breeze. Dan gazed out the window, taking it all in. There was something very earnest about life in these side streets. Undoubtedly tough with few luxuries, but honest and simple. Did these people even care about a fugitive from Beijing?

Eventually they pulled into a narrow side street that was not much wider than the van itself. Mr Feng picked his way down the alleyway avoiding dogs that lay in doorways on either side of them. At the end of the lane stood a dusty pale-blue metal gate that was about seven feet high. Mr Feng pulled up to the gate and stopped the van. He squeezed out and slid the gate open to one side. Dents in the metal made the gate rattle and groan as it moved through its posts, but it gave way to a large courtyard.

Once inside, Mr Feng closed the gate behind them. Although he should have felt safe, Dan now felt somehow conspicuous. He didn't belong here and became paranoid that he was being watched. Mr Feng opened the rickety wooden door to the building – a mud-coloured single-storey block of a house with a small window either side of the front entrance. The door had once been painted blue but only a few flecks of colour remained, peeled and flaked by the baking desert sun.

As Dan followed Mr Feng and Lisa into the house he was met by a large living room. On the back wall was a single row of kitchen units, a sink and a simple gas hob, the canister for which stood on the floor to the right. In one corner an old fridge that leaned to the left slightly suddenly rattled into life with a judder. Next to the sink there were pots and pans still waiting to be washed up from the last time they were used.

"When was the last time anyone was here?" Dan enquired.

"Mr Feng's brother left just this morning," Lisa replied without looking at him.

Her focus was on Mr Feng who had moved into a side room and was talking on his phone. Having no idea what was being said, Dan decided to have a look around the house. To the right of the front door was a small dingy room with light barely breaking through the dusted-up window. The floor was made of what looked like clay or rammed earth on top of which sat a number of overlapping rugs that stretched almost from wall to wall. It must have been freezing at night, Dan thought, as well as dirty.

Mr Feng's brother was not married. This was what a Turpan bachelor pad looked like. He ran a small enterprise transporting just about anything that anybody wanted between here and Urumqi. He had a truck into which he'd pile anything from scrap metal to crates of chickens, but he'd earned enough money to buy this plot of land and build himself a house. It wasn't large by any stretch of the imagination but Dan learned it was larger than the tiny apartment that Mr Feng, his wife and their eight-year-old son lived in in Urumqi.

Or at least that's what Dan thought Mr Feng's brother did.

At that moment, as Dan began to imagine how Mr Feng's brother felt the day he bought this place and how satisfying the feeling of his entrepreneurial hard work finally paying off must have been, Lisa put her head around the door.

"Feng's been on the phone to his brother," she said. "There are two roadblocks on the way between here and Urumqi, both manned twenty-four hours a day. There's a back route, but it adds three hours to the journey – doubling the time it'll take us. It's also pretty rough going. Feng's worried about the car as we need a bit more clearance than this van's got. I'm going out to get us some food. You stay here. Feng's going out for a drink and a game of pool with some friends and will be back later. We're spending the night here so make yourself comfortable."

"Wait. Does Mr Feng's brother know I'm here? Why is he talking about the check points?"

"No," Lisa lied. "It's just a pain in the ass for anyone driving between here and Urumqi – there are backlogs at both. Feng just said he had clients with him."

With that Lisa left. She opened the front door and she and Mr Feng went back into the courtyard. A chicken that had been scratching around in the dirt ran for cover behind a small and dusty tree that stood in one corner. Lisa opened the metal gate while Mr Feng turned the van around. As the gate rattled shut behind them Dan felt alone again for the first time in days. He looked at the hazy blue sky above him and breathed in through his nose. He held it in for several seconds before exhaling deeply, expelling almost all the air from his lungs. The weight on his shoulders, when he spent too long thinking about it, was almost too much to bear.

Dan turned back into the house and closed the door behind him. It was considerably cooler than the scorching desert heat outside. The house was dark and box-like but in the middle of the living room was a large, tatty cream-coloured leather sofa. Just below the front window a small Chinese-made television stood on a rickety brown coffee table. Dan lay down on the sofa. It smelled strangely of wet dog. It wasn't particularly comfortable and the springs nudged him in the back as he lay down. Within a minute or two of staring at the dark grey ceiling, he was asleep.

Several hours passed and it was mid-afternoon when he woke up. Lisa and Mr Feng were still not back and he woke up to pangs of hunger. He was thirsty too. Hauling himself off the sofa, Dan found a single mug in the pile of washing up in the kitchen and, in the absence of a sponge, washed it thoroughly using his hand. He filled the mug with water and gulped it down. Having sat in the pipes just under the back yard all day, the water was warm and did little to quench his thirst.

Suddenly there was a banging on the door behind him. Terrified and almost dropping the mug, he spun round.

"Sam! Sam! It's Lisa!" she cried, half shouting, half whispering.

Dan ran over and opened the door, his heart already racing.

"Feng's not back yet, right?" she asked breathlessly.

"No. I haven't seen him since you left," Dan replied hastily, wondering what the panic was for. "What's going on, Lisa?" he asked. "Do they know I'm here?"

"No, the total opposite," Lisa replied, trying to recover her breath. "They've arrested a guy down in Guizhou. He was backpacking through the villages down there when a local policeman noticed him coming out of a guesthouse. He was arrested by the policeman with the help of some local villagers," Lisa continued.

"Fuck," Dan replied, his eyes wide with disbelief. "Who the hell is he?"

"I don't know," Lisa replied, panting. "But that policeman is a national hero. People are already calling for him to be promoted to county chief. It's all over the news. He's doing interviews with every news channel going, saying how he found this guy hiding in a small guesthouse. They say he resisted arrest and tried to fight off the policeman. That's when the other villagers got involved. They drove him forty miles in the back of a truck to the nearest town, where he was handed over to police. They've just shown him on TV, being taken from a police van into the town police station. The poor guy looks scared shitless, but I have to say, he doesn't look much like you."

"Fucking hell," Dan said. "That's awful."

"It is for him, sure, but for us it means the roadblocks have been taken down. As far as they know, they've got their man. It's a massive result for the police, who have been getting it in the neck for not having caught you yet. It all backs up their belief that you are down there. We need to leave tonight. Perhaps we can get you to Urumqi Airport and out of here this evening while the guard is down."

This was a game-changing development and Lisa was right: if he could get a flight out of Urumqi this evening he could be out of China within a few hours. She was far more switched on than he was – always at least two steps ahead of him. It was almost as if Lisa had done this sort of thing before.

"I'm going to find Feng," she declared. "I need to stop him drinking any more. We leave as soon as it gets dark."

Lisa dropped her backpack on the floor of the living room and ran out of the house again. She'd left the metal gate to the courtyard open when she'd run in moments earlier. She sprinted out into the alleyway again and disappeared between two neighbouring houses.

Dan slumped back down on the sofa, numb from what he had just heard. The end was in sight. It was an incredible twist of fate but the thought of what the next few hours held filled him with dread. His throat ran dry again as he pictured himself having to walk into Urumqi Airport, produce his passport and purchase a ticket. If he got past those obstacles he would then have to pass through security, reveal his name again, his visa, his date and place of entry to China – everything about him would be laid bare in the scarcity of the airport. His head spinning, he lay comatose on the sofa, unable to move, staring at the ceiling.

Before long Dan heard the sound of an engine and Lisa and Mr Feng pulled back into the yard outside the house. Lisa got out and closed the metal gate behind them and Dan got up as they entered the house. Mr Feng nodded and said something to him in Chinese.

"You ready to go again?" Lisa translated.

"Absolutely," Dan replied. Lisa didn't translate. Mr Feng had already left the room and Lisa began gathering her belongings. She opened a thin plastic carrier bag that she had brought in from the car.

"Here," she said, pulling out a pack of six steamed *bao* bread buns. "Help yourself. I've got a packet for each of us."

Dan tore into the plastic and stuffed a bun into his mouth. They were soft and doughy but lacked both substance and much taste. He expected to be hungry again before they left Turpan. Lisa threw a packet to Mr Feng, who had re-emerged, and they all stood in the sandy courtyard eating in silence. The atmosphere seemed tense, but perhaps only Dan sensed it.

Lisa finished first and began pacing around the house, making sure she had everything they would need for the journey ahead. The sun was beginning to set over the rooftops that surrounded the courtyard and the sky was turning grey as the light faded. Before long the sun would be gone. It was time to leave.

Mr Feng threw a small holdall onto the passenger seat of the car. Lisa and Dan put their bags in the back and climbed in. Mr Feng drove slowly out of the gate before stopping to close it behind them one last time. Dan took a deep breath. They were about to embark on the final stage of the journey, the last chapter in the nightmare that his life had become. In a few hours' time he would be soaring out of China a free man once again. But he was about to enter the lion's den. A place where he would be scrutinised to within an inch of his life.

Picking their way through the suburban streets, they passed back through the busy centre of town, now lit in the dim glow of streetlights. It seemed like weeks ago since Dan had run into the yellow glow of the streetlights beyond the *hutong*s. His fateful encounter with Nancy seemed like a lifetime ago. He felt sick as he recalled how he had trusted her, convinced now that she was involved in his downfall.

After twenty or so minutes they emerged from the quietening streets of Turpan and back out into the desert. They were en route to Urumqi but nobody in the car had said a word since they had left. It seemed that everything that had needed to be said had been said. Or perhaps Lisa and Mr Feng just realised that they were entering dangerous territory. Dan sensed a strange feeling enveloping him. This felt like the final scene in a movie, just before the credits start rolling and the car is seen driving away into the fading sunset of the distance.

The road through the desert was straight and the landscape that evolved as they drove was flat and barren. It wasn't quite dark and Dan could make out rolling dune-like rock structures giving way to rugged mountains that glowed a pale orange in the fading light. The sun was low in the sky, skimming the mountains ahead of them as they drove west towards Urumqi.

Lisa broke the silence about half an hour into the drive. The sudden sound of her voice made Dan jump again.

"We'll probably have to crash at mine tonight. I doubt there's a flight anywhere this evening. We'll check out the options when we get there and try and get you a flight tomorrow."

"What time do you expect to get there?" Dan enquired, realising he no longer had any control whatsoever over his fate today. He wasn't even entirely sure where they were anymore, just that they were heading roughly north-west and all the time further and further from Beijing.

"We'll be there in a couple of hours' time. Around ten o'clock, I reckon," Lisa replied. "Get some rest, just in case there is a flight this evening."

"Thanks. I guess I'll have to fly somewhere that doesn't require a visa to get into…"

"That's true," Lisa replied without looking at him, turning her head to gaze out of the window again. There was a sad, almost lonely undertone to her voice. Dan looked at her quizzically. His eyes scanned her body up and down as she sat on the opposite side of the vehicle to him. She was just under six feet in height and when she spoke to him her eyes glimmered with a quiet intellect that simmered beneath the surface. When she smiled there was a cheeky playfulness to her smile that culminated in small and impossibly seductive dimples.

Dan knew that under different circumstances, perhaps at university, she would have been the kind of girl with whom there would be instant chemistry; the kind of connection that made going into classes every morning both exciting and nerve-wracking. She would be a clear and welcome distraction in any lecture, he mused. But here he was, hostage to his fate. Captive and entirely useless to Lisa he was as attractive a catch as an infectious disease. He brought her nothing but risk and danger. He felt entirely worthless.

He couldn't have been more wrong, but it would be several more days before Dan would learn that what he had in his possession was actually extremely valuable to her.

He looked at her now, gazing long into the depths of the darkness. Outside the windows the night was a thick, inky black. It was impossible to see beyond only the edge of the road, softly illuminated in the spill of the headlights as they sped through the desert towards Urumqi. Dan knew Lisa couldn't see anything through the window and that she was alone with her thoughts. He reflected on the loneliness in her voice. There was an undercurrent of sadness in it and his mind began to race to interpret it. For some reason he felt close to her as if they had known each other for years. He may have misread the situation, but he got the sense that the feeling was mutual. He sat there, confused, wondering how this might unfold if and when they got to Lisa's apartment in Urumqi.

Two hours or so after they left Turpan, a faint but distinct glow began to illuminate the sky like a halo over the city directly ahead of them. Within minutes they began to pick up the outer suburbs of Urumqi and before long the desert road gave way to a modern expressway that was busy with traffic. Dan's heart began to race again as they sped towards the city centre. He was back among people, police, authorities. They'd had no news since leaving Turpan as to whether the hunt for him had been reinstated or whether the authorities in the south of the country still truly believed they had caught their man. They hadn't encountered either of the check points that had been operational just hours earlier, but he wouldn't have to wait long to find out.

The increasing illumination of the streetlights and small businesses they passed suddenly seemed to jolt Lisa back into consciousness. She focused her eyes on the road ahead of them and said something to Mr Feng before turning to Dan.

"I've asked Feng to take us to my place. There's nothing else we can do tonight and I have the internet there, where we can check flights for you for tomorrow. I'll go out and grab us some food. We can eat at mine."

"You sure?" Dan replied tentatively, but without any other options to offer. "If you're OK with that, that'd be great."

Lisa returned a sympathetic smile and turned to stare out of the window again. Dan's heart and mind were racing, pulling in opposite directions. The whole sensation made him queasy and he swallowed hard, his throat tightening again.

By now they were well and truly in the thick of Urumqi. The suburbs had given way to endless rows of apartment blocks: great concrete monstrosities that stretched the length of the road and, in endless parallel rows beyond, housed thousands of people. Almost as ubiquitous as the apartment blocks themselves were the chimneys that punctured the skyline every hundred metres or so. Dan asked Lisa what they all were.

"Ha!" she replied. "I asked the very same question when I got to Urumqi for the first time. My guide looked at me with a sparkle in her eye and said, 'We have over a thousand chimneys in Urumqi,' as if it were something to be proud of!" Lisa continued. "In reality, they're just the chimneys from the heating systems for the apartments, but hell, it's part of the reason Urumqi has such a smog problem. You'd think they'd just slap some solar panels on the roofs and have done with it – we're in the middle of the goddamn desert after all!"

They wove through Urumqi's busy streets, picking their way through the cars, trucks and motorbikes that clogged the roads. Dan could see the lights of the CBD reach skywards in front of them as the traffic began to slow to a crawl. A small police truck pulled up in the lane to the right of the van, edging forward with the rest of the traffic. Dan looked out of the window to the left and felt the eyes of the police burning into the back of his head as he did.

"They've gone," Lisa muttered a few moments later.

Dan turned to her, surprised that she had noticed.

"Thanks," he sighed with a heavy resignation in his voice. She smiled and turned to look out of her window again.

"We're almost there. My place is just a couple of blocks from here. Feng will drop us off at the door and leave us. I'll warn you now, my apartment is not big. It's also a mess – I didn't think we were coming here!"

"Ha!" he spluttered in reflex response. She smiled at him with a glint in her eye and those irresistible dimples piercing her cheeks like needles in a pincushion. She turned to speak to Mr Feng again.

"We're here," she announced. "Grab your things out of the back – we need to get you inside ASAP."

Using a break in the traffic, Mr Feng slew a U-turn into the three lanes of oncoming traffic and veered over to the kerb on the furthest side of the road. As soon as they pulled up in the outside lane of the highway there was a sudden blaze of flashing blue and red lights and the screaming sound of sirens. Three police cars came tearing out of a lane no more than twenty metres from where they were parked. Dan was instantly terrified. His whole body became weak and he slid involuntarily down the seat almost into the foot well itself. The cars took off down the highway followed shortly after by two police motorbikes. From behind the front seat Dan watched as they disappeared down the highway until they were out of sight.

"Yeah, that's why we need to get you inside quickly," Lisa said. "I didn't tell you, there's a police station right next to my apartment. It's not big, but it's enough to give us a bit of hassle. I'll grab your bag and throw it inside. Once both our bags are in, you jump out and head inside. I'll hold the door open for you."

Lisa spoke with confidence that seemed unjustifiable to Dan at that moment. She said something to Mr Feng and quickly got out of the minivan. Dan heard the back door pop open as Lisa got a few things out and he watched as she entered a PIN code to her apartment block. The front door swung open and using one of the smaller bags to prop the door open she dropped her belongings inside. Returning to the car, Lisa opened the sliding side door and reached inside, first hauling her own bag out and dropping it inside the stairwell. She came back and whispered to Dan, "You go now. Get yourself inside. I'll close the car door behind you."

"OK," Dan replied, his voice shaking from the fear of what he was about to do. He got out of the car and walked as calmly as he could towards the apartment door. His legs felt as if he had been at sea, weak and uncertain. As he crossed the wide pavement to Lisa's apartment the heavy glass door began to close, pushing the makeshift doorstop out on to the street. The door clicked shut and Dan turned, wide-eyed, to look at Lisa, who was now closing the door of the van. She ran up and quickly punched the PIN in again. The door swung open, and they both fell inside the stairwell. Dan heaved a huge sigh, reinflating his lungs, which had become crushed under the weight of his stress-constricted chest.

Dan turned to make sure the coast was still clear only to see that Mr Feng had driven off and the traffic was flowing in all three lanes again. He didn't know it then but that was the last time he would see Mr Feng. As far as Dan knew, Mr Feng believed he had been trying to outrun a Xi'an drugs gang. But the feeling that Mr Feng knew who he really was nagged inside him. He could not imagine what the motivations for smuggling the most wanted man in China across two provinces could have been. Dan wasn't even sure he knew what Lisa's motivations were.

Unless there was something she wasn't telling him of course.

Lisa was gathering her things and began climbing the stairs to her apartment.

"Come on. We can't sit in front of the window."

Dan picked himself up and hauled his backpack onto his shoulder. It felt like days since he had carried his bag and for a blissful moment it felt like he was simply backpacking once again. For those few seconds he wasn't a fugitive on the run, hiding out in the middle of the largest city in China's western interior. But he knew that getting out of here would be like a fox escaping a den surrounded by more than four million hounds. The fleeting moment of escapism was over and he climbed the stairs to Lisa's apartment.

"Don't you have a lift? An elevator?" he panted as they reached her apartment on the fourth floor.

"Yes," she replied, "but it has security cameras."

Lisa was so much better at this than he was. Again, he felt embarrassed by her superior aptitude for what it takes to be a fugitive. She was smart and switched on and had already repeatedly saved his life.

Lisa was right – her apartment was a mess: food wrappers lay scattered around the sitting room into which they had walked and her bed lay unmade, the sheets lying on the floor where they had fallen the last time she got up. Dan stepped over an empty plastic Coke bottle while Lisa closed the door behind him.

"Sorry – I'll tidy up now. Dump your stuff on the couch – you can sleep there tonight."

She pointed to a three-seater sofa with dark-brown cushions and a wooden frame. Dan dropped his bag on the floor beside it.

"I'll give you a hand," he said and began picking discarded wrappers off the floor. A pile of dirty crockery lay on a glass coffee table in the middle of the room. Lisa thanked him as she appeared from the small kitchen with a black plastic bag for the rubbish and they set about tidying up.

"No-one ever comes here!" She laughed. "I didn't realise it was so bad!"

Once the apartment was clean, Lisa and Dan slumped onto the sofa, exhausted after a long day on the road. Lisa picked up the television remote and turned it on, flicking through a few channels until she found the local news.

A rockfall on the Karakoram Highway had killed a number of Han migrants who had been working on resurfacing the road that led from Kashgar across the border into Pakistan. Lisa told him that the finger was already being pointed at Uighur separatists as an act of sabotage, even though it was most likely the rain that had brought the rocks down. The ethnic tensions in this part of China were on a knife-edge, with the Han Chinese accusing the Uighurs for anything and everything. The Uighurs opposed what they saw as the invasion of the Han into their homeland. It had been going on for decades but the tension had increased significantly in the last few years as Beijing sought to reinforce its control over this restive western province. It seemed that the long-sought-after independent Uighur state was slipping further out of reach than even that of the Tibetans.

The next news item began with police in Beijing and Dan's stomach churned nauseously in an instant. This was him. He couldn't understand a word of what was being said but Lisa's silence spoke volumes. She sat glued to the screen, her face turning increasingly ashen as the news continued. Lisa said nothing as she just sat and watched for what felt like an eternity.

"They've released the guy down south," she said after a minute or so. "They've realised he wasn't you and they've let him go. The police officer who arrested him has been suspended, pending an investigation. The humiliation is too much for the Party to bear without consequences," she continued. "Worse still, they said they know you've been in Dunhuang, but they believe you're still there. We're not going to get you to the airport tomorrow, I'm afraid."

His heart was racing again. It hadn't been pounding quite like this for some time now and he felt his throat tightening as he watched the video of a police helicopter circling over Dunhuang. The photo of him from Beijing sat in the bottom right-hand corner of the screen, the faces of the two girls on either side of him blurred out. The determination to escape crept back, stronger than he had felt it for days.

As the piece finished Lisa switched the television off and turned to Dan, her face devoid of all its colour. Dan realised then that this was the first time the two of them had been together to watch the news. Until now, she'd only had updates from the radio and Mr Feng. The cold, stark reality of seeing his face on national news was proving difficult to stomach. Dan saw her swallow hard. She rested her face in her hands, fingers covering her eyes. He looked at her, lost for words, unable to offer any sort of reassurance.

Dan clenched his teeth, angry that he was in this situation and that he was still captive within the cage-like borders of this country. He felt the anger rise in him and once again turn into that determination to escape. Dan stood up and moved over to Lisa, crouching in front of her as she sat, head in hands, motionless.

"Lisa," Dan said softly by firmly, "let me stay here tonight and I'll leave in the morning. It's unfair of me to stay here any longer than that. You don't need to be part of this. I'll get out of Urumqi somehow and you can forget that I was ever here. I just need to sleep this evening and I'll leave in the early hours, before you're even awake. I'll be gone before sunrise."

Lisa slowed lifted her head out of her hands and looked at him. She stared straight into his eyes, her own glistening with tears. She gave him a sympathetic, big-eyed look and swallowed hard again. Dan could tell she was struggling to find the right words to communicate what she was thinking. Her eyes searched across his face for the answer. He put his hands on her knees as her elbows rested on her legs. She ran her tongue around her lips – lips that had become dry with the intensity of the moment.

"I want to help you," she said at last. "I fucking want to help you get out of this. I love this country but at the same time I fucking hate it. I hate that a guy can come to see all the beautiful things this incredible country has to offer but end up running for his life. I feel like the human race hasn't moved on since the Middle Ages and we're still being fucking cruel to each other. Sam, I'm going to help you get out of here and fuck, I might just come with you."

His eyes widened as Lisa's last comment spilled from her lips. This thought had never even crossed his mind until now.

Lisa would come with him to Kyrgyzstan. From his perspective it wasn't a ridiculous idea and the more he thought about it the more it made sense: to have her with him would be the most incredible asset both practically and emotionally. His mind raced, trying to compute all the scenarios, outcomes and risks associated with Lisa joining him on his run. From her perspective, however, it was even more insane than harbouring him in her apartment, which until now he'd thought was the most dangerous thing she could possibly have done.

Still staring at him, waiting for him to respond, Lisa sat back in the sofa and placed her hands on her head. Dan got the feeling she felt a certain sense of relief herself at the thought of crossing that border into the vast meadows of Kyrgyzstan. Perhaps they were both pursing the same release from China.

Dan frowned as it became his turn to struggle to find the words. After several minutes of silence, he looked up and spoke.

"Are you serious? You're going to come with me to Kyrgyz? Really?"

"Why not, man?" she responded immediately. "I need an adventure and this is the best fucking excuse I'm ever going to get."

Realising that Lisa was serious, he softened his tone. "Lisa. This is not just some adventure. This is as real as it comes. I don't want you to put yourself in any more danger for me. You don't have to do this. You shouldn't be wrapped up in this as it is. You've been incredible these last couple of days – you've helped me more than I could possibly have hoped. I'm in Urumqi; the Tian Shan Mountains are now just beyond the city and almost within touching distance. I'm so close, and you can still walk away from all this with your freedom intact. I already owe you my life. Don't risk yours because you feel sorry for me. This time last week, you didn't even know me."

Lisa realised that what he was saying made sense, even if the last part wasn't strictly true.

"Feng has to go back to Turpan tomorrow. He has family business to attend to. But you know he said his brother was up here somewhere? Well, he's just picked up a truckload of scrap metal that needs to go somewhere. He can sell it in either Turpan or Kashgar. Although Kashgar is about six times further, he can get at least twice the money for it, he says. If we pay his gas money, he'll take us – it'll be worth his while for twice the money. He's at a funeral tomorrow but leaving for Turpan in the evening. If I catch him in time, he'll take us both to Kashgar. Don't worry – I'll pay for it so we don't have to use your card. I need a couple hours tomorrow morning to sort a few things out. You stay here and I'll be back once everything is done."

Lisa's thought process was unfolding itself in front of Dan as fast as she could speak. She leaned forward and stared deep into his eyes again.

"Let's get out of here."

8

CROSSING THE TAKLAMAKAN

Dan woke the following morning to the sound of the shower running. Lisa was up. He curled into the foetal position on the sofa, chilly and hungry. Pulling the thin blanket over his head he made a cocoon and filled it with his warm breath. His throat was dry but he was too tired to get up for a glass of water. He hadn't slept properly for what felt like days and it was a luxury to simply be horizontal.

Lisa came out of the shower, her hair wet and a towel wrapped around her body. She walked into the living room where Dan was lying and he could see her through the blanket. He watched as she poured herself a glass of water from the simple kitchen that stretched across the opposite wall of the sitting room. Facing away from him, she adjusted her towel, letting it drop slightly to reveal her lower back as she dried her body. Despite the adolescent urge to keep watching, Dan closed his eyes. This girl had saved his life several times over the last couple of days and was now his newfound travelling companion. He cleared his mind and refocused on what complications might lie on the journey ahead.

The next thing he heard was Lisa waking him up. He sat up as she began to speak.

"I'm heading out; I have a few things to organise. I'll grab us some breakfast on the way back. I won't be long. You OK here? Help yourself to anything you can find – I'm not going to need any of it after all. There should be hot water for the shower. If not, just wait a few minutes for it to reheat. Don't open the door to anyone. I'm taking my key so I won't need to knock when I get back. I've taken your cash card from your wallet – I'm going to post it to a friend in Xi'an to throw them off the scent. I'll be an hour or so. We're not leaving until this evening so take your time. Catch up on some sleep if you need to. I can't guarantee you'll get much in the next couple of days."

With that Lisa picked up a rucksack that had been sitting in the middle of the living room floor and swung it over her shoulder. She picked her mobile phone off the glass coffee table and grabbed her keys from a shelf beside the door. As she left, she closed the door quietly leaving Dan in silence save for the traffic noise outside. The latch clicked shut in the lock and he was alone.

Dan looked at his wallet lying open on the coffee table and lay back on the sofa, alone with his thoughts, staring at the ceiling. Barely blinking, he allowed his mind to spin as he recalled what had happened over the last few days, how far he had come from Beijing, everything he had done to evade the police and where he was now. Urumqi. A city he'd never even heard of until shortly after he'd met Lisa. He was, for the time being at least, relatively safe inside Lisa's apartment. This would be a needle in a haystack even if they knew he was in Urumqi. He would never make it out of the city if they did, but he couldn't help but think that the longer he hid, the greater the chance of the truth coming out. Dan then began to think that running from the police was probably a crime in itself, and either way his situation was now pretty dire. His mind spinning, he fell asleep, exhausted.

He woke up some time later. Lisa was still not back. Hauling himself up into the sitting position, Dan stretched the aches and creases out of his body. The vertebrae in his neck clicked as he rolled his head from side to side. He yawned and exhaled deeply. The next stage of his run was about to begin.

The warm water of the shower once again soothed his aching body as the steam filled his lungs. Dan closed his eyes, imagining he was in the spa on a beach somewhere idyllic. In reality he was in hell and about as far from the sea as it is possible to get. He dried himself off in the living room and changed into the cleanest clothes he could find in his bag. Crumpled and damp, they negated much of the benefit of the shower, and sand spilled from his pockets onto the floor as he turned them inside out. Dan swept the little pile of Gobi desert under the sofa with the grubby sock he was wearing. Lisa was leaving and would never find it anyway.

As Dan began to put his things back into his backpack, there was a click at the front door and his heart jumped. He turned his head towards the sound and froze. The door opened and Lisa walked in. His shoulders dropped with relief, and he muttered a feeble, nervous "Hey".

Lisa said nothing until the door was closed behind her. He'd forgotten how much better she was at all this than him.

"Hey. You're up. You were crashed out when I got up this morning. You feeling better?"

"A little, thanks," Dan replied. "I needed it."

"Everything is set for later. Feng's brother is going to pick us up at eight o'clock tonight. To keep the story the same, I've told him you are a friend of mine, running away from a Xi'an drugs gang. There's a courtyard out back and he'll bring his truck in there so we don't have to go back out onto the street. Since the trail for you reached Dunhuang, it's the main news up here too. People will probably recognise you, even without your hair. Especially if you're wearing the same T-shirt as in the only photo they've got of you…"

"Dammit," he said, feeling stupid. "I'll change."

"I've sent your cash card to a friend of mine in Xi'an. A guide called Iris. I've told her to wear gloves as she opens the letter and to withdraw four hundred dollars in cash that she can keep for the trouble. She's then going to find an alley away from any CCTV and 'lose' your card. She's a good friend of mine. She won't ask any questions and four hundred dollars is a small fortune over here. If we can keep the search yo-yoing between Dunhuang, Xi'an, Beijing and the south, we might just make it across the border."

At that point Dan's stomach grumbled so loudly that both of them looked down at it in surprise.

"Ha! You must be starving!" Lisa remarked. "Here, I bought you an egg and bacon sandwich from a western food shop down the road. It won't be quite like you're used to – the pork out here is different somehow. Richer. It's pretty good."

Lisa produced a baguette about eight inches in length stuffed with sliced egg and bacon that was so deep red in colour it looked like it had been stained with beetroot. Dan had never seen bacon quite like this but gratitude seeped from his salivary glands with every mouthful.

Lisa left him to it and disappeared into her room. Dan realised she was packing her backpack with the things she was going to need for their journey.

"If I'm not coming back I'm going to need these things," Lisa said as she picked up a couple of books and a photo of her parents from the living room. Removing it from its frame, she paused to look at it before returning to her bedroom.

The hours passed and afternoon turned into evening. Lisa's apartment was starting to look less lived-in and more abandoned-in-a-hurry. Dan and Lisa sat and chatted about their pasts. Dan learned that Lisa had lost her mother in a car crash eleven years earlier. She had been fourteen at the time and it had shattered her world. Her father was a lawyer in the US and following the death of her mother he had encouraged Lisa to see the world. She'd been backpacking in South East Asia for twelve months before she'd arrived in China. Lisa had fallen in love with the culture in the south-western province of Yunnan and decided to learn the language. She'd returned to the States and studied Mandarin and Chinese history at university before finding her job as a tour guide for high-paying western oil and gas companies. She was earning decent money but longed to go travelling again. She'd set her sights on South America but found herself stuck working here in western China. It wasn't what she wanted to be doing and the desolate, sandy expanse of Xinjiang, despite its beauty, was not the lush green, mountainous landscape of Yunnan that had first caught her imagination. She missed the colourful minority cultures, the clean air and the incredible food.

She told him about the time she'd travelled for fifteen hours over mountains by bus to get to a beautiful lake that sits on the north-west Yunnan Plateau. It forms part of the border between Sichuan and Yunnan province – the highest lake in the region and home to the Mosuo tribe, a sub-group of the Naxi people – just one of the fifty-six officially recognised ethnic groups in China today. Dan listened intently as she told him how the Mosuo are famous as one of the last matrilineal societies in the world. Lisa had been fascinated by the culture and after arriving, spent four months living among the Mosuo, learning their language and customs. Dan was genuinely fascinated and could have spent hours listening to her regale stories from the south. As she spoke, he was again struck by the sadness that he would probably never get to visit those places – the places that when he first landed in Beijing he thought he'd see – even if he was ever proven innocent he wouldn't risk coming back to China. Dan longed to see the green hills that Lisa described, to meet the people Lisa had met and breathe that clean air of freedom once again.

All too quickly the evening became night and it was time to leave the haven that was Lisa's apartment. Her phone rang, making both of them jump. It was Feng's brother and he was outside.

"It's time to go," Lisa said poignantly.

Dan nodded his head in slow, reluctant agreement, knowing that he probably wouldn't rest again for several days. They hadn't even discussed what was going to happen when they got to Kashgar or how they were actually going to get across the border itself. Dan had no idea how long all this was going to take or what Lisa had planned for them. All he knew was that Mr Feng's brother was driving them to Kashgar in the truck he used to haul scrap metal around Xinjiang. How exactly this was all going to work, Lisa hadn't told him. But he was about to find out.

"Just remember not to show your face," Lisa reminded Dan as they left her apartment and walked down the stairs to the door that led into the courtyard at the back of the building.

Filling the alleyway was a blue and grey truck that was old, battered and showing all the signs of a lifetime of toil, plying the sand-blasted roads of Xinjiang. It was piled high with great shards of corrugated sheet metal – the kind of machine that had simultaneously scared and fascinated the hell out of him as a boy. As they approached, Mr Feng's brother was busy tightening the ropes that held some of the largest pieces of metal in place on the far side of the truck. Lisa went round to see him. They chatted loudly for a few seconds while Dan awaited his instructions.

Lisa reappeared.

"There's a table at the back of the truck, up against the cab, for you to lie under. It'll protect you from the metal we're going to put on top of it. I'm going to be in the cab with him, but you can't be seen. You're going to have to climb up the side of the truck and drop down inside. Under the table, you'll find a mattress that Feng's brother has put in there for you to lie on. Climb up here," Lisa said, pointing to a series of footholds that scaled the back of the cab where it met the trailer.

Dan looked at Lisa warily. "Really? Is that the plan?" he asked hesitantly, cautious at the thought of travelling the next fifteen hundred kilometres buried under a pile of scrap metal.

"It is," Lisa replied bluntly. "If you've got a better one you're welcome to share it now. Get in. I'll pass your bag up when you get to the top. It'll be your pillow until we get to Kashgar."

"OK then," Dan said, realising that Lisa was not going to take any hassle from him. He got the feeling she would go to Kashgar without him if he didn't climb into that truck right then.

Dan picked his way to the top of the cab and caught his backpack as Lisa threw it up to him. Dropping it inside a narrow void among the piles of metal in the truck, Dan lowered himself in. The back of his T-shirt ripped on a jagged piece of casing from an old washing machine. At the bottom of the truck Dan found the table Lisa had told him about and there was the mattress he was to lie on until they got to Kashgar. In the dim light, Dan could make out that it was old, thin and stained with large brown watermarks. He had to contort his body to get under the old metal table that was so low there was barely even room to sit up. He pushed his backpack in ahead of him and crawled in. As Dan struggled to get comfortable there was an ear-piercing scraping sound and everything went dark. Mr Feng's brother was back-filling the void with a large industrial oil drum; Dan could hear more metal being piled on top of it.

Suddenly, he heard Lisa's voice. It was clear but he couldn't tell where it was coming from. Dan searched around in the dark.

"I'm here," Lisa said softly, her voice filling his right ear. "There's a hole in the side of the truck. You can't see me and I can't see you. We're leaving for Kashgar now," she continued. "We'll stop in a few hours for a break so you can stretch your legs. It's almost eight o'clock. If we stop around midnight, the roads should be clearer and we should be well away from most towns and cities. To your left you should find a bottle of water and some snacks. We'll stop for more supplies some time tomorrow morning. If you need to speak to me, bang on the back of the truck while we're moving. I can't guarantee I'll hear you, but I'll try to keep my ears open. Whatever you do, do not bang when the truck isn't moving. Have a good journey and see you in a few hours."

With that, Lisa left. Dan could barely stretch his legs out straight and could already feel the large corrugations of the hard metal through the thin mattress below him. This was going to be arduous. There had not been a time since he'd left Beijing that he felt more alone, more on the run and more vulnerable than he did right then. This was as real as he imagined it could get. This was people trafficking. This was almost professional.

As he struggled to get comfortable, the truck started with a violent shake. As they edged forward out of the narrow alleyway Dan could hear pieces of scrap metal moving and falling into place. He tucked his legs up into the foetal position under the table afraid that something would fall and trap them. The truck bumped heavily as they drove off a kerb and more pieces of metal settled into empty spaces. Within a few minutes Dan could tell they were on open highway as the roar from the road all around him became deafening. For the most part the going was smooth, save for potholes here and there that jolted his spine as they sped into the darkness.

A few moments into the journey Dan began to realise that the space where he was lying was getting hot. Not the sort of heat from the desert – he was almost used to that by now. This was different. This was engine heat. The base of the truck was starting to warm up and he searched around in the darkness, trying to find the edge of the mattress. When he found it the metal base of the truck was hot; almost too hot to touch. His fingertips flinched away from it. The mattress was insulating him from the worst of it but that too was starting to get warm. Dan began to panic that the heat would become dangerously high, perhaps even unsurvivable. They had only been driving for around fifteen minutes or so and Lisa had said they would stop "in a few hours". Before long Dan felt his back beginning to sweat and it soon became itchy on the grubby mattress. His brow began to dampen and felt sweat running into his hair as he lay motionless. He felt scared, disgusting and vulnerable.

Mr Feng's brother kept on driving, unaware of the trouble Dan was in. They were going at good speed and didn't stop for over three hours. All the time, Dan struggled to breathe in the suffocating heat of the claustrophobically small space in which he was hiding. He'd drained the bottle of water Lisa had left for him within the first forty-five minutes. It was the closest to death he had ever come.

Eventually the truck swerved to the left and the road became rough and uneven. Mr Feng's brother braked, and they came to a gradual halt. A couple of moments later Dan heard the click of the cab doors opening on both sides and the sounds of people climbing out. Lisa spoke to him.

"We're going to take a break. We're in the middle of the

desert so we're safe here. We'll just move the stuff off, then you can climb out for a bit."

Dan could hear Mr Feng's brother climbing up the side of the truck and this time the scraping sound of the barrel being hauled out was more than welcome. Dan didn't wait for the all-clear; he writhed his body around and twisted it up into the narrow standing space created by removing the barrel. As he stood up he gasped at the fresh air as it filled his lungs. Weak, he struggled to climb up the side of the truck but found a tiny foothold on top of the table that had been his refuge for the last couple of hours. Scrambling back to the lip of the truck, the cold night air filled his bronchioles with life-giving oxygen. It was beautiful, fresh and clean.

Although his back was stiff, Dan dropped from the top of the truck with the agility of an eager schoolboy. He landed nimbly in the cool desert sand and felt the heat of the truck radiating onto his back. The coldness of the desert night had never felt so wonderful.

"How you doing back there? You OK?" Lisa enquired.

"Not great to be honest," Dan replied. "It's roasting hot, dangerously hot. I finished all that water in about forty-five minutes. Have been dying of thirst for the last hour or so. I'm not complaining really, but the mattress isn't doing much to stop the bumps from the road. It's like I'm lying on the hot truck bed itself."

"Yeah, I know. It's not great. Obviously, had we had a little more time…" Lisa tailed off. She knew the whole set-up wasn't ideal but there was nothing either of them could do about it now. "If it helps," she continued, "we've already covered three hundred kilometres. We're a fifth of the way there."

Dan was surprised they'd covered that much distance. He looked at his watch. Mr Feng's brother must have been going almost a hundred kilometres an hour since they'd left. Dan looked around for their driver but he had disappeared into the scrub and was only visible by the glowing trail his cigarette left in the darkness.

"That helps to know," Dan replied. "If I can just get used to the heat or sort it out somehow that would be better."

"We've got plenty of water up front. I'll give you a new bottle now. I won't give you any more for the time being if it's just going to get hot in there but there should be enough to see us through to the next truck stop. We'll stock up again then. I'll make sure we stop every couple of hours even if it's just to give you a new bottle of water. You'll be OK," Lisa said.

"Thanks," Dan replied somewhat vaguely. The thought of climbing back into that void in a few minutes' time had taken away any of the sincerity he had intended.

Lisa gave him a new two-litre bottle of water that was tepid from having sat in the foot well for the last three hours. She also gave him some more food and a packet of biscuits.

Mr Feng's brother was back and had stubbed his cigarette out in the desert dust. He looked a lot like his brother, but better built and without the moustache. He was the younger of the two by almost three years, and the dirty white T-shirt he was wearing revealed strong arms and the physique of someone engaged in manual labour. He exchanged a few words with Lisa before she turned to Dan and told him it was time to get moving again. Reluctantly, Dan climbed back up to the top of the truck and slid down inside, being careful not to catch his T-shirt on the jagged metal. Lisa had climbed up behind him and passed the water and food. Dan put them on the floor at his feet and began to worm his way back under the table. He was barely under it when Mr Feng's brother appeared at the top and dropped the barrel into the gap. Dan heard two or three more pieces of metal being lowered on top of it and found himself sealed in once again. It would be impossible to get out in a hurry if he needed to for any reason. He felt like he'd just crawled into his own coffin, and it was still stiflingly hot.

They pulled back onto the road and before long the droning roar of the asphalt returned. Dan imagined them hurtling through the Taklamakan at a hundred kilometres an hour, alone in the desert night with nothing but endless straight roads leading into the blackness ahead of them. Recalling the map in his guidebook, he knew that they were passing through some incredible scenery. To the north the snow-capped Tian Shan Mountains would soon be coming into view. To the south the vast expanse of the Tarim Basin. Beyond that, the Kunlun Mountains rose steep and high before giving way to the Qinghai-Tibetan Plateau.

They were travelling along the northern Silk Route – a series of tracks that had been traversed by travellers for centuries before this truck came tearing through. All journeys along the Silk Route had been dangerous; extreme weather conditions and bandits made these journeys perilous for all who had trodden these paths before them. For Dan, his journey was a matter of freedom or imprisonment, although he had actively sought this remote part of China for the relative safety he'd thought it might offer. In doing so, he joined the ranks of the thousands of travellers over the centuries whose journeys through these parts had been fraught with risk.

As the heat in the back of the truck rose again and his mind wandered way out into the desert night, Dan began to drift off. The steady and constant noise of the tarmac below eventually lulled him to sleep.

A couple of hours later Dan woke, dripping with sweat. He reached for his water bottle in the pitch black and drank around a quarter of it. The truck was slowing down again and he looked at his watch. They'd been going for another three hours and it was early morning. They pulled off the road and into a rough layby.

Before long the scraping sound of metal being dragged up and out of the truck returned and a gust of fresh air filled the void under the table as Mr Feng's brother lifted the barrel out of place. Dan squirmed his way free and climbed to the top of the truck. His back stiffer than ever, he took a moment or two to stretch it out as he sat and surveyed their surroundings, the gloriously starry desert night overhead easily the most brilliant he had ever seen. He climbed down the truck and dropped into the desert sand again.

It was bitterly cold and the frigid desert air quickly cooled his sweat-soaked T-shirt, causing him to shiver. Lisa too was cold so this would only be a quick stop. She gave Dan a new bottle of water before he climbed back into the truck. This time, the heat from the engine was strangely welcoming and it was nice to be warm again. Yet the mattress was damp and sticky from his sweat and lying back down on it was unpleasant. Mr Feng's brother replaced the metal and they were off into the desert once more, continuing their journey to the famous market city of Kashgar. Dan wondered how many times Mr Feng's brother had done this journey and whether he ever needed to sleep. As far as Dan knew, Mr Feng's brother had been awake for most of the day and had now been driving for almost seven hours.

The cold desert air had woken Dan up and he lay on the mattress staring into the inky blackness, unable to see a thing in front of him. He put his hand up to feel the table above him. The top of it was wooden although the legs were made of metal. He imagined it to be a large old office table or desk. Now it was the only thing stopping him being crushed by the tonnes of metal that lay all around him.

It wasn't long before Dan began wondering about the next part of his journey again. Where would he stay once he got to Kashgar? How long would he be there before making an attempt at the border? How was he actually going to get across into Kyrgyzstan? Was he going to go via the official route or was he to pick his way through the mountains on foot and slip over the border unnoticed? Was that even possible? If he did that, what would happen at Bishkek Airport when they checked his passport and visa status?

Damn. Visas. Dan realised he would probably need a visa to get into Kyrgyzstan. That meant he would have to apply for one in Kashgar, but that would be impossible. If he was to take the official route into Kyrgyzstan he was going to need a new passport altogether. If he were going to hike an unofficial path into Kyrgyzstan he'd still need a visa to avoid complications when he left the country. But how long would that walk take? Days, probably. Dan's mind raced and his heart began to beat faster with panic. He hadn't thought about all of this until now, but it seemed he was going to be holed up in Kashgar for some time. Given that Lisa would also need a visa to cross the border, he hoped she had thought this all through.

Of course she had.

Days ago.

Dan was awake for the entire duration of that leg of the journey before he sensed the truck slowing down again. He felt them pull off the road but this time something was different. There was no rough desert surface. They were still on tarmac. Judging by his watch it was now early morning and the sun would probably be up already. Travelling during the day threatened to be even hotter than overnight and that in itself was concerning.

As the truck stopped Dan heard the cab door open. Suddenly, as if from nowhere, there were voices. Three or four male voices all speaking Chinese. They seemed to be buzzing around the cab from one side to the other. Dan desperately held his breath. Was this the police? Had they just been pulled over? Was he about to be discovered? If so he was in the most incriminating position he could ever have been in – hiding like a coward in a void under piles of scrap metal clearly hoping never to be found. The talking became louder and somewhat agitated. Dan's heart thumped in his chest and he struggled to calm it down, fearful that he could be heard. He lay there, trying desperately not to make a sound, listening to the voices and trying to work out what was going on.

Then, as if right beside him, he heard someone playing with a part of the truck near his head. There was a clunky metal-on-metal sound and second or two later his ear pressed to the bottom of the truck bed, Dan heard the sound of liquid gushing below him followed by the smell of diesel fumes and he breathed a huge sigh of relief: Mr Feng's brother was filling the tank with fuel. They must have pulled into a petrol station somewhere. With his heart racing, Dan lay there listening to the fuel tank steadily fill below him.

Ten minutes after they'd stopped they were off again. Dan looked at his watch. It was 07:35. There were a couple of holes in the side of the truck he hadn't noticed before through which he could now see tiny glimpses of daylight. It was still swelteringly hot, although he knew it would only get hotter as the sun rose in the sky and the road began to heat up. He drank another half bottle of water. The next time they would stop he wouldn't have the cover of darkness and they would be out in the open desert. Dan tried hard to imagine just how remote this part of the world was and whether there was much risk of seeing anyone else out here. It seemed impossible that they wouldn't see another soul, so any subsequent stops would have to be carefully planned.

Dan was exhausted and his head was busy. He lay on his back, increasingly wet with sweat, staring into the inky blackness that enveloped him. Aside from the few narrow slivers of light that shone through from the wall of the truck behind him, he was in total darkness. Muscle fatigue was beginning to set in and he desperately needed to stretch out. The most comfortable position he could find was lying on his back with his legs bent at the knees, feet in the air, resting on the underside of the desk. He had stopped hearing the roar of the road below him, just as he had stopped hearing the roar of plane engines mid-flight on his way to Beijing. Dan was alone with his thoughts, crossing the Taklamakan desert, only glimpses of which he would ever get to see.

He drifted in and out of sleep again but woke up as the truck juddered violently, skipping over rough ground. This time it went on for much longer at than previous stops. Sitting as upright as he could, Dan listened intently to what was going on outside.

Eventually the truck came to a halt and here was a pause before the cab doors opened. Dan listened to the footsteps of someone climbing the side of the truck and waited for the welcome sound of the metal being removed. It was blissful to hear and his spine tingled with excitement. As Mr Feng's brother lifted the barrel out of place and onto the desert floor, an incredible shaft of sunlight filled the void as if someone had poured liquid gold into the deep well. For the first time Dan could now see the various machine fragments, household appliances and vehicle parts that had surrounded him all the way from Urumqi. He rested momentarily as he took in the liquid sunlight and breathed the abundant fresh air. He squinted hard, his eyes struggling to adapt from the pitch-black, tomb-like enclosure to what he thought must be some of the brightest sunlight on earth. There was no shade to be seen for miles and with the sun almost directly overheard the truck offered little respite.

Dan used his arm to shade his face and searched through narrowed eyes for Lisa. She wasn't anywhere to be seen. In fact, he couldn't see anybody. As his eyes slowly adjusted to the intense light he realised they were entirely surrounded by desert. Looking towards the back of the truck he spotted Mr Feng's brother walking off into the sand dunes around fifty metres away, carrying a roll of toilet paper with him.

At that moment Lisa put her head out of the cab window, making Dan jump.

"Hey, get in here. It's too bright out there without sunglasses on. You'll go blind!"

Dan dropped down to the hot sands below and climbed back up into the truck. It was warm but considerably cooler than where he had been lying, and Lisa had moved over to the middle of the three seats. She gave Dan another bottle of water and some bread buns filled with meat and green peas.

"We picked these up when we stopped for gas a couple of hours ago. They're a real treat. We've got plenty so help yourself if you're hungry."

"So we *did* stop for gas," Dan replied. "I almost shat myself when I heard people talking. I thought we'd been pulled over or something."

"Ah, yeah, sorry. Feng's brother was bartering over the price of the gas. Anything goes out here and they'll rip you off if you're not careful – they know they're the only gas for several hundred kilometres so can charge pretty much what they like. Feng's brother's a pro as well, though – he won't be taken for a ride. He knows them here as well, which helps. He offered to buy twenty of those buns off them to sweeten the deal a little. They wondered why the two of us needed so many but he told them we were picking someone else up in Aksu – the town we passed about an hour ago."

"Ha! I like it," Dan replied between mouthfuls. The buns were good and he ate six between several welcome glugs of cold water that they had bought at the same time.

"We've done just over a thousand kilometres," Lisa told him. "Less than five hundred more to go: the home straight. We're making good time. How you holding up in the back?"

"Wow, a thousand kilometres already?" Dan replied, choosing to resist the opportunity to complain about the heat in the back of the truck. "That's good going. I don't know how

Mr Feng's brother does it – a thousand kilometres straight without much of a break. I guess it's what he does for a living, but it's still impressive. He must be a machine."

"Yeah, we're going to take a bit of a rest here actually," Lisa replied. "It'll give him a break and means we can avoid the worst of the sun. We'll set off again in a couple of hours. Feel free to get some rest, go for a walk or something. Feng's brother will sleep under the truck once it's cooled down a little. There's plenty of space under there if you do want to get some sleep. I'm going to stretch out in here."

Having finished what would turn out to be both his breakfast and his lunch, Dan climbed out of the truck. Mr Feng's brother had returned and left the toilet paper in the space behind the cab. Sure enough, he was settling down to sleep in the shade under the truck. Scooping together a pile of sand onto which he rested his head, Mr Feng's brother lay directly on the desert floor. Dan watched him from the corner of his eye and within a few minutes their driver was asleep. The ability to seemingly switch your body off and lapse straight into sleep was perhaps the one trait Dan envied most in people. It was something his girlfriend had been able to do but a skill he had never mastered himself.

Deciding to take the remainder of the toilet paper and go for his own walk into the desert, Dan set off in the opposite direction from where Mr Feng's brother had reappeared. As he walked it dawned on him again that he was, to a certain extent, still relatively free. If he had wanted to, he could probably have run off into the desert on his own. He wouldn't have survived for long in the intense heat of the day but at least the choice would have been his.

Dan walked for several minutes, picking his way through the rough grass-like shrubs that littered the desert. The sand was baked hard by the sun and broke into thin plates underfoot. He turned round to see how far he had walked and the truck was just a speck behind a couple of small undulations in the distance. This was probably far enough, he thought, so choose a large rock among a scattering of small stones just in front of him.

As he approached what he thought must be the most remote and isolated latrine in the world, he was greeted by a small pile of tattered white toilet paper flapping in the desert breeze.

"Ha! Bloody typical!" Dan thought. "In the middle of the Taklamakan desert, miles and miles from anywhere, away from the main road and I'm not even the first person to have been here! In China you're never far from the next human! Not even out here."

He made his way to another rock, where there was no evidence of previous visitors, and stopped to look out across the vast, inhospitable terrain that stretched for miles into the hazy distance.

Several minutes later, his contribution to this malnourished ecosystem complete, he made his way back to the truck. Copying Mr Feng's brother's example, Dan made a small pillow for himself and settled down for a nap, the shade of the truck making the temperature more than comfortable. Before long, he too was asleep, breathing the fresh desert air and the freedom it brought with it.

Dan dozed for just over two hours before being woken by the sound of Mr Feng's brother crawling out from under the truck. He opened the cab door and spoke with Lisa, who had also just woken up. Dan made his way out and stretched his back, arms and legs, knowing that in a few moments' time he was likely to be back in the confines of the truck bed.

Lisa came and spoke to him.

"We need to be moving again. We've got about another five hundred kilometres to go but as we get nearer to Kashgar there will be fewer places we can stop safely enough to get you out. It's about five hours of driving. We're best to try and get there without stopping now, if we can."

"That makes sense," Dan agreed. "As long as I've got water, I should be OK." Lisa continued "We'll stop in a couple of hours' time, but we won't get out. I'll just jump out and tap on the side of the truck three times. It literally means 'OK. Question mark'. All you need to do is tap twice in reply: 'OK'. Don't try and talk to me unless I talk to you. If you're not OK, tap three times 'NOT OK'. Does that make sense? If there's no reply from you, we'll just keep driving and sort it out when we get to Kashgar!"

"Ha," Dan replied. "That's true, I guess. Yes, it makes perfect sense. Let's just try and get there now. I'll try to sleep again."

Dan climbed the side wall of the truck for what he hoped would be the last time, wishing he hadn't just had two hours' sleep. Dropping down inside the cavity Lisa passed him another two bottles of water and he wriggled into the space under the table. Immediately he realised he should have put the mattress out to dry in the sun. It felt sticky as he crawled across it and lay down again. The large metal drum was lowered into place and before long they were turning around in the desert, jostling their way back towards the main road.

Five hours seemed impossibly long and Dan tried to shut his thought processes down so as to rest his mind. He wondered when Lisa had come up with the code of "OK" and "NOT OK" as a series of taps on the side of the truck. He couldn't help but think she had done this all before. It seemed too well rehearsed, too smooth and too well co-ordinated. He would ask her once they'd crossed the border into Kyrgyzstan.

He lay awake for the rest of the journey, rocked backwards and forwards by the movement of the truck. Eventually they began to slow from the speed of the open highway to what Dan imagined to be smaller roads on the outermost outskirts of Kashgar and for the first time since leaving Urumqi he could hear other traffic on the roads around them. After half an hour or so of this slower pace they turned off the smooth asphalt road again and onto a bumpy track. They drove for a few minutes before coming to a stop. Dan heard the cab door open and a couple of seconds later there was a "tap, tap, tap" on the side of the truck. Dan reached around behind him and returned the signal. He was OK.

Lisa then spoke, whispering through the crack in the side of the truck.

"Change of plan. This is where you need to get out. But you need to be quick: it's broad daylight and there are people around. When we open the back, pass me your rucksack and then climb out. Jump down and run around to the other side the truck. There's a car waiting to take us into to Kashgar. Get in the back and shut the door."

"Got it," Dan replied, his heart now beginning to race again. He hadn't known they were swapping vehicles. The change of plan was unnerving, but he didn't have time to think. Mr Feng's brother was removing the barrel and again the sunlight flooded the void. Dan slid forward, dragging his backpack behind him. As he stood up in the narrow opening, he saw Lisa's hand reaching down. She took his bag from him, threw it to the ground and jumped down. Dan followed, again dazzled by the bright sunlight as he surfaced. He jumped from the truck and ran round the other side as Lisa had instructed. They were in a valley surrounded by rugged, towering snow-capped mountains. Wooden picnic tables sat among short pine trees and Dan could see that there were pathways leading into the woods at the bottom of the mountains. The fleeting glances he got as he ran to the waiting car were beautiful. Were these the Tian Shan Mountains?

At the back of the truck a black sedan car was waiting for him, engine running. Lisa had already thrown his backpack into the boot and was holding the rear door open. It was a smart-looking car of Chinese make that had white net curtains across all the rear windows – the type that might otherwise be used to transport diplomats or government officials. Dan jumped in the back and Lisa followed, closing the door behind her.

In the driver's seat sat a small Uighur man with dark-brown leathery skin. He wore a beautifully embroidered *doppa*, turquoise in colour and decorated with a pattern of white lines interspersed with red dots. His hair was grey, suggesting a man in his late fifties or early sixties. He smiled a warm, reassuring smile as Dan and Lisa got in the car.

Next to him in the passenger seat was a young man who Dan guessed to be in his late twenties. He was slim and smartly dressed in a white shirt tucked into black trousers. He turned to Dan and spoke.

"Hello, my friend. My name is Ali and I am your guide in Kashgar. I am a friend of Lisa's. A friend of Lisa's is a friend of mine. You are welcome in Kashgar. I hear your story from Lisa. You are safe here in my city. We look after you, so please relax. We fight against the Han Chinese, so you are in good company with Uighurs!"

Ali's face seemed to light up as he smiled at Dan. He was a handsome young man with green eyes that sparkled as he spoke. Tall and slim with a youthful complexion, he too wore a colourful *doppa* and his skin was the same olive brown. Where his *doppa* met his face there was a narrow margin of lighter skin that had obviously avoided the intense tanning effects of the Xinjiang sun. Ali turned back round and nodded and the driver began to move off.

Dan realised then that he hadn't had a chance to thank Mr Feng's brother. That was two Feng brothers in a row he had neglected to thank.

"Will we see Mr Feng's brother again?" he asked Lisa.

"No," she replied.

"Please thank him for me next time you speak."

Back on the main road the car turned right towards Kashgar. On either side, wooden shacks and rickety stalls sold a variety of street food from piles of fresh fruit to bags of what looked like spices. Whole goat carcasses hung drying in the sun covered in swarms of black flies. The roadsides were busy: families walked in small groups, people bought and sold at the roadside stalls and old men sat watching the day go by. Dan felt relatively safe here. Seventy percent of the population was Uighur and, as Ali had said, most resented the presence of the Han Chinese. Dan felt surrounded by friend and allies.

Just under an hour later they reached Kashgar proper. White-tiled buildings sat beside buildings of light brown clay. These were interspersed with tall, straight poplar trees with green leaves covered in the light brown dusting of sand that had seemed to follow Dan since he'd first arrived in the desert. He began to sink back into his seat to avoid being seen. Ali seemed to sense his anxiety.

"This car is for VIP guests in the government," Ali said as he looked over his shoulder at Dan. "Not even the Han Chinese will give us trouble in this car," he continued reassuringly.

That was good to know. Dan relaxed a little but still sat as far back in his seat as he could.

They made their way through the outskirts of Kashgar and into increasingly narrow streets that were barely a vehicle's width wide. On all sides were clay-bricked buildings that had few windows. Ornate wooden doors broke up the monotony of the seemingly endless walls. Again, dust and sand lay gathered in neat windblown piles everywhere he looked.

"This is Kashgar Old Town," Lisa said. "You're going to be staying here. Ali has a spare room in his house where you can sleep."

"Really? Wow, that's great. Thanks, Ali," Dan replied, somewhat surprised. Lisa really did have this all worked out. Ali smiled and nodded in response but said nothing as he directed the driver through the maze of streets. People moved into doorways to let then past and small children scattered barefooted ahead of them, laughing as they tried to outrun the car.

After several minutes of navigating their way through the narrow alleyways, the car stopped at a double doorway surrounded by a heavy, ornate wooden frame. Ali squeezed out of the car and, producing a key from his pocket, opened the two doors. The driver turned the car into a small alleyway opposite and reversed back into the open doorway. Dan and Lisa found themselves in a courtyard that was open to the sky save for five wooden beams that stretched horizontally from one wall to the other. A grape vine grew up one wall and had reached the wooden nearest beam. It would grow to cover much of the courtyard in a few years' time, providing shade from the intense Kashgar sun.

Dan had made it to Kashgar. Against all odds he was now almost four thousand kilometres from Beijing. His journey had taken him westwards into the desert by train, through the shifting sands of the Gobi by night and through the endless and inhospitable Taklamakan desert hidden under tonnes of scrap metal. Most importantly, however, he was now just two hundred kilometres from the Kyrgyz border and his final run was imminent.

9

THE COUNTERFEITERS' WORK

Inside his house, Ali showed Dan the bathroom – a small, windowless room with a long-drop toilet and wooden plank with a round hole in it that served as a seat. A roll of paper sat at one end. From the adjacent wall protruded a small tap and short length of hosepipe that was to be used for both washing hands and keeping the wooden plank clean.

Next door, a small bedroom housed a single bed, dark wooden wardrobe and a three-drawer chest of drawers on which sat a Chinese-made television. A frameless old mirror, so aged that most of the reflective surface was gone, hung on the wall. The bed was made with thin white sheets but given the scorching temperatures Dan didn't expect to need much else. High in the top corner of one wall was a small window about eighteen inches square covered by an ornate grille of Islamic design. Dan could see the wooden beams of the courtyard through it.

Ali passed Dan a bottle of cold water as they joined Lisa and their driver outside again. Dan sat and gazed up at the clear blue sky, watching birds wheel freely high over the city.

Standing up to leave, the driver shook Dan's hand. It was unusually sincere and Dan was taken aback by the gesture. Perhaps the driver recognised his battle against the aggression of the Han Chinese. Perhaps Lisa had fabricated a different story entirely. Dan still didn't understand her motivations.

"We need to talk about our next moves," Lisa announced as the driver pulled out of the courtyard and back into the labyrinth of Kashgar's Old Town. "Ali is heading out to get some food for you so let's go into your room. We can't be overheard speaking English out here."

The two went inside and sat on the edge of the bed, facing each other. Lisa spoke first. "Have you thought about how we get across the border? I must admit, having never done this before, I'm a bit out of my depth here," Lisa lied. "I was OK getting us this far only because we happened to be driving to Urumqi when you and I met and then, by pure coincidence, Feng's brother was available to bring us down here. Beyond this point, I'm far less certain."

"How do you know Ali?" Dan enquired. "And when did you set up the switchover?"

"Ali's a good friend of mine," Lisa explained. "We used to work for a tour company here in Kashgar a while back. He's a great guy. He's one of the modern young Uighurs: up-to-date with what's going on in the world, internet-savvy and reasonably well educated. Don't get him wrong, he's passionate about his opposition to the Han Chinese being here in what he sees at the Uighur homeland, and he's just as militant as the generation before him. I called him on that last stint of the journey. He's been out of work since the authorities closed down the company he was working for six weeks ago, accusing them of spreading anti-Chinese sentiment among international visitors. I knew he'd be available to help. The driver is his uncle, who has driven for the local government for almost forty years. I must admit, I wasn't expecting a car with diplomatic immunity," she lied again. "But Ali never fails to surprise me! If he could, Ali would love to travel to Europe. He's a big soccer fan and he learned much of his English from watching matches on TV. It's impressive, but he's a smart guy."

"Wow. That *is* impressive," Dan responded, wondering how anyone gained much of a lexicon from watching football.

"OK," Dan continued. "I think we need to try and cross at the legitimate border point on the Torugart Pass. I wondered whether we try to cross the mountains undetected somewhere else, but truthfully I think that would just be dangerous if not impossible. It might also mean we have problems in Kyrgyzstan if we don't have correct documentation, even if we did survive the mountains. We're going to have to fly out of there at some point, after all."

"I agree," Lisa replied. "To be honest, I hadn't even considered going any other way."

"Good. In that case the main problem I see is my passport. It's me they're looking for and it has my name printed across it in indelible ink. The chances of getting through would be slim to zero. I *assume* they're still looking for me, of course…"

"They are," Lisa noted. "It was on the radio in the truck. They're still hunting for you around Dunhuang. Any time now Iris – remember? The girl I know in Xi'an? – will get your card in the post. That should throw them off the scent a little, assuming they trace your card, of course, and buy us some time. But I agree – I wouldn't like to try crossing the border with your own passport. I'll speak to Ali when he gets back to see what the options are. See if he can come up with something."

"I think," Dan continued cautiously, "I need a new passport. A counterfeit with a new name. I wouldn't know where to get one. I'm out of my depth here as well."

"I don't think it will be too hard," Lisa said. "You can get pretty much anything you want here in China, and certainly in Kashgar. With Pakistan about four hundred kilometres from here and Tajikistan just two hundred and fifty, the black market is big business. I don't think we'll have many problems. The only thing might be the time it takes, but I'll ask Ali."

At that moment Ali returned, opening the large wooden doors with a heavy *clunk*. Lisa stood up to leave the room and Dan followed. As they got to the door Lisa turned and whispered, "Hey." She put her right hand on Dan's cheek and, closing her eyes momentarily, kissed him softly on the lips.

Dan was completely taken aback and didn't move; he hadn't seen this coming at all. Lisa pulled away, looked deep into Dan's eyes for a second and gestured to him with a flick of her head that they needed to go outside. Without a word they walked into the courtyard where Ali was waiting. He had brought several shashlik skewers and a number of small round flatbreads. Despite not drinking alcohol himself, Ali had bought Dan a bottle of cold Wusu beer – the local brew.

Ali passed him the food and Dan sat down on the ledge.

"Ali, thank you so much," Dan said gratefully. "You must let me know how much this all cost. I want to pay for it."

"Don't worry about that right now," Lisa chipped in as she picked her bag up from the courtyard floor and swung it over her shoulder. "We'll sort it out. I'm not staying here tonight," she continued. "I'm staying with a friend while we're in Kashgar. I'll come back in the morning – we'll sort out your passport et cetera then. Sleep well – nice to not be in the back of the truck, I'm sure."

With that, Lisa spoke to Ali in Mandarin, and left. He followed her to the door, watching as she made her way into the alleyway and closed the door quietly behind her.

That night Dan slept soundly. The room was cool but not cold as the heat of the day seeped out from the brickwork, and the mattress was considerably more comfortable than the last one he'd slept on. The silence of the Old Town was blissful compared to the roar of the road he had endured the night before. All things considered, it was beautiful.

The following morning Dan was woken by the call to prayer as it reverberated around the city and bounced along the walls of the Old Town alleys. It was a haunting sound, particularly at this hour, but one that Dan loved. It was five a.m. and once the adhan had finished, Dan could hear the early-morning chatter of birds from the rooftops around him. As he lay quietly in bed he heard the sound of approaching hooves and a number of donkey-pulled carts rattled past. He lay in bed for the next couple of hours listening as the Old Town woke up. He could hear babies crying and children laughing. Occasionally a car would pick its way along the lane outside Ali's house.

At around seven-thirty Lisa arrived. She had brought breakfast for all three of them and Ali proceeded to make a pot of tea on a small stove he had brought into the courtyard. The three sat in silence as they clenched the small, warm teacups tightly in the chilly morning air.

"Sam needs a new passport," Lisa announced suddenly but softly. "One without his real name in so that we can get across the border without problems. Do you know where we could get one?" she continued, pretending not to know.

"Yes, no problem at all. I have a friend who can arrange passports. You need British passport, yes? They are easy. It will take some days and they will want to see your passport for some informations, but I think it is no problem."

"That would be perfect, thanks, Ali," Lisa replied. "Sam, you OK to give Ali your passport? Ali is well connected in Kashgar. He knows everyone and everyone knows him. He can get us literally anything we need."

"Sure thing, of course. I'll grab it in a sec," Dan replied, turning to Ali as he spoke. "So how does it work?" he continued, switching his glances between the two of them. "I guess I'll have to come up with a new name, date of birth et cetera. Do I get a new nationality as well? What about the stamps in my passport? Will they copy those, or use those somehow?"

Ali replied, "They can do whatever we want. I have two friends who are master at forgery. It is their job to do what customers ask from them. I think you should keep your details similar to your real information, in case you are asked for it at the border. I think you should stay from England and maybe exactly one year older. Older people are more trustful than young men in China! Yes, you make a new name for yourself. Who you going to be? Arnold Schwarzenegger? David Hasselhoff? You can be anyone you like when you change your passport!"

"Ha!" Dan laughed. He liked Ali; he liked his humour. He made him feel at ease hidden here in the depths of Kashgar's Old Town while the rest of China hunted for him.

"I take you to see them tomorrow," Ali continued. "They are good friends of mine."

"You can take me to *see* them?" Dan replied, surprised that such people would accept visitors.

"Only I know where they work, and they trust me. You travelled from Urumqi in the back of scrap metal truck for twenty-four hours. I believe you are not joking to me, right?"

Ali's tone had turned serious as this rhetorical question hung in the steadily warming air of the courtyard. "You are a long way from the border still. Any problems and you cannot make it from China on your own."

This sounded more than a little threatening and Dan frowned as he replied to Ali, his furrowed brow expressing the seriousness he now felt in every aching muscle of his body.

"No trouble, Ali; I need your help. I need to get out of China. I need to escape."

Ali relaxed. "OK. We will help you. Lisa is a good friend of mine and she told me you need my help. It is no problem. I think we can do this easily."

Dan started to worry about how seriously Ali was taking this. Did he realise that there was a bounty on his head? Did he realise how long this had been going on, how far he had come and what he had been through to get to Kashgar? Dan began to worry that Ali would be the weak link in his escape plans. He needed to speak to Lisa.

Ali stood up, gathered the teacups and took them inside, leaving Lisa and Dan sitting in silence. Lisa gazed up at the sky, her eyes closed, soaking up the sunlight. Ali reappeared a few minutes later and spoke softly. "I am going out. I need to see my friends. I ask them how long to make a new passport, then I come back. From there, we make a plan."

He left, leaving the door to the courtyard to close gently behind him. Dan waited a few moments to ensure Ali was no longer within earshot, then turned to Lisa. "Lisa, how well do you know Ali? He's so laid-back about this whole thing, I'm worried he's underestimating the situation here."

"He's a good friend," she replied. "I've known him for years. We've been guiding together ever since I got out here, pretty much. He's a laid-back kinda guy, but he's sincere. He will help us get across the border. He also has contacts in Kyrgyz who can meet us at the border and drive us up to Bishkek. If we want we can buy our flight tickets out of Bishkek now. It might make getting through immigration easier, if they have to check that sort of thing when we get there. Don't worry. Ali will take care of us. I'm coming with you, don't forget. He won't let us down."

Dan nodded his head slowly but didn't reply, recognising that he once again seemed to have very little say in what happened hereafter. He was now, again, stuck in the middle of a sprawling Chinese city with very little chance of escaping unaided. Dan looked at Lisa from the corner of his eye, still wondering what her motivation was. Could he really trust her? He remained confused; she had got him this far, helped him beyond anything he had ever experienced before and, so far, all at her own expense.

Or that was his understanding, at least.

At that moment Lisa's mobile phone rang. She pulled it from her pocket, looked at the name that had flashed up and answered it in Mandarin. She spoke for several minutes before hanging up and turning to Dan with a smile.

"That was my friend Iris, from Xi'an. She got your card in the post this morning and has taken the money out. She disposed of your card in a side street near a bar that's popular with the local police. She's expecting them to find it this evening, which should buy us some more time. They'll either think you're in Xi'an or be very confused! She's done a good job for us."

"Wow, cool! Thank you. That should throw them off our scent for a while," Dan replied, using the word "our" deliberately to remind Lisa that she was in the thick of this too.

She looked at him with a gentle frown that soon broke into a warm smile.

Ali had been gone for almost two hours when he suddenly burst through the door in such a hurry that Lisa and Dan both instinctively jumped to their feet.

"Sorry," Ali spluttered. "We have to go now. My friends have a break in their work for today only, so we can start your new passport right now. Please get your real passport and come with me."

Dan looked at Lisa, who nodded back at him. He ran into his room and grabbed his passport, returning to the courtyard half expecting to see the car waiting for him. Instead Ali reappeared a moment or two later holding a long, white, gown-like garment and an ornate *doppa*.

"We can only walk to the counterfeiters' place," Ali said resolutely, urging Dan to change into the clothes he now held out in front of him. Dan was instantly anxious; he would look nothing like a Uighur – his pale skin and Caucasian features would surely give him away.

"It's not far – you'll be OK," Ali reassured.

Dan's heart began to race as the thought of stepping out into the streets of Kashgar, a city with an unusually high police presence at the best of times, filled him with absolute dread.

Lisa, who Dan guessed had been aware of the idea, had disappeared into the street outside for a cigarette. The smell of tobacco smoke drifted into the courtyard as Dan stood rooted to the spot running his options through his mind. He wasn't happy with the plan.

"Do I have to come with you? Can't I just give you my passport?"

"No. My friends will do your new passport for cheap price but they want to meet you. They know your story and want to see the man who escaped from the Chinese police for so long. If you don't come, they won't do it."

"I can pay them," Dan protested in reply.

"It will take three thousand dollars for a new passport in short time. I believe actually you don't have any money because Iris in Xi'an has your card!"

Ali was right – he was penniless and it hit him then like a punch in the face. Lisa has posted his bankcard to Xi'an on the morning they had left Urumqi but, being caught up in the whirlwind of events of the last few days, he hadn't, until this point, realised that that left him without access to any money whatsoever. He was confused. Confused at how Lisa thought he was going to survive in Kyrgyzstan without any money. She was coming with him but he couldn't expect her to pay for everything. He still didn't know why she'd paid out as much as she had done to get him this far.

It would be several days before he learned that Lisa needed him penniless and dependent.

"Please hurry. They are not patient men," Ali insisted.

Dan could read the urgency in Ali's agitated body language.

"OK. But we must hurry. I don't want to be in the streets for any longer than I have to be," Dan replied cautiously. He felt as conspicuous as a man on the run ever could.

Lisa finished her cigarette and returned to the courtyard. She looked Dan up and down with curiosity and amusement. Without looking at Ali, she spoke to him in Mandarin, to which he laughed a deep laugh that Dan hadn't heard from him before.

Lisa spun on her feet to leave but Dan caught her arm and stopped her.

"What did you say, Lisa? What did you just say to Ali?" he demanded.

"I said we need to walk fast!" she replied with a wry smile before stepping over the wooden threshold of the gate back into the street. Dan followed with Ali behind him. The lane was quiet and the hot sun was now high overhead.

The Old Town was built almost exclusively of red-brown clay bricks although some buildings had been rendered with grey concrete. A tangle of telephone wires criss-crossed the lanes at certain points, culminating in web-like masses around the tall telegraph poles. White plastic air conditioning pipes hung out of walls like cannon from warships, the dripping water forming puddles of damp dust immediately beneath them. Dan noticed that some of the houses had overhanging balconies on the upper floors, creating both outside space and shade for the windows below them. The narrow streets, paved with hexagonal bricks, were barely the width of a modern motorcar. The three turned left, right, left again and left again until Dan was well and truly disorientated. Just as he was about to question where they were going, Ali spoke up, softly but deliberately.

"We're here."

They hadn't passed another person in the five minutes or so it had taken to reach the counterfeiters' workshop and Dan sighed with relief to have reached it so quickly. His heart hadn't stopped pounding since they'd left Ali's house and he was breathing heavily as Ali knocked on the nondescript wooden door in front of them. A few seconds later the door creaked open a small way and Dan heard a language he wasn't familiar with. Ali replied quietly and it opened fully.

He entered the house first, followed by Lisa. Dan walked in last and, copying Ali, removed his *doppa* as he stepped into the house. The door was low and he had to duck to avoid cracking his head on the old wood frame. Inside, the house was cool and dark and Dan found himself directly in front of a window that looked out over the city of Kashgar itself.

The door had been opened by a young Uighur woman who Dan guessed to be in her mid-twenties. She was wearing a blue dress with red sleeves and embroidered flowers at the cuffs. Her hair was hidden under a loosely tied pale beige headscarf. She smiled nervously as the unusual trio entered the room and, making sure they hadn't been followed, shut the door quietly behind them. As the door closed, another young woman appeared from a back room carrying a small teapot and three cups. She set them on the table in the centre of the room and began pouring drinks for the visitors. Ali was speaking what Dan assumed to be a Turkic Uighur language to the first woman and their conversation seemed warm and friendly as the group stood and drank the tea. Dan exchanged a few glances with Lisa who only responded with a discreet, reassuring nod.

Dan sensed they were somewhere that didn't receive many visitors. Of the five of them in the room only Ali really looked relaxed, oblivious, it seemed, to the tension the other four appeared to sense. Dan got the uncomfortable feeling that Lisa had met these women before.

After they'd finished with the tea, the first woman uttered something to Ali and promptly left the room through a door at the rear of the house.

"Please," Ali said, ushering Dan towards the same door.

Dan followed the young woman out of the room into a small, rudimentary kitchen and through another door that led outside to a walkway under a white canvas sunshade that was strung between two wooden rafters. A steep set of fifteen or so clay steps led down the side of the building and the path at the bottom stretched away between two adjacent buildings in front of them. But the young woman doubled back and edged along a narrow path that Dan hadn't noticed initially. It was so narrow that he had to pull his arms together in front of him to ensure his shoulders didn't scrape along the walls. Lisa and Ali followed closely behind, both doing the same.

On the right-hand side at the end of the short path was a small doorway in the wall little bigger than the door on a kitchen cupboard. The woman knocked gently and whispered quietly. A second or two later the door opened. The woman stood aside and ushered Dan into the darkness. He looked back at Lisa, who nodded for him to enter.

As he stooped low, his heart racing, Dan could see a dimly glowing light bulb hanging in the darkness. A hand appeared and guided his foot onto a small wooden ladder. Dan steadied himself on the sides of the doorway as he eased himself in. There was just enough light from the bulb to see that he was about two feet off the floor so he jumped down, landing on the hardened clay floor. He moved out of the way so that Lisa and Ali could follow. Dan guessed that they were now somewhere under the house itself. A basement, perhaps. As his eyes began to adjust to the dark, he found himself in an empty room. The floor was hard and cold and the walls were bare clay. As Ali joined them, the young woman closed the door behind and Dan could hear her footsteps walking away, leaving them in the semi-light. In front of them stood a man with thick, scruffy dark hair, a short-trimmed beard and gaunt, chiselled face. He wore khaki green military-style fatigues and heavy black boots.

The brief silence was broken by the man, who spoke softly but with a thick Russian accent.

"Come," he said and pushed open another door in the wall adjacent to where they had come in. Dan could hear the muffled sounds of machines at work as he followed the silhouette of the man through the door into a much larger room. He was convinced that they were now fully under the house, possibly even directly under the room where they had drunk tea a few moments earlier. As his eyes grew accustomed to the changing light he could see that they had walked into a crack house of criminality; on the wall immediately to his right were floor-to-ceiling shelves piled high with boxes of what looked like blank passports of all nationalities. On the adjacent wall were two massive state-of-the-art industrial-sized printers that were churning out reams of legal documents, ready to be signed and passed off as genuine. In the middle of the room was a large wooden table about three metres in length and almost two metres deep. On the left-hand side of it was an architect's drawing board, propped up so high that Dan couldn't see beyond it. To the right of that was a large cutting board, scarred with deep cuts from years of precise scalpel incisions. A small desk lamp provided the only light in the room. On the floor a waste paper bin stood overflowing with offcuts that also covered much of the room like sawdust on the floor of an old butcher's shop.

As Dan gazed around in a combination of awe and dread, a man stood up from behind the drawing board. He was wearing a head-mounted magnifying glass that momentarily made one of his eyes look enormous before he removed it. He was a slim man, almost clean-shaven, with dark eyes. He gave Dan a warm smile as he extended a handshake. As Dan moved closer he noticed the man had the stubbly start of a moustache and goatee and a few erratic whiskers that were much longer than the rest of the hair on his face. His dishevelled appearance suggested he hadn't left the room for a number of days.

"My name is Karim," he said nervously, clearly uneasy speaking English. He shook Dan's hand firmly before returning to his work behind the drawing board.

The first man now spoke to Dan. "And my name is Atash," he said confidently in a strong Russian accent. "I am glad to meet you. Ali told me your story. It is like Hollywood movie!"

As Atash spoke, Dan noticed his piercing blue eyes, so iridescent that they appeared to have no pupil at the centre. He was a scruffy-looking man with a full but relatively short beard and messy dark-brown, almost black, hair. His skin was pale white with at least two scars on the bridge of his nose that he had received in a fight. Despite their incredible colour, his eyes were narrow and cold. He was a career criminal and Dan was glad to be on friendly terms with him.

"My friend is Karim. He is from Kyrgyzstan. He is best counterfeiter in Xinjiang; I am making promise to you. I am from Tajikistan. Together we can make any document you need, in good time and good money. It will not be problem when you want to use one of our passport. We make perfect copy for you, my friend."

Dan stood listening to this man, who appeared younger but infinitely more dangerous than his colleague, unsure of how to reply.

"You need passport, yes?" Atash continued. "What you need? America passport, UK passport, China passport? Or we make you camouflage passport for like New Grenada. Anything you want. We have here."

"What is a camouflage passport?" Dan asked curiously, surprised at the fluency with which the words left his own mouth.

Atash turned to Ali and started speak that unfamiliar language Dan had heard upstairs. Ali listened intently, clearly learning something new. When Atash had finished talking, Ali turned to Dan.

"A camouflage passport is a passport for a..." He paused and turned to Lisa, asking her for a Mandarin word in English.

"Pretend," she replied.

"A pretend country," Ali continued. "They make up a country, like New Grenada, and make a passport for you. It makes you not enemy of any country, so you cross the border easily!"

Both Lisa and Dan laughed. It was a clever idea and something he had never thought of before: a passport with truly international neutrality.

"I think it is safest if I have a UK passport with a new name and photo. Perhaps change some of my details. I am from England, so I cannot pretend to be American for long. I need the border crossing to be quick and easy, with no problems."

"OK. You are my customer. I make what you need," Atash replied without debate. "You have your passport here now?"

"I do," Dan replied, reaching under the long white gown and producing the passport from his back pocket. He passed it to Atash who scrutinised every page with the intent of an expert examining a previously unseen scientific specimen. It made Dan's skin tingle when he realised at that point that Atash was the only other person in the room who knew his real name.

"No problem. This is easy job," Atash said, looking firmly into Dan's eyes. "I give you special price because you are friend of Ali. I give you three hundreds fifty America dollar and three days. In three days you will have new passport and you can go to Kyrgyzstan. I do visa for you for including in price."

Dan looked at Lisa, again aware that he didn't have any money. She spoke to Atash directly.

"That is good. Thank you, Atash. I will pay you for this when we collect it if we are happy with the job you have done."

Atash glared back at Lisa, offended to his very core.

"We do best job in Xinjiang!" he snapped. "You cannot find a better passport. If you don't like my work, you leave now, OK?" It was the loudest anyone had spoken since they'd arrived at the house.

Lisa stood firm, unfazed by Atash's reaction. She knew how to get a reaction from him. Atash scowled at Lisa and turned to Dan.

"OK. I need details from you. What you want new name? What your birthday? Where you born? You tell me, I write. You not change when we make passport so make good choice, OK?" he said. "You want us to start today?"

"Yes, please. I need to get out of China as soon as possible. I need to get into Kyrgyzstan. I want you to copy my passport exactly, with all the stamps that are in there, on those dates so if I need to talk about any of them, I can. Please change the China entry date to two days after the real one. Everything else, the same. And yes, I need a Kyrgyz visa. Can you do all that for me, including the visa?"

"Sure," Atash replied almost arrogantly. "I have big pile of visas ready for you already. So, what name you choose?"

"I've been thinking about this one. I'm going to go with Mason Hunter," he replied. "First name Mason – M.A.S.O.N. Family name Hunter – H.U.N.T.E.R."

"That's an interesting name!" Lisa interrupted sarcastically.

"It's an anagram," Dan replied, giving her no further information. Immediately he could see Lisa's starting to rearrange the letters in her mind, frowning as she computed the various possible combinations.

"OK, what birthday you want?" Atash continued.

"Eighth of August 1980," Dan replied. "Eight is a lucky number in China. I could do with some luck and hopefully it will be a nice innocent talking point at the border if I need it, rather than whether I am that bloke off the news or not."

Lisa replied, "You've been thinking about this. I'm impressed."

Ali had moved around to the other side of the drawing board and was watching Karim meticulously extract a photo from another passport. Next to him was a pile of twenty or so passports held together with an elastic band waiting for the same treatment. This was big business.

"Good." Atash said. "And where you born in England?"

"Let's go for Oxford," he replied. "Maybe they have heard of the university and think I am an academic or something."

"Yes, that is good choice," Atash responded. "I think that is a good place. If I am intelligent man, one day I want to go to Oxford University!" he continued, breaking into a laugh. Lisa laughed with him and proceedings were back on track.

"Last thing. We need a new photo for you, Mr Hunter. Luckily, I take your photo here. It is not in the normal service we do for our customers. This place is a secret, you know. Please. Come over here."

Atash beckoned Dan over to a corner of the wall that had been painted grey. From the darkness Atash pulled out a studio light on an adjustable stand and reflector that he positioned on the floor. He switched the light on, causing Dan to squint as the intense brightness burned deep into his retinas. He tried to shade his eyes from the light as they adjusted to it. Meanwhile, Atash had produced a large digital camera and connected it to his Apple laptop. Clearly no expense had been spared in the equipment Karim and Atash surrounded themselves with – he'd never even seen a professional digital camera before. Dan wondered just how much money exchanged hands here and how vast the network they operated in really was. Standing in the darkened basement beneath the streets of Kashgar's Old Town, about as far from anywhere as it is possible to get, the depravity of the criminal organisation he was currently caught up in was not something Dan wished to dwell on.

He stood there, oblivious to everything, unaware of just how hard the four other people in the room had worked to get him there.

Atash took three photos of Dan that appeared almost instantly on the laptop. Without consultation Atash chose one and rejected the other two. There was nothing sentimental about this operation. A moment later the photo emerged from the printer on perfect glossy paper. Atash put it on a pile of other photos waiting to be cut out by Karim.

"OK. We done here," Atash announced. "We have everything we need. Please leave with us and will make passport for you in three days, no problem. I send to Ali's house by boy. You pay him the money for very good job."

Lisa and Ali had gathered by the doorway and Dan joined them. Karim peered round from behind the drawing board, his amiable face lit up by the light from his desk lamp.

"Goodbye and good luck, my friend. We wait to hear from Ali your good news." He waved a friendly goodbye as he spoke before burying his head back into the pile of work on his desk.

Atash opened the internal door and led the group back into the first empty room they had entered. Dan heard a lock click into place as Atash shut the door behind them. In the dim light of this small room the external door was invisible. Not a photon of light leaked through and there was no handle on this side. Dan didn't know how she knew they were ready, but the young woman now opened the small door in the wall and Ali climbed out, followed by Lisa. Dan turned, shook Atash's hand to ensure they left on good terms and climbed the short ladder out of the basement into the bright sunlight of Kashgar. Dan pulled his *doppa* on and straightened out the gown to ensure it fully covered his legs. The woman led them down the path again and ushered them into a narrow lane that led back out into a lower level of the Old Town. She spoke to Ali and they exchanged nods of friendship before she turned and left them alone in the alleyway.

Ali suggested they head straight back to his house, to which Dan agreed without hesitation.

En route Lisa turned to him. "I've worked it out. I've worked out your anagram – 'Sam on the run'! Very clever," she said. The sparkle in her eye as she looked into his made Dan's stomach somersault.

They arrived back at Ali's house without any hassle, passing just a handful of people on the way. None of them even looked at Dan or his implausibly white skin. Once safely back inside the courtyard, Dan removed the *doppa* and gown and returned them to Ali.

"Keep them for now," he said. "You might need them if we leave my house again or if we have unexpected visitor."

Dan said nothing, the thought of unexpected visitors reminding him of the precarious situation he was still very much in.

The next three days were spent mostly lying on his bed in Ali's house, trying to keep out of the searing Xinjiang heat, contemplating the border crossing into Kyrgyzstan and how strange it was that a largely forgotten corner of the former Soviet Union promised him sanctuary and freedom. Dan longed for the lush green meadows he imagined Kyrgyzstan to offer and to be able to speak to people without fear of being turned over to the police. Here in Kashgar, the Old Town was mostly quiet but the number of people in the street outside seemed to peak at the beginning and ends of the day as they went about their business in the relative cool. They had no idea that the most wanted man in China lay just the other side of that thick clay wall.

Dan didn't see much of Lisa over those three days. He wrongly assumed she was spending most of her time visiting friends in and around Kashgar before they left the country. In reality she was still working. He only saw her late in the evenings, when she brought him hot food. The rest of the time he ate the flatbreads and shashlik that Ali provided, still hostage to the two young women he had encountered in Beijing.

Dan missed Lisa. He missed her girl-next-door face, the smell of her skin and the sparkle in her eyes. He missed her voice and her company. He looked forward to being alone with her in Kyrgyzstan when the two of them would be free from the entrapment of China. Alone with his thoughts, his mind wandered and his imagination escalated.

On the second evening Lisa came to tell Dan that she had arranged for them to be met on the Kyrgyz side of the border by a driver and guide who would take them to the capital, Bishkek, from where they could fly out.

The thought of "we" was comforting solace within the otherwise lonely four walls of the small room in Ali's house, as grateful as Dan was for them. In a few days' time he would be backpacking through Kyrgyzstan with Lisa, a free man once again: free to roam, free from fear, free to tell Lisa that he was falling in love with her.

10

THE HIGH PASS

Around ten o'clock in the morning, three days after the encounter with Atash and Karim, a young boy arrived at Ali's house. He was small and slim wearing a brown tunic over black nylon tracksuit trousers and white trainers. He was only slightly out of breath as he knocked on the open door and waited politely. Ali emerged and greeted the boy. They chatted for around thirty seconds and Dan noticed Ali give the boy a bundle of folded US dollar notes bound by an elastic band, followed by a handful of yuan notes. The boy beamed gratefully and passed Ali a small paper package, bowed his head gently and darted off back into the dusty lanes of the Old Town from where he had come. Dan's new passport had arrived.

Ali spotted Dan watching from the doorway and held the package out to him. Dan walked out into the courtyard and took hold of the parcel that contained both his original passport and his brand-new counterfeit.

"Thank you, Ali," Dan said. "Let's have a look, then."

Dan sat down on the stone ledge to flick through the pages of his new passport. It appeared to be a perfect replica of his original. Karim and Atash had even aged it slightly so it didn't look so obviously new. All his old stamps appeared to be there just as hoped so Dan flicked to the photo page. There was the image Atash had taken of him against the neutral grey background that made the image look like it had been taken in a photo booth back in the UK. His short hair was very different to the shoulder-length hair in his original passport. His name had been changed to Mason Hunter and he was now born on the eighteenth of August 1980. Not quite the eighth of August he had asked for, but close enough. He was now Oxford-born and had an entirely new passport number. He didn't know it at that point, of course, but those nine digits were about to become a significant factor in his attempt to cross the border into Kyrgyzstan.

"It's good," Dan said, looking up at Ali, who stood about a metre from him watching him inspect the passport. Dan held the pages at different angles, looking for the holograms and hidden printing that he knew a genuine passport had. They were all there. "It's *very* good."

"I am glad to hear it," Ali replied. "My friends Atash and Karim are best in business. I don't know how they do it, but I never ask! I only see one fake passport before and he could not tell it is real or fake. They are professionals like master artist."

Dan hadn't thought of it that way before and a strange and unexpected feeling of admiration washed over him as he looked at the perfect but entirely fake passport as a piece of art. Though he could not deny the criminality involved, he respected the level of care, the attention to detail and the skill with which his passport had been replicated. The various stamps had been meticulously recreated, the passport was slightly dog-eared at the corners and the gold emblem on the front had been rubbed off in a number of places. There were creases along the spine as if the passport had been held open and stamped by immigration officials several times before. It really was a beautiful piece of work.

Dan looked up at Ali again, nodding contemplatively.

"You are right, Ali. This is a piece of art. It's incredible to look at, to hold in my hand. You are right. They are artists."

Ali smiled, glad that Dan saw it that way.

"Now you need to decide what you do with your real passport. If they look your bags and find it, I think big problem. But, you don't have Kyrgyzstan visa in it, so you must use your new passport to get out of Bishkek. When you get to UK, you have to choose: do you use real passport or fake passport? If they see fake passport, you have problems. If you use real passport, maybe they ask where is your Kyrgyzstan visa. I leave you now, for a few hours. Tomorrow, we drive to Kyrgyzstan. I need to tell my driver."

With that, Ali opened the door and stepped out into the street. Closing it quietly behind him, Dan was left sitting staring emptily at the closed wooden door, with the words "tomorrow we drive to Kyrgyzstan" ringing in his ears. He felt his throat tightening again – something he hadn't felt for several days and he began to feel thirsty. The day was already scorchingly hot but his palms now began to sweat. After everything he had been through since fleeing Beijing, after the thousands of miles he had travelled and the scares he had had along the way, his run was almost at an end. This time tomorrow it was possible that he would be in Kyrgyzstan, breathing the fresh mountain air of freedom. The other side of the Tian Shan, the Celestial Mountains, really would feel like heaven.

On the other hand, it could all be over. He could be locked up in a cell here in Kashgar, the chief of Beijing police on the next flight via Urumqi. Dan would then be interrogated, perhaps even tortured, over the coming few days. These could be his last few hours of freedom. He had run from the police, evaded them for days, engaged with criminals and embarrassed them on a national scale. His life depended on the intelligence of the Chinese border guards standing between him and Kyrgyzstan. Ali was right. If they *did* search his bags and find his original passport it would be game over. But he hadn't considered using his fake passport to get back into the UK. He had always imagined that he would use his real passport.

Dan retreated to the cool shade of his room and lay on the bed, running the options through his mind. Should he leave his passport here in China so that he could never be caught with it? Should he destroy in entirely, burn it perhaps? Or should he take it with him, hiding it somewhere deep in his luggage and simply hoping it was never discovered? Before drifting off to sleep, he decided to keep it with him. If he *was* arrested at the border he might need it to identify himself to the British consulate. If he did make it through and all the way back to the UK he would re-enter on his original passport. The risk of trying to enter the UK on a fake passport was too great. The thought of stumbling at the final hurdle, just as his troubles would be all but over, convinced him to take it with him, hidden in the depths of his backpack.

He woke up a couple of hours later to the sound of Lisa whispering to him. "Sam. Sam, wake up," she said softly. "Ali called me. He said you have your passport so we can leave for the border tomorrow morning."

As he came to, Dan saw Lisa's face close to his, her large eyes watching him return to life. She put her hand on his cheek and smiled. "It's almost time to leave this shit behind us."

Dan laughed and sat up on the edge of the bed beside Lisa.

"How do you feel?" she asked.

"If I'm honest, nervous," Dan replied. "This could go one of two ways. You know what those are. This time tomorrow I'll either be a free man enjoying the vistas of the Kyrgyz steppe or a prisoner here in China. Locked up in a cage beginning to rot with the other unmentionables."

Lisa picked Dan's new passport up from the chest of drawers and began flicking her way through it just as he had done earlier.

"Wow. It's good," she commented. "I don't really know what I'm looking for, but you cannot tell that it's a fake. Ali has told me about Karim and Atash's work before, but I've never seen it in the flesh," she lied. "It's incredible."

There was a moment or two of silence between them as Lisa looked ponderingly through the passport, turning it round to read the upside-down stamp he had been given on his entry into Slovenia a couple of years earlier. She put the passport down and turned to Dan.

"You're going to be OK. You're going to make it. You've come this far, you've escaped everything they've thrown at you and you're still going. This is the last challenge. I am confident they're not going to spot the fake passport – it's too good a copy. You look nothing like your old self or the photo they are circulating on the TV. I just don't think there's going to be an issue," Lisa said.

"I hope you're right," Dan replied cautiously.

With that, Lisa lay down on the bed, squeezing into the narrow space between Dan and the wall. She arched her back and shuffled up the bed to rest her head on his pillow. Dan turned to look at her, the beautifully round tops of her breasts just visible in the V-neck of her tight white top. She looked back at Dan, gazing deep into his eyes. A seriousness spread across her face as they looked at each other for what felt like a lifetime. Dan was lost in the unspoken exchange entirely.

A moment later, still gazing at him, Lisa slipped off her top and lay on the bed in her jeans and bra, eyes glistening as she looked deep into Dan's, inextricably pulling him in. Dan lay next to Lisa, his head propped up on his left arm, heart racing, before gently placing his right hand on her flat stomach. He moved his palm up the contours of her body and onto her ribcage, wrapping his fingers around her side and he went. Her warm skin was soft and smooth as Dan ran his hand slowly back down the length of Lisa's body and over her stomach again, pulling her slightly closer as he did. She looked beautiful lying there on the bed next to him and he could now smell her hair and her skin. It was intoxicating, and Dan's heart was pounding. But this wasn't the panicked racing that had enveloped him so many times since running from the Lu Yuan. No, this was different. This was an intense fluttering that he felt in his chest and stomach simultaneously such that it almost stole the breath from his lungs. His body felt heavy and weightless all at the same time and the world seemed to melt around him as he leaned in and kissed Lisa deeply on the lips.

It was late afternoon as Dan and Lisa made love. Warm, sweaty, passionate but loving sex. This wasn't an emotionless encounter. There was love between them as they became lost in each other until the sun had set outside.

Lisa drifted off to sleep as they both lay there naked on the bed, entwined. Dan pulled the sheet over them and lay staring at the ceiling as he had done for so many hours over the last few days. Lisa's head rested on his arm as he cradled her against his body. His own head was a mess of emotions: scared, exhilarated, in love, nervous, uncertain. Another couple of hours passed as all these thoughts ran havoc inside his mind.

At around nine o'clock, Lisa's phone pinged with a text message. She woke up slowly, kissed Dan on the lips and sat up. She pulled on her top and reached for her phone, her legs covered by the white bed sheets. Dan watched her read her message, looking at the seductive curves of her braless breasts. She was beautiful.

A second message arrived and Lisa got up abruptly and switched the television on. Dan sat up, realising this could only be about him. Lisa flicked through a couple of channels and found the news. Getting dressed as she watched intently, she began to translate. "It's about you, Sam," she said excitedly. "They've found your card in Xi'an and have worked out that you withdrew money a couple of days ago. They've sealed off the city and are going from district to district looking for you! This is incredible! Far, far better than I could have imagined. Wow. The two girls are still in hospital in Beijing, apparently, but this all really helps you tomorrow. The Torugart is the last place they will be expecting you to turn up!"

"Fucking hell," Dan said as he watched footage of hotels being raided and foreigners being questioned in front of crowds of television cameras.

"I still don't understand why this got so big. Surely this kind of thing happens all the time in country of this size."

"Sam, you do know, don't you?" Lisa remarked as she turned to him, suddenly sounding concerned.

"Know what?" Dan replied hesitantly. "I know it involves some Beijing politician somehow, and something about corruption, but I have no idea who or why!"

"He's not just some Beijing politician, Sam!" Lisa continued. "The girl to your left in the photo just happens to be the daughter of Zhou Jun – a senior member of the Central Committee of the Communist Party – one of the most powerful men in China, widely tipped to be a future leader of the country. He is the former Minister for Housing and Development. However, he's in the middle of a party investigation into corruption, which, if proven, would be a political nuke.

"Zhou's brother-in-law is Secretary for Xinjiang and *his* son just happens to run a construction company out here – XinCivil. Apparently, last year Zhou signed off two massive new dam projects on the Irtysh river, north of Urumqi, without going through the full tender process, with, predictably, the secretary's son winning the contracts to build both. None of it is particularly subtle, but it was all over the news the week before you got here. They might have got away with it if it wasn't for Uighur separatists who bombed the XinCivil offices in Urumqi when word got out that Uighur prisoners were to be used as forced labour to build the dams. The bombing made national news, of course, and it all unravelled from there, especially when international human rights groups picked up on the story, too. The last thing China wants is prying international eyes out here. I don't know whether you running to Xinjiang is genius or crazy, but it sounds like you had no idea you've just run into the fire itself."

Dan listened dumbstruck as Lisa continued. "And the Chief of Police is pretty much fighting for survival. If he doesn't find and convict you, he will have failed in what is probably his most important assignment ever, because if word gets out that this has all been made up, to detract from the corruption investigation that was due to conclude any day now, heads will roll. Including that of this Zhou Jun. It will bring massive embarrassment upon the whole Communist Party; they're battling with corruption and diminishing public trust as it is. It's a major political scandal now, blown out of all proportion because of the people involved and that you haven't been caught yet. The media love it. There are documentaries starting to appear on TV about the whole thing. The news is enjoying its highest ratings ever."

Lisa looked at Dan and realised that he hadn't known any of this.

He sat in front her, silent, stunned. He understood it all now. It all suddenly made sense. If they caught him, Zhou Jun would ensure Dan didn't stand a chance at justice; he would be incarcerated in a heartbeat. Finding Dan and convicting him would be a sure-fire route to promotion, wealth and celebrity status for the police involved and the troubled politician would get to spend time with his traumatised daughter, diverting the spotlight and garnering the sympathy of the nation. It was dog eat dog. East versus West. Career police chief versus foreign young backpacker. It was ugly and Dan was at the very centre of the storm.

"Fuck them all," Dan said eventually. "I get it." He lay back on the bed in disbelief. "I fucking need to get out of here tomorrow," he said resolutely.

"Yeah, it's pretty fucked up, huh? I know you're innocent, Sam. From the moment I met you I knew you were innocent," Lisa replied, almost letting her story slip. "I need to get my stuff packed up for tomorrow. We're going to leave early. The border opens at eight o'clock and with a bit of luck we'll find them groggy and off the pace when we get there. We need to arrive right as it opens. It's also a busy time of day so they'll be flustered and keen to get people through quickly. We leave here at seven o'clock. You OK with that?"

"Um, yeah. Yeah," Dan replied, not really able to compute everything he was hearing. His head was spinning.

"Sam," Lisa said sharply, "I'll see you first thing in the morning." She leaned over and kissed him again.

Dan held her head close to his and kissed her deeply. "This time tomorrow we'll be star-gazing on the Kyrgyz side of the border carefree and together," he promised her confidently.

Lisa smiled warmly at him and left. Ali had just returned and Dan heard the two of them talking in the courtyard. He got dressed quickly, straightened himself up in the small mirror and waited for Lisa to leave. As he heard the door close, Dan went out to see Ali.

"My driver come tomorrow morning early," Ali said. "We leave before the city is busy and the border people wake up. I think you will cross the border easily at that time," he reassured Dan. "Now, I sleep because I wake up early."

With that Ali smiled and sauntered into his room. Dan wasn't tired so spent his last evening in China lying on the ledge in the courtyard watching the sky. Despite being in the middle of Kashgar, the night was surprisingly dark and the stars were clear overhead. The temperature was dropping but it was pleasantly warm late into the evening. Around midnight Dan packed his bags, placing his original passport at the bottom of his backpack along with the scroll painting he had bought in Beijing.

The following morning, Dan woke early. The sun was only just coming up and the air was chilly. He washed his face and went to sit in the courtyard with his belongings, anxiously contemplating the day ahead. Ali woke up shortly afterwards and joined him in the courtyard. "You ready, my friend?" he asked.

"As ready as I'll ever be," Dan replied.

They sat in silence for around half an hour exchanging only occasional words, the anticipation on both sides hanging heavily in the morning air. Ali knew this was a big day. Dan knew this was possibly the most dangerous thing he had done so far and the outcome was far from guaranteed.

Just before seven a.m., Lisa arrived. She smiled at Dan and threw her bag on the ground. Their driver arrived several minutes later and backed the car into the courtyard. The three discussed logistics for a few moments before Lisa turned to Dan to fill him in.

"Shall we? Our driver's ready. He's going to drive you and me to the border. Here's the story: we don't speak any

Chinese. Ali is our guide here and we're just a couple of tourists backpacking our way into Kyrgyzstan. Nothing more complicated than that. We'll go through passport control at the entrance to the Torugart road, about an hour from the city. After that, we hit a gravel road that takes us up to the border post at the top of the pass. That road takes a couple of hours, I believe. At the top, we leave Ali and the driver as we walk across the border with our bags. On the other side our Kyrgyz driver and guide will be waiting. Ali and our driver return to Kashgar and we continue on to a place call Tash Rabat – a yurt camp in the mountains. We have food and accommodation waiting and we should be there by nightfall, all being well."

"That sounds good to me," Dan replied enthusiastically.

It *did* sound good. It sounded like a concrete and straightforward plan. Dan put his bag into the boot of the car and joined Lisa in the back seats. Ali stood by the open gates, waiting to close them as they left.

One last time the car picked its way through the narrow streets of the Old Town that was now waking up to the start of the new day. Lisa and Dan pulled the white net curtains around the rear windows of the car as they joined the early-morning traffic on the streets of Kashgar. There were only a few cars around but there was a noticeable police presence. Most major junctions seemed to be overlooked by a policeman and there were patrol cars parked along all the main roads. Lisa assured Dan this was normal for Kashgar, where ethnic tensions frequently spilled over into trouble.

Before long they were in the outskirts of the city and making their way through agricultural land. The roads were dusty and all along the route poplar trees stood covered in the familiar sandy yellow-grey film. Stallholders were setting up their roadside kiosks for another day of business and schoolchildren ran along the roads, their backpacks bouncing on their backs as they went.

Dan's nerves were starting to get the better of him and he began to fidget. He got his new passport out and reviewed his new name and date of birth, familiarising himself with his new identity just in case he was questioned on any of it. He flicked through the pages as he looked for the details page.

He found his upside-down Slovenia stamp, his Morocco entry and exit stamps and various other stamps. He reminisced about some of the more enjoyable trips he'd had, mostly with friends and his ex.

Then, with the border post in view, Dan's heart stopped. He scrabbled backwards and forward through his passport several times, frantically turning the pages.

"Lisa!" he shouted with such alarm that Ali turned round and the driver looked at him in his rear-view mirror. "Lisa! I don't have a China visa in here!" he gasped. "Fuck. They've fucking missed it out."

Lisa took the passport from him and began flicking through the pages. She went through the entire document three times and saw that he was right. Dan clutched at his head with both hands in disbelief. Lisa called to the driver to stop and he pulled off the road into a small layby just two hundred metres from the border. Lisa gave the passport to Ali. He flicked through the ornate pages and looked back gravely at Lisa, speechless, their eyes locking for several moments.

"We have to go back," Dan said, panicked. "I cannot get out of China without a visa in there. They'll haul me over the coals. We need to get your friends to put a visa in. Fuck! Why would they miss it out and why didn't I notice it? Are you sure we can trust these guys? Are you sure this wasn't a set-up?"

Dan's hands were shaking as he spoke and he had broken into a sweat. They were within sight of the first border post and he had nearly blown it.

"Fuck," Lisa said, realising there was no alternative. "Sam's right. We'll have to go back. There's no way we can try and get through if he hasn't got a visa. Ali, tell the driver to turn around. We'll need to get back to yours."

Dan sank back into the seat, his head pressing deeply into the headrest in intense frustration. He couldn't believe this was happening; he was so close to getting out of China but he had also just come excruciatingly close to disaster. He closed his eyes and listened to his racing heart thumping in his chest.

The driver turned round in the road and they made their way back to Kashgar. The four sat in silence for the entire journey, each unsure of where the blame lay. Should Dan have spotted it? Was Ali responsible for having recommended Atash and Karim? Was Lisa responsible as this whole thing had been of her planning?

The city was much busier now, the last half an hour making all the difference to the number of people on the streets. Dan shook his head incredulously as they pulled back into the Old Town. Back where they had started. He was angry, although he was unsure who he was angry with.

Back in the courtyard of Ali's small house, Dan sat down on the ledge with his head in his hands while Lisa stood opposite. Ali was pacing backwards and forwards in one corner.

"We need to get Atash to do a visa today. Tomorrow is Friday and the border is closed at the weekend. The longer we stay here, the greater the chance of something going wrong," Dan said. "Ali, I need you to take my passport back to Atash today and get him to do it," he continued, taking charge of the situation.

Ali looked at Lisa and she nodded slowly in agreement. There really was no other option. Ali took both of Dan's passports off him reluctantly and agreed to go back to Atash's place. Ali was unsure whether Atash and Karim had ever had work returned to them before so he would go with a certain amount of trepidation. With that, Ali left and Dan sat shaking his head, looking at Lisa without speaking. She knew exactly what he was thinking, but stayed silent. She sat there looking at the sky between the beams above the courtyard.

A few moments later, she spoke. "I need to go back to mine for a bit. I won't be long. A couple of hours, tops. We'll have to try again tomorrow, but I'll come back later with some food. I'm sorry about today."

With that she picked her bag up and opened the door.

"Lisa," Dan called out, "I don't blame you. I should have spotted it. I just don't understand why they would miss it out, particularly as I specifically asked them to put a different date on it. Atash wrote it down, didn't he? It's not your fault."

Lisa smiled at him gratefully and left. Today had been a disaster and everyone knew it. Dan went back into his room and fell onto the bed, shattered from the adrenaline and frustration of the last hour, seething about what had happened. Atash and Karim were supposedly the best in the business, and they had made what appeared to him to be an unbelievable oversight. It was such an oversight that Dan could only assume it had been deliberate. He was angry at having trusted them with such a fundamental part of his whole run to the border and that he had allowed them to let him down. He was angry with himself for not having spotted it either. He was angry that Lisa wasn't with him at that very moment. He breathed deeply and heavily, trying to slow his heartrate. He found himself staring at the ceiling once more.

Just before midday, the sound of the door closing on the courtyard made Dan jump up. Ali had returned. With a heavy sigh, Ali handed the passports to Dan and nodded slowly. The visa had been done.

"Not good. Atash was not happy with his mistake. He say sorry to you for your trouble today," uttered Ali wearily.

He looked exhausted and Dan wondered what he had just been through. Given the way Atash reacted when Lisa questioned the quality of his work, Dan suspected he had been furious that Ali had had to take the passport back. Atash was a proud man and today would have been intolerably humiliating for him. Dan sensed that there was something Ali wasn't telling him.

Lisa arrived back in the early evening and, as promised, had brought food with her. Dan slowly picked his way through the food as the sun went down, ending what had been a spectacular failure of a day. This time yesterday he had been imagining that this time today he would be sitting under the stars in Kyrgyzstan, watching the Milky Way roll by overhead with Lisa at his side, a free man. Tomorrow, they would have to try for the border again. Today had been a day to forget.

Lisa left soon after and Ali went out for a walk, he said, to reflect on the day's events. Alone, Dan retired to bed early, exhausted from the trauma he had been through that morning. The disappointment and frustration of the day had drained him emotionally, but he couldn't shake the "*what if...?*" question. He was lucky to be back in Ali's house; it could have been a whole lot worse.

The next morning Dan woke early again. There was something about this border crossing that caused him to wake before sunrise. His stomach was churning as he sat on the edge of the bed and rubbed his eyes into the new day. He stood up and stretched, reaching the ceiling with the tips of his fingers. He caught a glimpse of himself in the mirror and psyched himself up once more. Today they would succeed. There was nothing within their power that would let them down now. They had done everything they had to do and everything was in place.

Ali was already up, hunched over a small cup of tea, a blanket around his shoulders as protection from the chilly, cloudless desert dawn.

"Hey," Dan greeted him disconsolately. The failure of yesterday still hanging heavily over both of them.

"Hi, Sam," Ali replied. "You sleep OK?"

"Yeah, I did. Thanks. You?"

"Not bad," Ali replied.

It was just before five o'clock and the sky over Kashgar was turning from the darkness of night into the inky, velvety-blue of the very early morning. The call to prayer had just finished. Ali poured Dan a cup of tea as he sat down opposite, sipping at the edge of the boiling water. The steam filled Dan's eyes with a pleasant and moisturising warmth. The next time he looked up, the sky was turning the bluey-grey of cigarette smoke and a few wispy bands of cloud now streaked the crisp Friday morning air.

At six-thirty Lisa arrived. She was quiet. Daunted no doubt, Dan assumed. He reminded himself that not only was she about to help the most wanted man in China to escape over the border into a corner of the former USSR, but she was also coming with him, giving up everything for the biggest unknown of her life.

Lisa smiled at Dan.

"Ready? You'll get across today. Today we make it happen," she said.

He didn't know it then, but this seemingly casual phrase would ring in his ears for days to come.

"Yeah, all good," Dan replied to the girl he was rapidly falling for. "Ready to get going when you are."

"Sure thing. We'll be off soon," Lisa responded.

Just before seven a.m. the driver appeared. Again, he, Lisa and Ali discussed logistics. The conversation was much more serious than it had been the day before.

"Same plan, same story as yesterday," Lisa said to Dan as she opened the car door. Lisa let Dan get in first. She seemed nervous, which was out of character for the woman who had been so strong for so long. Dan wrongly dismissed it as nothing more than the thought of the border crossing that lay ahead of them.

Once again the car made its way out of Kashgar, the streets once more coming to life. They passed the same groups of children skipping their way to school and before long they were on the road out to the border. Dan gripped the armrest in the door with his right hand and put his left hand on Lisa's leg.

She looked at him with sympathetic eyes and touched his hand momentarily. She still seemed on edge.

"You OK?" Dan whispered to her.

"Yeah, sorry, Sam," she replied quietly. "I just want to get through this first border post. We're almost there."

"I know. Me too," Dan replied, as he turned to gaze out of the window.

As they approached the border, the road narrowed to a single lane, forced to half its normal width by a vast line of trucks that Dan suspected had been queuing for a number of days, waiting for clearance to cross into Kyrgyzstan. Many had their cab doors open and their drivers asleep across the seats. Dan had flashbacks of the journey he had made to Kashgar a few days earlier in the back of the truck, crammed into that void under the table. He remembered Mr Feng before that and how he had never had the chance to thank him.

The driver slowed to a crawl as they pulled up behind a line of stationary cars. They were fifth in the queue and Dan could see police and immigration officials ahead of them. As they inched forward, the driver wound down his window and as they reached the front of the queue one of the immigration officials peered into the car. Ali spoke and explained who his passengers were, pointing to Lisa and Dan in the back of the car. Lisa held Dan's hand, reinforcing the guise of them being a couple. The immigration official said something to the driver, who proceeded to drive forward. Into the lion's den once more.

He parked the car up in a rudimentary and dusty parking area at the front of the immigration post and Ali turned to Lisa and Dan.

"OK, we need to go into the immigration office with your passport and they check these things. This is normal process. No problem," he assured them.

Shoulder to shoulder, the three walked into the immigration office. It was an ugly, white-tiled building with reflective, blue-mirrored glass windows across the top. Large golden Chinese characters emblazoned the front facia of the building and Zeng Liansong's Five-Star Red Flag fluttered in the katabatic Tian Shan winds. Dan was now standing at the foot of the Celestial Mountains that had been nothing more than a distant dream away as he had fled Beijing.

If the sight of these mountains ahead of him hadn't been so breathtaking, he would have perhaps been more nervous about being out in the open, surrounded by police and immigration officials. As it was, his heart was racing and his palms were sweaty, but he felt calm. He tried to act like the slightly bemused backpacker that he was supposed to be. The police, he noticed, were mostly concerned with the new cars that were arriving and were not paying much attention to those they had already waved through. Despite the police presence, the area was awash with money-changers and fake watch hawkers, haggling with drivers and tourists alike for business. It was a filthy, lawless scene of desperation and dishonesty. As they walked, Dan wondered what purpose the police here really served.

Inside the immigration building an early-morning argument was under way between a young official in dark green uniform and a truck driver who looked like he had been sleeping in his truck for weeks. The driver was shaking his papers in the face of the official on the other side of the desk, who sat stoically, shaking his head in return. Eventually, the driver reached into his jacket pocket and produced a scrap of pink paper. The official took it, looked it over several times and stamped it. The driver sunk in relief, nodded his head and collected his papers. Dan couldn't understand what had really been going on but it seemed bureaucratic in the extreme.

Another couple of truck drivers ahead of them passed through without issue and Lisa and Dan shuffled their way to the front of the queue. Ali spoke with the guard in Chinese as Lisa stood there listening, forgetting that she wasn't supposed to understand any of their conversation. Nervously, Dan handed over his new passport. The official thumbed his way through it and found the page with the visa. Dan's heart was pounding. A second or two later the man opened the details page with Dan's improbably recent photo on it. He stopped momentarily to read the details. Dan saw the young man swallow hard as he looked at the passport. Looking up, he squinted, straining to look beyond Dan's eyes and into his soul. It was an excruciatingly uneasy moment.

He flicked back to the visa page and without hesitation stamped the exit date on to it. He did the same to Lisa's without even looking at her photo page. They were free to go. Dan couldn't believe it had been so simple.

It was all a little too easy.

Back in the car and leaving Kashgar and the chaos, uncertainty and dubious currency changers behind them, the driver tore into the rough gravel road of the Torugart Pass, sending a spray of small stones skitter-scattering out from behind the increasingly impractical sedan. Oncoming trucks showered the windscreen with dust as they rattled past.

The border into Kyrgyzstan, normally just a steady stream of trucks carrying goods and scrap metal between the two countries, had just become a path to freedom. The beginnings of a wave of excitement began to wash over Dan. He turned to Lisa and smiled as they climbed the gravel road into the rugged mountain pass. She held his hand as they climbed higher and higher. On either side of the road marmots scurried for cover on short, stout legs as the car hurtled past, their large backsides clearly giving them away in the stubby grass.

The road wove its way into the mountains, climbing slowly at first but steepening as they approached the border itself. The flat grassy foothills were miles behind them as the terrain became progressively rocky and rugged. Eventually they were surrounded by snow-capped peaks, the sudden temperature drop tangible even inside the car. Dan felt himself starting to become breathless as they gained altitude and the air thinned. For much of the journey they had sat in silence, but Dan was tantalisingly close to freedom and his skin began to tingle at the prospect. Lisa gazed out of the window, occasionally looking up at the rocky cliff faces as they skimmed past. A flurry of snowfall that lasted around ten minutes briefly threatened to scupper their plans yet again.

Before the two hours were up, the driver began to slow. The road took one last steep hairpin turn and then almost levelled out into wide, flat plateau of land. Looking out the window to his right, Dan could see mountaintop after mountaintop, stretching as far as the eye could see. He was in the heart of the Tian Shan. It was a breathtakingly beautiful sight. He was at the top of the high pass.

Ali turned to his passengers and spoke. "We're here. This is the border. We show your passport one more time and they open the gate. You have to walk with your bag for a few metres. Your new driver and guide are coming on the other side. Congratulations, Sam. We are here."

They were poignant words and Dan felt dizzy, unsure what to do with them. He felt like a convict about to be released from prison. A trapped man about to breathe the fresh air of freedom that he had craved for so long. His palms were sweaty. Ali got out of the car and opened the door for him.

The driver opened the boot of the car and Dan reached into pick his backpack out. Instantly it struck him.

"Lisa!" Dan gasped. "Where's your bag? Where's all your stuff?"

He was confused and looked again for Lisa's bag. It wasn't there.

"Lisa. What's going on?" he cried breathlessly in the thin air. He heaved deeply for what felt like an eternity, before Lisa finally replied.

"Sam, I'm not coming with you. I'm so sorry. I'm not coming with you," she said, looking up at him and choking on her words, her eyes welling up. "I can't. I can't leave everything here in China. This is where I belong. I don't know you. We only just met. You need to go by yourself. Go and get out of here. It makes no sense to come with you. I have too much to lose."

Dan was lost for words and felt sick to his stomach. He searched for a response but could find no words. His mind flashed back to earlier this morning. He hadn't seen her put her bag into the car. She hadn't done it. She'd had no intention of joining him. He couldn't understand why she wouldn't be coming with him. Dan hadn't even considered this for a second. It wasn't supposed to be happening like this.

"You need to go now," she continued. "Cross the border. The guards are waiting for you. You don't have time to waste here. You need to go. I'm so sorry, Sam. Please forgive me. One day this will all make sense."

Dan's head was spinning. Lisa, Ali and the driver were all stood facing him as Ali urged him towards the border, speaking sympathetically. "Sam, they are waiting for you. We have to leave you here now. You must cross the border. Your guide is coming for you."

His voice was soft and encouraging. The gentle authority that he exuded somehow forced Dan forwards. With his bag slung over his shoulder, his legs shaking, weak and heavy, Dan shuffled through the powdered gravel towards the gate. One of the two young soldiers on duty at the remote outpost stepped forward and took Dan's outstretched passport. Dan didn't remember much about those next few moments; his head was foggy with confusion. The soldier looked at the photo and stared Dan up and down before his face fell ashen. He passed Dan's passport back to him and said something to the colleague standing beside him, who immediately stepped forward and lifted the bar that formed the crude border between China and Kyrgyzstan. As Dan began to walk forwards, he felt Lisa's hand on his arm.

"Sam. I need you to give these to your guide. They are instructions for the next part of your journey. Do not open them – the guards cannot see the contents and your guide needs them straight away."

She pushed two envelopes into Dan's hand, one white and the other a pale blue. Both had Chinese writing vertically down the left-hand side. One was thin, containing little more than a letter but the other was full and felt padded. Dan put them inside his passport and clutched it tightly. Lisa was still holding his arm.

"I'm sorry, Sam."

She looked up at him with large, wet eyes. Dan looked back at her, longing for an "I love you" that never came. He moved to kiss her, craving one last touch of her lips. She recoiled slowly but deliberately, letting go of his arm. That was the last time Lisa ever touched him. She took a couple of steps backwards and swallowed hard before turning and walking back to the car. That was the last time he ever saw Lisa's face. The driver had turned the car around and was now holding the rear door open. Lisa got in.

Ali pointed a short distance just beyond the border post behind Dan. A car was approaching, a cloud of dust billowing in its wake. A young Kyrgyz man in pale denim jeans and leather jacket got out. He waved to Ali, who returned the gesture.

"There is your guide, Sam. I know him," Ali said, walking towards to him. "His name is Dastan. He take great care of you, my friend."

Dan could hardly hear the words Ali was saying. A swirling cloud of confusion had smothered him, and he felt dizzy and faint. Dastan had walked as close as he was allowed and was smiling broadly, waiting for Dan to cross into his country.

For all the time he had been running, in all the terrifying moments in the last two weeks, it had never crossed Dan's mind that when the time came he would be reluctant to cross the border out of China. Dan longed for Lisa, his heart torn clean in half. But she was gone.

With a deep breath Dan's shook Ali's hand, thanked him, took two steps forward and left China.

11

UNDERSTANDING

On the other side of the border, Dastan's shook Dan's hand firmly and vigorously, and welcomed him to Kyrgyzstan in his thick but boyish Russian accent. Dastan was fresh-faced with blonde hair that was shaved short around the sides, leading to slightly longer hair on top. His pale Caucasian complexion was markedly different to the faces Dan had been among for the last week or so and Dan subconsciously noted that this represented a fork in the road in his pursuit of freedom.

Dastan took Dan's backpack from him and opened the rear door of the car. Dan slumped into the back seat. The driver turned the car around and they started to head away from the border. As they left, Dan turned to look out of the rear window only to see Lisa, Ali and their driver heading back down the Torugart road towards Kashgar. That was the last time he ever saw Lisa. He watched out of the window until the car was out of sight and then turned, his stomach concave with grief, as the border post disappeared into a cloud of dust behind them. Dan sank into the seat as Dastan gave him an introduction to Kyrgyzstan that he cared too little about to hear. He was out of China. He was free. But his emotions were shot.

Just a few moments after they had set off, the car rounded a corner and pulled up in front of a large metal link gate topped with coils of razor wire.

"What's going on?" Dan asked, his heart starting to race.

"It is lunch time," Dastan replied. "The border is closed. These men need their lunch or they will not be happy. And you don't want to meet them when they are not happy!"

Dastan's English was almost fluent and Dan could tell he was a good person, but he struggled not to blame him for the pain he was feeling. Dan didn't want to be in Kyrgyzstan. He wanted to be in Kashgar. With Lisa. It wasn't Dastan's fault but for some reason Dan felt an unshakeable resentment towards him.

"I brought you food," Dastan continued. "Are you hungry?"

Dan hadn't thought about it, but he was. He nodded in quiet agreement and Dastan passed him a thin blue and white striped polythene bag, containing shiny bread-like buns that Dastan explained were called *manti*, and a packet of biscuits. Despite his hunger it took Dan twenty-five minutes or so to finish the four buns. The sadness he felt at having lost Lisa so terminally began to swell into more strange feelings of anger. His mind wandered as he recalled what had happened over the last couple of days. He remembered seeing her put her bag in the back of the car yesterday morning – the day they first attempted the border crossing. It started to make sense now why Lisa had been so uncharacteristically nervous around him this morning. That is why she'd said, "You'll get across today.

Today we make it happen." She hadn't said, "*We'll* get across." The question of whether she would have joined him had they made it across on the first attempt was one that would pain him for days to come.

Just under an hour after Dan's party had arrived at the gate, a Kyrgyz official emerged from a side building and walked towards them wearing long green military trench coat, a dark fur *ushsanka* on his head and a Kalashnikov rifle over his left shoulder. His heavy black boots scuffed the surface of the compacted gravel road as he marched towards them and unlocked the gate. The driver wound down his window and the two spoke for a good couple of minutes before the guard pointed to a squat, two-storey building to the right of the road. Dan tried to work out what was going on as his heart began to race again. He assumed this was Kyrgyz immigration and tried to convince himself he had nothing to fear.

It was at that point that Dan remembered the passport in his hand was fake, and he began to panic. What would the consequences of trying to enter Kyrgyzstan on a fake passport be? What if the Kyrgyz authorities had been told to look out for him and return him to China? How had his passage across the border been so easy? He reminded himself that his journey was still wrought with danger, and he still had several hurdles to cross before he could truly consider himself free again. Kyrgyz immigration was just the next of them.

Dan looked down at his passport and suddenly remembered the envelopes that he was still clutching in his hand. He gave them both to Dastan.

"These are from my friend Lisa, in China. She said I need to give them to you."

"*Da*. Thank you. I need this informations. After this passport check, I don't call you Mason, but I use your real name, Sam. Is this OK?"

"That's fine," Dan replied, having forgotten that his passport gave his name as Mason Hunter. He barely even picked up on Dastan suggesting his real name was Sam. It had become a comfortable alias ever since he had first met Lisa all those thousands of miles away in Jiayuguan.

The three climbed out of the car and the driver opened the boot. The guard opened Dan's backpack and looked inside. He plunged a hand down into the contents and rummaged around. Satisfied that there was no contraband, he gestured to Dan to close it all up again and follow him into the squat, whitewashed building. It was badly weathered from years of harsh winters and biting winds, the corners of the building crumbling on all sides. As they walked to the building, Dan got his first taste of the Kyrgyz landscape. Up here it was barren, rocky and bleak and a cold wind whipped around them as they walked the short distance into the building. Another guard passed them in the opposite direction, going to take up his post at the gate.

They were led into the office, but it was not what Dan had expected: the first room was entirely empty. The walls were bare concrete and there was just one tiny window in the far corner. It was dark, cold and prison-like. The guard led them through a door on the far side of the room and into another similarly cold and dark space. They turned ninety degrees and walked through another empty room. This one had bars at the window and scribbling on the wall. They turned another ninety degrees and Dan began to feel disorientated. He began to worry that this was deliberate. His pulse began to quicken as they entered a fifth room. This was also empty save for two old wooden chairs that sat up against the exposed concrete wall. The guard signalled for Dan to sit as he and Dastan stood in the corner of the room and lit cigarettes. They spoke in Russian as Dan sat on one of the chairs, anxiously wondering what was going on. A doorway diagonally opposite him spilled a faint pool of light into the cell-like room but nothing more than a dim puddle on the floor.

Suddenly, a voice from the neighbouring room broke the silence, causing all three men to jump. The guard watching over them quickly dropped his Chinese-made cigarette to the ground and stamped it out with his heavy Russian-made boot. He ordered Dan up, and he obligingly jumped to his feet. The guard put his meaty hand on Dan's right arm and manhandled him through the door into the next room.

In front of him there was a large wooden desk that filled most of the small room Dan now found himself in. On the edge of the table there was a glass ashtray out of which a faint wisp of smoke rose from the pile of dying embers of a recently extinguished cigarette butt.

Behind the desk was the most intimidating-looking man Dan had ever encountered; he was almost half as wide as the desk itself, with the largest arms Dan had ever been in the presence of. The man's neck was short and thick, nothing more than a roll of fat squeezed in between his head and his vast shoulders. He wore military fatigues, army-issue black sunglasses despite the gloomy room and a black woollen hat that was rolled up at the sides so that it sat on the top of his head. He had no hair, save for the minimal stubble of a freshly shaven head. He looked like a thug. He was a Bond villain, a terrifying ball-breaker of a man.

He spoke to Dan in badly broken English, barely comprehensible under the largely unintelligible Russian accent.

"Show me passport," the man growled. "England, *da*?"

"Yes, England," Dan replied nervously. The other guard stood beside Dan, one hand clutched on the rifle that he now held in front of him.

The man took Dan's passport and thumbed through it. He looked intently at his Kyrgyz visa as Dan willed him not to find a mistake or suspect it was anything other than genuine. The man looked him up and down. He wrote notes on a blank piece of paper beside him before filling in his details on a small green piece of paper. He took his time, labouring over every character. He was either just slow or enjoying the tension he created. Dan felt his brow begin to dampen despite the chilly mountain air. He swallowed hard several times as the man completed his paperwork.

Then, without warning, the man stood up abruptly and Dan could now see that he was well over six feet tall. The man took Dan's passport in his left hand and waved it in the air in front of him. He sneered at Dan, staring right through him. Dan was petrified. This is what "game up" actually feels like, he thought. The man knew it was a fake and Dan was now in serious trouble. He felt stupid for having thought he could get away with it.

Taking Dan completely by surprise, the man shot his right hand out in front of him, his short, fat fingers barely able to move for his large fat hand. Dan looked down at it, extended in front of him. The man's face cracked into a smile of surprisingly white teeth.

"Welcome to Kyrgyzstan!" he proclaimed with a guttural laugh that shook the room.

"Fuck!" Dan thought as he shook the man's hand almost in reflex response. It was massive and flabby. His sausage-like fingers protruded straight out his hand, unable to bend enough to grip Dan's.

"Welcome to my country."

Dan realised that a tourist was probably rare entertainment in this loneliest of places and these poor men were probably grateful for the distraction. Dan suspected the whole thing was an act, designed to intimidate unsuspecting and nervous fresh-faced foreigners that passed their windswept door. He imagined them laughing as he drove off into the distance, scoring the success of the latest tourist intimidation. And, to be honest, he couldn't blame them.

As Dan pulled his hand out of the handshake, the man returned his passport and spoke to Dastan in Russian.

"He wants photo with you." Dastan laughed, turning to Dan. "He takes his photo with all foreigners just in case he meets a famous one but doesn't recognise them!"

The man laughed with Dastan. Dan moved round to the other side of the desk and the man clamped one of those massive arms on Dan's shoulders. It was so heavy Dan had to reposition his feet to accommodate it. The guard produced a small Olympus camera from his coat pocket and took two photos of them. The man shook Dan's hand again and pointed to a door that led to a long, straight corridor. At the end of it Dan could see the road outside and realised that being led through the maze of cell-like rooms a few minutes earlier was all part of the game. Dastan gestured to Dan to leave, so, checking the passport in his hand, he thanked both of the men and walked outside into the bright sunlight at the top of the Torugart Pass. He was through immigration and well and truly into Kyrgyzstan and could finally start to enjoy it. He appreciated the sense of humour, the pantomime characters, and he began to love its remoteness. He forgave Dastan for the grief of losing Lisa – it wasn't his fault. He hadn't been returned to China after all and he was free to enjoy the liberty and pleasure of travelling in Central Asia. All he had to do now was make it to Bishkek and fly home.

Back in the car, they left the immigration officials, who had come outside to wave them off behind. They were heading for Tash Rabat, a caravanserai that had stood in this remote and little-visited corner of the world since the fifteenth century. At three thousand, two hundred metres above sea level, they would be over half a kilometre lower than the Torugart itself, yet still at altitude. Dan couldn't wait to see the stars that night. He had dreamt of lying in the meadows of Kyrgyzstan, gazing up at the Milky Way a free man ever since he had made the decision to run from Beijing and cross the border almost two weeks ago. He missed Lisa.

The road was far rougher than on the Chinese side of the border. On that side that road had been powered into a sandy, gravel-like surface, but this side was rocky. Dan could see large stones sticking out of the road as they bumped along the tops of them at high speed. He was surprised the car was in as good condition as it was considering it had already driven this road at least once just to meet him. Before long he forgot about the constant bumping and the roar of the tyres on the hard road surface. He was lost, gazing at the incredible scenery that was laid out before him. The flat, grassy plateau of land stretched several kilometres into the distance only to end at a ring of snow-capped mountains that encircled them.

They had been driving for about an hour when the driver suddenly slowed to a crawl. Ahead Dan could see what looked like a truck lying on its roof in a ditch to the side of the road. As they approached, Dan saw that that's exactly what it was – all twelve sets of wheels up in the air. The driver was sitting in the upside-down cab, blood streaming down the left side of his face. The windscreen was completely smashed, although somehow it had remained in place, but the load of scrap metal was lying strewn throughout the grass on the side of the road. The driver stopped the car and they all got out. A flurry of sleet blew horizontally from right to left, and the wind was bitingly cold. Dastan and his colleague spoke to the Kyrgyz truck driver, who was clearly shaken. He'd fallen asleep at the wheel and the truck had simply veered off the road and into the ditch, where it had rolled right over onto its roof. It had happened only a few minutes before they had arrived. Dan gave the driver the packet of biscuits Dastan had given him and he took them gratefully, his arm shaking from the adrenalin that still coursed through his body. The truck driver explained that he'd already called for help and that another driver from the nearest town, Naryn, was on his way and would be here in around three hours' time. The air was frigid, but the driver seemed not to notice. With a tissue, he wiped the blood that was running down his face. The three men spoke for ten minutes or so before the truck driver urged them to continue on their way.

As they got back in the car Dastan explained to Dan that trucks leaving the road here was a frequent occurrence; some of these drivers drove for days through the mountain passes of Central Asia, sleeping wherever they could and usually not very well. The long, straight roads and continuous vibrations from the rough surfaces were exhausting and accidents happened almost weekly.

"There is bad accident not far from here. The truck rolled long way downhill. The poor driver survive, but die two days later from cold when nobody find him. The truck is still there, rusting. We will see it from the road."

Almost three hours after leaving the Torugart, they turned off to the right and onto a track that soon began to wind up into the hills, fording a rocky stream as they went. They headed deeper into what became a verdant, grassy valley rising up on either side of the road. Nestled into one hillside was a domed brick building surrounded by a low wall that gave it the appearance of a small fortress.

"We are here – this is Tash Rabat," explained Dastan. "It is old caravanserai, a place for travellers to rest when they cross the Torugart Pass. It is many hundreds of years old. For me, I think this is real Silk Route."

Dan looked out of the window in awe at the beauty of the surroundings. He couldn't wait to get out and explore Tash Rabat and the hills around it. This was the kind of travelling he had expected to be doing in China before everything had gone so spectacularly wrong. They pulled up to a cluster of traditional round tents that stood scattered in a meadow of alpine flowers. A young man with short dark hair, rosy red cheeks and a heavy woollen sweater emerged from an old caravan that stood rusting a short distance from the tents. Dastan got out of the car and Dan followed, a rush of fresh, cold and crisp mountain air filling his lungs. It was beautiful and instantly invigorating. He had travelled almost two hundred miles on rough, unsealed roads to get here today but hadn't expected the reward to be so beautiful. He wished Lisa was here to see it.

Dastan greeted the young man with a firm handshake while the driver stood next to his car and lit a cigarette. He appeared unfazed by the splendour of the scenery that surrounded them as Dan walked up a small hill nearby. A herd of scrawny-looking goats trotted off to join a group of horses that grazed further across the hillside. As Dan reached the top, he gasped; laid out in front of him as far as he could see was green hill after green hill, leading to snow-capped, rocky mountains far in the distance. The sky was a brilliant blue colour with billowing white clouds, adding scale and drama to the breathtaking panorama. He sat down to take it all in and as he did, he felt the stresses of the past two weeks draining from his body. He had finally collapsed, exhausted, drained and finished. He had escaped from China. He was free again and he was on his way home. Dan lay down, gazing at the blue and white sky that drifted past above him. He inhaled and exhaled the clinically pure alpine air as the aches and pains in his limbs seeped into the ground around him. He struggled to comprehend everything that had gone on in the past two weeks. The miles he had run and the scrapes he had been in. Lisa. He recalled the people who had helped him: Mr Feng and his brother. Ali, Karim and Atash. Lisa. Beijing felt like a lifetime ago. Nancy. He was convinced she had something to do with what had happened after they had first met. His mind wandered along the route he had travelled to get here: Xi'an, Lanzhou, the point at which he had jumped off the train and walked across the tracks at Jiayuguan.

Inevitably his head returned to thoughts of Lisa again. He had never met anyone quite like her before. He had fallen for her intellect first. He loved that she spoke fluent Chinese. He loved that she knew at every turn what needed to be done to get him safely from one place to the next. She had been in control and he loved that about her. He loved that she had instructed their various drivers to smuggle him through some of the most heavily populated parts of the planet. He loved that she had set each step of the journey up for him. Since he had met her in Jiayuguan, she had taken charge of his escape and he lay here now, looking up at the Kyrgyz sky, a free man thanks to her. His gratitude began to mix itself into grief and a profound sense of loss as tears came to his eyes.

As he lay there on his back, the sweet smell of alpine grasses all around him, Dan's eyes became heavy and he started to drift off. Over and over in his mind, as the sound of wind in the hills became distant, the thought played out: if, just *if*, they had made it over the border on that first attempt, would Lisa be here with him now?

He was woken sometime later to find the sun was setting and the sky was an eerie purple-grey. Several bright stars had appeared and it was significantly colder than when they had first arrived. He heard Dastan calling him. "Sam! Sam! Where are you? We have food now. Sam!"

Dan saw Dastan as soon as he stood up. He waved and began to scramble back down the steep hillside to the tents in the meadow at the bottom.

"Sam. We have food now. Our host make good dinner for us tired traveller!" Dastan said as Dan approached. A glorious waft of home cooking hung in the still air of the valley. Dan could see steam and smoke rising from a chimney that emerged from the top of one of the tents.

"Please." Dastan gestured. "This is the food yurt where all guests eat together like big friends and family do." He pointed to one of the round tents that had an open doorway at the front. A roll of material had been gathered up at the top of the door and tied in place using two sashes. Inside, candle-lit lanterns dimly illuminated one large table that stretched almost the diameter of the tent. As he walked inside, Dan was surprised to see a small group of Europeans already eating. He hadn't seen another western face, other than Lisa's, for almost two weeks. It was a strange moment of culture shock and one he was wholly unprepared for. The group looked over at him and one young man, with a couple of weeks' worth of stubble, a red fleece jacket and striped woollen hat, smiled and said, "Hello," in a heavy Scandinavian accent. Dan returned the greeting and sat down next to one of the group.

They introduced themselves one by one: Anna, Erik, Henrik, Solveig, Leila. The guy who had spoken to him first introduced himself as Omar. They were here in Kyrgyzstan on a trekking holiday and were four weeks into a five-week trip. Dan listened to them recall stories of the hikes they had done in the valleys of Altyn Arashan and Ala Archa and how they had camped on the shores of lake Song Kol – a high alpine lake and the second largest in Kyrgyzstan.

There had been another member of their party, a man called Mats, but he had fallen and broken his leg while climbing in Ala Archa at the start of their trip. He'd been taken back to Bishkek, where he was in hospital. They would collect him on the way home and fly back to Oslo together. Dan liked the

Scandinavian pragmatism, but the thought of being left alone to languish in a Kyrgyz hospital for the best part of a month was not one he relished.

Dan guessed the group to be in their late thirties and they were good company. He'd introduced himself as Sam. It felt good to be Sam again; he felt liberated and somehow younger. They spent the evening eating the delicious mutton and vegetable stew with rice fried in what he understood to be cottonseed oil, and drinking beer that the Norwegians had brought with them from Bishkek. The young man who had cooked the food left them to it at around ten o'clock and Dastan and their driver retired to their yurt about thirty minutes later. Dan avoided much talk of his travels in China save to say he had travelled along the Silk Route to get here. He learned that the group had hoped to see snow leopards but, despite having been in some of the best parts of the country to see them, had thus far been unlucky.

Eventually the conversation died out and one of the girls accidentally nodded off at the end of the table, to much laughter from her travelling companions. At that point they called it a night. Dastan, who had heard them stop talking, came back to show Dan to his yurt. As they walked from the food tent to his, Dan noticed the spectacular night sky above him. All around the night was pitch black and he couldn't see a single hill or mountaintop anywhere. But the Milky Way was clearly visible, just as he had imagined, stretched like an iridescent scar across the heavens, magnificent and humbling. He felt small and insignificant. Lisa was supposed to be here with him but she was now hundreds of miles away, locked in the prison-like constraints of China.

Inside, the yurt was beautifully ornate. There were colourful rugs on the floors and walls. At one side was a full wood-framed bed with a mattress, again covered in beautifully colourful blankets and topped with a light brown sheepskin. Although the air outside was frigid, the yurt itself was toastily warm. Dastan had put Dan's bag at the foot of the bed and there was a bowl of warm water on a small bedside table for him to wash his face before going to sleep. The numerous wooden spoke-like beams that made up the roof reminded Dan of traditional Japanese *wagasa* umbrellas. The structure was truly picturesque.

Unaware at this point of the shocking truths that the following morning would bring, Dan slept well that night. The combination of good food, beer, mountain air and freedom conspired to give him eight hours of deep, uninterrupted sleep. He woke the next morning to the sounds of goats bleating outside his yurt and a dog barking somewhere nearby. Dan could tell that the morning was already sunny for light crept in through a few gaps around the simple door.

He sat up in his bed and stretched the aches out of his arms and back. The bed had been warm but there was a chill in the morning mountain air. He could hear the group from last night and sat and listened to them for a few minutes before their voices began to grow faint. They were heading off on another hike and he wouldn't see them again. Dan got out of bed, washed his face in the now briskly cold water and got dressed. As he opened the door to his yurt, the blinding sunlight hit his eyes and Dan had to squint hard as he shielded them with his hand. As his pupils adjusted, he was once again met by the glorious sight of green hills, endless blue sky and snow-capped mountains. There was barely a cloud in sight.

He left his yurt and wandered out into the open. A cluster of horses was grazing nearby, goats wandered aimlessly up and down the grassy hillsides and skinny dogs lay in the warm sunshine. The car was still there, which Dan was both relieved and disappointed to see; he could quite easily have stayed here in Tash Rabat for a few days longer.

He made his way over to the food tent – the only other place he really knew in this small settlement. The door was open and as he peered inside he saw Dastan playing cards with the young Kyrgyz man he had seen the evening before. He noticed Dan in the doorway and gestured for him to come inside. The young man stood up and walked over to the stove; he lifted the lid on a large pot, from which billowed great clouds of steam. He ladled several large scoops of a broth-like liquid into a bowl and brought it over to the table for Dan before producing a plate of flatbreads and what looked like samosas. They were warm and filled with minced meat and vegetables and smelled delicious in the morning sun. Dan thanked the man and sat down to eat.

"Did you have a good sleep?" Dastan enquired.

"I did. I slept really well," Dan replied. "Please tell the man that it is the best sleep I have had in weeks."

Dastan translated for him. The man smiled and nodded his head in acknowledgement. He said something to Dastan and then left the two of them in the tent by themselves. As Dan ate, Dastan spoke to him.

"We should go for a walk today. I have some things I want to tell you. But not here in case there are people who listen to us."

Dan stopped eating and looked at Dastan with a mix of intrigue and concern.

"OK…" he replied. "Is everything OK, Dastan?"

"Yes, yes. OK. No problem. It is safe in Kyrgyzstan but there is things I want to tell you about the people who help you in China, because I think you don't know that yet. But I don't tell you here. When you finish, we go for walk."

"Sure," Dan replied nervously. He finished his breakfast quickly and looked at Dastan who seemed calm and in no hurry to go for this walk.

"Shall we go?" Dan announced. "I want to know what you have to tell me."

"OK, let's go. I get us some water then we go for walk." Dastan replied.

Outside the tent, Dastan filled two plastic bottles with water and they set off down a rock-strewn track on the far side of the settlement. Ahead of them rolling green hills lay before rugged mountain outcrops. The sun illuminated the lush green grass on one side of the hills while the lee sides remained in shadow. A few goats dotting the hillsides ahead of them scampered away as the two men approached. They had been walking for several minutes before Dastan began to talk. He appeared nervous and looked around him before speaking.

"OK. I think you do not know, so I want to tell you. I think you need to know because it will make more sense to you if you know."

Dan said nothing. He listened intently.

"The men you met in Kashgar, Atash and Karim, they are, how do you say? Like a gangster. You know mafia? They are like Kashgar mafia. Especially Atash. He is like the boss in Kashgar mafia. He is very dangerous man."

Dan was silent. Although surprised, what Dastan was telling him instantly made sense. It had been naïve of Dan to think they just ran a counterfeiting operation.

Dastan continued. "Atash has many men killed in Xinjiang. He is well known in that part of China and here in Kyrgyzstan. I never met him, but I hear his name often. But I don't know why he helped you. And who is that girl? I do not know her. I never saw her before and I do not know her name. Is she friend of yours?"

"Not really. I only met her last week," Dan replied. "Her name is Lisa. She is a guide in China. Do you know why I am here?" he asked curiously, wondering how much Dastan knew about what had happened in China.

"Yes, I hear you are running from police in China. I hear you are also running from drugs gang in Xi'an." Dastan answered.

"Something like that," Dan replied, being cautious not to tell Dastan too much, having just found out he had been wrapped up with the Kashgar mafia for the last few days. As far as he knew, Dastan was trying to trick him into openly talking about the group.

"The man, Ali, he called me some days ago and asked me to meet you at the border," Dastan continued. "He told me Atash himself ask me to meet you. He said to make sure no problems leaving China. You know, last year a border guard was killed by murder at the pass the day after he stopped one of Atash's men to cross the border. They drove up at night and cut his throat while he was sleeping. Everybody up here knows that story. Atash has friends on the Kyrgyzstan side and he pay not money, but favours to the guards. When they want something from China, he send it. You know, cigarettes, alcohol and sometimes even Chinese girl. They send them up for the night and then the next day they drive back down to Kashgar. In exchange, they let anyone across the border with what they carry, if you understand me."

Dan understood.

"But he not have control of China army," Dastan continued, "so he must *show* big power there. That is why they kill the soldier last year. Since then, no problems crossing the border. There is a code, but I ask nobody to tell me. I do not want to know how they work. I just meet the people who need me and bring them to Bishkek or where they want to go. I get money, only money for this job."

Dan was both captivated and terrified by Dastan's story. This gave extra impetus to the burning desire to get back to England. He felt like there could be snipers behind any of the hills around them, tracking him in their crosshairs as he walked. Dan drank a large swig of water from his bottle, trying to take in what Dastan was saying and trying to recall everything that had happened in the last few days. Was there anything else he had missed that would now make sense given the newfound context of the set-up in Kashgar?

Dastan spoke again. "Do you know why Atash help you?" he asked.

"Honestly, I am not sure. Maybe he is a friend of Lisa's," Dan replied. "I only met her by chance. Maybe she knows him. Actually, she said Ali is her friend, so maybe that is the connection."

There was silence between them as they both considered what they had just learned. Dan's head was spinning as he strained to remember everything that had happened since arriving into Kashgar: the things Ali had said to him, the meeting with Atash in that basement, anything Lisa had said or done. Nothing came back to him except for the persistent question of whether Lisa would have joined him here if they had been able to cross the border on the first attempt. He tried hard to ignore that most nagging of questions, but it persisted.

A few moments later, the two came across a stream and Dastan sat down on a grassy bank beside it. Dan joined him. The water was sparklingly clear and clean enough to drink. It babbled away in front of them, jumping and splashing over the rocks and pebbles that lay strewn across the riverbed. Dan picked up a small stone and threw it into the middle of the stream. It made a satisfying *plunk* as it disappeared into the glass-like water.

They had been sitting watching the stream for five minutes or so when Dastan reached into the inside pocket of his jacket and produced an envelope. He passed it slowly to Dan, offering it out to him to take. Looking down, Dan realised it was the pale-blue envelope that Lisa had asked him to give to Dastan just before he had crossed the border yesterday. The Chinese writing down the right-hand side was unmistakable. It was the more padded of the two that he had passed to Dastan.

"This is for you. Inside is enough US dollars to buy ticket from Bishkek back to London. I think you don't have any money for a ticket, right?"

Dan took the envelope and opened it carefully. Inside was a thick wad of one hundred dollar notes. There were fifteen of them, tatty from years of changing hands and now bound together by a thick, brown elastic band. Dan took the pile of money out and examined it. It looked genuine to him, but then, what did he really know?

"I will help you buy a ticket in Bishkek. I know a good travel agent where we can go. You can pay US dollars no problem here in Kyrgyzstan."

"Thank you," Dan replied. "When do you think we will get to Bishkek?"

"We will stay here for one more night, then we drive tomorrow. We will have one night in Bishkek and then you can fly back to London after that next day. I think you have to fly to Istanbul first, but I check for you."

Dan was now just forty-eight hours or so from a flight back to the UK. After all the miles he had travelled, the end was finally in sight. He put the money back in the envelope and tucked it safely in the inside pocket of his own jacket.

Dastan and Dan sat without speaking for half an hour or so, watching almost hypnotised as the stream flowed gently and endlessly past them. Occasionally a goat would wander aimlessly into view on the hillock on the other side of the stream. They'd both watch it eat the short, tough grass apparently unaware as to their presence. Dan picked up another stone and threw it into the water just in front of them. It seemed to stir Dastan back into life and he looked at Dan.

"Time to go?" he enquired.

"I guess we could," Dan replied without much thought. There was nothing to do back at the camp other than to go for another walk or sleep.

Dastan slowly got to his feet and offered Dan his hand. He took it and Dastan pulled him up, grasping Dan's hand with his rough, weathered grip. He looked at Dan and said,

"It is incredible story, Sam. I think you don't know yet how incredible your story is."

"Thank you, Dastan," Dan replied sincerely. "I still need your help. I've got the money now, but I don't know where to buy a flight ticket or get out of here. I still very much need your help!"

It would be another two days before Dan really understood the true extent of what Dastan had just said, but the words would echo in his ears that evening. They walked back to the yurts in almost total silence, other than when Dastan pointed out an eagle or two that circled overhead, hunting for marmots. They got back to camp far quicker than Dan was expecting but there was nobody else around other than two undernourished dogs that were play-fighting in the short grass.

Dastan left Dan as they arrived back at the tents and went to find his driver to make plans for the drive to Bishkek the following day. Left alone, Dan decided to head into his yurt to pack up his things and dwell on what Dastan had just told him. As he sat on his bed under the umbrella-like yurt, Dan tried to recall everything that had happened since he'd met Lisa. He'd met her outside the restaurant in Jiayuguan and they had travelled overland all the way to Kashgar. Dastan seemed to know Ali and Atash but didn't know who Lisa was. It made no sense. Dan couldn't work out how she fitted into everything. Running various scenarios around in his head for several minutes, he came to the conclusion that only once she had realised who he was did she contact the people she knew in Kashgar. Only once it had become too dangerous for her to continue to shelter him alone did she call on their help. She had screamed at him when she found out that he was the most wanted man in China and he assumed it was shortly after that that Ali and Atash became involved.

He didn't know it then, of course, but he couldn't have been more wrong.

12

THE KYRGYZ CAPITAL

After a hearty breakfast of fried eggs and goat meat, Dan, Dastan and their driver left the verdant hills of Tash Rabat and began the journey towards the Kyrgyz capital, Bishkek. The mountain air was crisp and clear and the light blue sky held only a few wisps of cloud on a gentle, chilly breeze. As they picked their way down the rocky track back to the main road, Dan heaved a sigh of relief – they were finally on their way to the capital and he was within a hair's breadth of the flight to freedom that had felt unobtainable for so long. Once airborne, he would be en route to London and the safety of home.

There was little chat in the car save for a few short conversations between Dastan and the driver but the further they drove into the interior of Kyrgyzstan the smoother the road became. Welcome relief from the rubble of the Torugart road.

Around an hour and a half after setting off, they pulled into the small and forlorn-looking town of Naryn that sat at the bottom of a bowl of dusty red mountains. Architecturally the town was unmistakably Soviet and its largely empty streets had seen little investment since the early days of the USSR. An old blue and white electric bus trundled by with two weary-looking passengers on board. It tracked a spider's web of power lines overhead via a flimsy-looking pantograph that appeared to have been fashioned from an old clothes hanger.

In the centre of town they crossed a bridge over the churning Naryn River, the waters of which would eventually merge with the Syr Darya and flow westwards through neighbouring Uzbekistan all the way to the rapidly diminishing Aral Sea. All around, rugged mountains loomed tall, their snow-capped peaks glistening in the bright mid-morning sunlight yet despite the beautiful setting this was a run-down and depressing place. The few people that Dan saw seemed to be elderly, left behind perhaps after the town's halcyon days, now shuffling along the dusty roadsides in thick fur coats carrying plastic bags full of root vegetables.

Beyond the city the road climbed steeply, giving way to breathtaking views of the river valley behind them. Kyrgyzstan was certainly far more beautiful than Dan had ever imagined. A monument to the Kyrgyz poet Astanbek came and went as Dan gazed out of the car window, a passenger and no longer a fugitive.

The road surface had changed from dust and broken rocks to thin, faded and tired asphalt. There were no kerbs at the edges and the road was deteriorating from the outside in such that it was unclear where the asphalt stopped and the dusty, rocky scrub on either side of the road began. Weaving their way higher and higher into the mountains, Dan's driver made steady progress north towards Bishkek.

As they approached a line of lorries struggling with the mountain ascent, Dastan spoke for the first time in what felt like hours. "We are nearly at Dolon Pass. It is high pass between Naryn and Bishkek. You see a sign soon, at three thousand thirty metres. There is always bad traffics on this road here! And these trucks, they drive from China all the way to Russia. It is crazy long way. I think these men are heroes that nobody know about."

One by one the trucks made it to the top of the hill and over the pass. Dan saw the blue sign that Dastan had mentioned. The air felt thin again, just as it had when they had crossed the Torugart a couple of days earlier. Dan sat back in his seat, taking deep breaths to fill his lungs as best he could. The driver sped past the line of trucks in one manoeuvre that seemed to take forever to complete as the trucks accelerated down the hill on the other side. Had there been any oncoming traffic there would have been no way of avoiding it.

The road opened to spectacular scenery on either side. On his left Dan could see the Songköl Too mountains and to the right the Bayduluu Range. The Dolon Pass carved its way right between the two.

Around ten kilometres north of the pass, the road converged with another that joined them from the left. Dastan told him that that road led to Song Kol – the lake the Norwegians had been to a few weeks earlier.

Just as Dan was starting to lose himself in the gaze across the mountains, Dastan suddenly began to panic. "Sam! We have polices coming! Get down! Get down!"

His heart racing, Dan slid down the seat as far as he could so as not to be visible to the approaching cars. The driver slowed to a crawl and Dastan spoke quietly, keeping his eyes fixed on the road ahead.

"There are two cars coming our direction. I do not know if they come for us or just drive past us but I see the blue flashing lights coming down the road. It is good thing we have mountains roads to see long way like this."

As he crouched behind the driver, Dan realised that this was the first time Dastan had made any reference to him being a fugitive. He wasn't even supposed to be a fugitive in this country. For the first time in days, Dan began to panic and his mind raced with all the same old questions. What if this was it? What if the game was finally up? Would he be deported back to China? Would he get consular access to the UK here in Kyrgyzstan? Would he be *locked up* here in Kyrgyzstan?

"OK, they come, they come," Dastan warned. Dan heard the two police cars approach, the rattling of their engines sounding more like tractors as they pulled up next to his car. He heard the driver wind down his window and exchange a few words before the two police cars drove on.

Dastan turned to Dan. "OK, you can come back again. The police is passing now."

Dan sat back up in his seat and brushed himself down. Looking out of the back window, he could see the two white police cars disappearing into the distance.

"What was that all about?" Dan enquired.

"I do not really know, you know. They say they are looking for foreigner on motorbike. They ask if we seen him, but we say no. They say he came from China two days before now, carrying cocaine or something."

His heart still racing, Dan sat back and breathed a sigh of relief. Dastan's behaviour had been odd – panicked, like nobody else he had encountered in the thousands of miles he had either travelled or had been smuggled. It was almost as if he too had expected to be caught at that moment. Perhaps it was just that Dan was so poorly hidden in the back seat of the car. All it would have taken is for one of the police to look through the window for all of them to be in serious trouble there on the roadside. What might have followed didn't bear thinking about.

As they approached the edge of Bishkek the roads became busier and people filled the streets. It was almost nightfall and the agricultural land on the outskirts of the city inevitably gave way to an increasing density of buildings until Dan found himself in the thick of the Kyrgyz capital. Wide tree-lined streets hosted row after row of ornate white buildings, reminiscent of the Soviet heydays. They passed a vast open piazza surrounded by grandiose government buildings. It instantly reminded Dan of Tiananmen Square, where he had been shortly before that fateful photograph. It made him shudder as he recalled seeing himself on the news for the first time that evening.

Bishkek, however, seemed more civilised than Beijing, more orderly and far less chaotic than the Chinese capital had been. Dan recalled his run through the *hutong*s and his escape on the train. He pictured the scores of police who must have been looking for him that night as he fled.

As his mind wandered back through the harrowing events of the past couple of weeks, the car turned right off the main road and left into a side street, slaloming through endless raised drain and manhole covers that made for a nauseous few minutes. It was now almost completely dark as the driver picked his way between the cars that were parked on either side of the road and into a small gravel car park at the end of the street. They had arrived at their hotel. Weathered gold lettering above the door spelled out "Silk Road".

The driver opened the boot of the car and stood back so that Dan could haul his backpack out. He knew Dan was no ordinary tourist. As Dan lifted his bag onto his shoulder, the driver closed the boot and lit a cigarette. He turned around to rest on the back of the car and puffed small clouds of smoke into the light evening breeze. Dastan made his way up the steps to the front door stretching the creases from his shoulders as he went.

The hotel itself was a tall, grey monstrosity, looming ominously above the gardens and statuesque pine trees like something from a horror movie. Its walls were a faceless rendered concrete that gave it the air of a sanatorium. If the manicured gardens had been any less welcoming, Dan would seriously have questioned Dastan's choice of accommodation. Instead, he followed him into the hotel lobby, where a young Kyrgyz woman greeted Dastan in Russian and Dan in English.

"Welcome to Bishkek Silk Road Lodge, Mr Mason Hunter. I hope you will enjoy your stay here. How long you stay with us?"

Dan glanced at Dastan, unsure what to answer. "Just one night," Dastan replied.

As the words spilled from Dastan's lips, Dan's world slowed to a crawl: tomorrow he would be flying out of Bishkek. The end of this torment now seemed tantalisingly close, and his head began to spin at the thought of boarding the plane. It was still spinning as the woman took him through the hotel introduction: where his room was and what time breakfast would be served. Dan heard none of it other than a distant droning sound that bounced around his eardrums and faded into background noise.

As the woman put his room key on the counter in front of him, Dan snapped out of his thoughts. He smiled at the woman and picked it up, noting the room number, 525. He picked his bag up off the floor and swung it over his shoulder as Dastan pointed to the direction of the lift.

"I join you tomorrow morning for breakfast," he added. "Have good sleep. See you in the morning at nine o'clock. Tomorrow we buy you ticket to England."

Those words seemed to hang in the lift as it scraped and rattled its way slowly to the fifth floor.

Room 525 was large but tired-looking. The walls were adorned with large-print wallpaper in an uninspiring shade of beige. Faded orange curtains hung limply at the window, in front of which stood a cheap wooden desk with a tattered old lampshade and torn black office chair. To the left-hand side of the room was a single metal bed that sagged ominously in the middle. An orange bedspread made of a shiny cotton–polyester mix lay across the top of it. As Dan dropped his bag onto the bed it made a conspicuously loud creaking sound.

The rest of the room was largely empty other than a small black safe on a shelf next to the door. The bathroom was disproportionately large, with faded plastic fittings. The bathtub had a large crack along the length of the front panel and the mildew on the opaque shower curtain was visible on both sides.

But Dan was exhausted. The long drives of the past few days coupled with living in almost constant fear of being caught were taking their toll on him. Various moments from his run flashed through his mind: one minute he was driving along the edge of the Qilian Mountains, the next he was claustrophobically curled up in the back of Mr Feng's brother's truck, feeling every bump in the road as it hurtled him through the Taklamakan desert. Then almost instantly he was lying on the grass at Tash Rabat watching the clouds drift overhead. Dan lay on the bed, his head once again spinning as he recalled the dizzying events of the past two weeks.

Outside, there was little noise other than the occasional car driving along the lane beside the hotel. From time to time headlights would illuminate the curtains as another car arrived at the hotel before leaving again, returning the room to semi-darkness. Dan heard male voices talking on the front steps and the unmistakable smell of cigarette smoke somehow made its way through a gap in the window.

All of a sudden the quiet was shattered by the distinctive crackling sound of gunfire. A short burst of six rounds echoed around the walls of the hotel. Dan froze rigid, gripping the bed with both hands. His heart was racing but he attempted to slow his breathing so that he could hear what was going on outside. Was this a raid on the hotel? As he lay there waiting he heard the sounds of two or three people running past. There was shouting. Thirty seconds or so later there was another burst of gunfire: ten or so rounds, much closer than before and seemingly right outside the hotel.

Then there was silence. Dan waited, hardly daring to move. He could hear his heart pounding in his chest, thumping on his rib cage. He wondered how many more times he would have to go through this before this ordeal would be over. There was no more gunfire after that. Noticeably, there were no police cars or sirens. Dan got up and moved carefully towards the window, cautiously pulling the curtain back an inch or two. The lights were off in his room and he was confident he couldn't be seen. Outside, the road was lit by a solitary streetlight that gave off an eerie yellow-orange glow, lighting only a small patch of the road around it. Dan couldn't see any people and, other than for a scrawny-looking dog that trotted fox-like down the lane looking for scraps in the bushes, the street was quiet again.

Dan left the window, took off his jeans and climbed into the rickety bed. Every time he moved the metal springs emitted a dubious creaking sound. He tried to lie as still as possible, aware that the people in the room downstairs could probably hear every suspicious groan that the bed frame made. It wasn't easy – the mattress was thin and broken and he could feel every spring within it. Before long he fell asleep, exhausted.

The next morning he was woken by the sounds of a garbage truck doing its rounds. The sound of bins being emptied must be the same the world over, Dan thought deliriously to himself. He lay in bed picturing what might happen in the hours ahead. A flight ticket, check-in and security at the airport, waiting for the flight, taking off and the deep breath of freedom that he had been gasping for for so long. The dread of the hurdles he was about to jump was outweighed by the thought of that plane taking off from Bishkek Airport. The sun was streaming in through a gap in the faded orange curtains which Dan pulled open to reveal a glorious clear blue sky. He paused to admire the line of mountains in the distance overlooking the city. There was snow on the very tops and the slopes were a light grey-green. Bishkek was waking up around him.

Dan showered and got his things together. This time he avoided the lift and took the stairs down to the ground floor. He found the unassuming breakfast room dotted with small tables covered with the same plastic wipe-clean tablecloths found in cheap hotels the world over. In one corner of the room, two large men in baggy, ill-fitting suits sat talking conspicuously quietly. They were speaking Russian and although Dan had no idea what they were discussing he became paranoid that there was something sinister about their behaviour. The man closest turned to look at Dan, studying him up and down as he made his way to a table at the far end of the room. Satisfied that Dan was not Russian, the two men continued talking, glancing over at him from time to time.

Dastan arrived a few moments later and waved to Dan as he entered the room. He acknowledged the two men in Russian and joined Dan at his table.

"Did you sleep OK?" Dastan asked.

"I did," Dan replied. "You?"

"Yes, good sleep."

"Did you hear the gunfire outside last night?" Dan continued.

"Gunfire?" Dastan queried. "No. I went to drinking bar with my cousin last night. You mean outside here?"

"Yes," Dan replied. "Right outside the hotel."

"Maybe just a fight. I hear nothing on the news this morning," Dastan assured him.

As they talked, a young man walked in carrying two plates of scrambled eggs, bacon, sausages and toast. There was no choice of breakfast here. Dastan and Dan tucked in with little chat, but as they finished Dastan spoke about the day ahead.

"When we finish, we go to flight travel agency to buy your ticket for flight today. Lisa gave you money for that ticket. Please bring it with you. We must pay in cash. Lisa already pay for this hotel, so no problem there."

"Thanks Dastan. I have everything with me here so we can leave when we are ready."

Outside the driver was waiting by the car. He had the engine running and got out to open the boot as they approached. Dan threw his backpack into the car for one last time and climbed into the back seat. Dastan took up his place in the passenger seat again and spoke to the driver as they headed back out into the streets of Bishkek. It was an attractive city, clean with more trees than Dan could recall seeing in a city before. They drove for around fifteen minutes, picking their way through the cosmopolitan morning traffic of cars, donkey-drawn carts and bicycles. Momentarily forgetting that he was still a fugitive, Dan took in the sights and sounds of the Kyrgyz capital with the wide eyes of every other tourist.

Eventually, the driver made a series of turns into narrow side streets and pulled up outside a small inconspicuous kiosk that was sandwiched between a café that was still closed and what looked like a snooker hall that didn't open until the evening. The small booth, little more than a metre wide, was staffed by a young woman with pale complexion, red cheeks and heavy eyebrows.

In badly faded paint, Dan could just about make out the words "Travel Agency" in English, with what he assumed was the equivalent in Russian above it. Dastan could not be serious. This was not where he was going to hand over the only monies he had access to. This could not possibly be his route to freedom.

Dastan looked over the seat at Dan.

"OK, we here. This is my friend. She will give us a very good price for your ticket to London. I know her a very long time. Please bring your passport and your cash with you."

So this really was it. Feeling as helpless now as he had done running through the *hutong*s in Beijing, Dan entrusted his fate to Dastan and his friend.

As Dastan got out of the car the young woman suddenly became animated. She greeted him with a large smile and reached over the kiosk counter to hug him. They spoke in Russian for a few seconds as Dan hesitantly approached. Dastan turned to him, unexpectedly put his arm around his shoulder and said in English, "This is my friend Mr Mason Hunter. He needs to go back to England today."

The woman looked at Dan and smiled.

"Ah, England. *Da*. No problem. There is a flight to Istanbul and from there you continue to England. I check availability and prices for you now," she replied in almost perfect English.

"Then you give us great price!" Dastan chipped in flirtatiously.

"Ha! I do my best for you!" the woman laughed in reply as she tapped the keys on her keyboard, eyes darting about her screen as she worked.

"OK, there is flight tomorrow morning at 07:55 to Istanbul. Turkish Airlines flight number TK349. From there, you connect to London. That is the first flight and best one. It is five hundred and fifty American dollars. Is that OK?"

"Is there not a flight today?" Dan enquired, anxious to be on a plane home as soon as possible.

"No, that is next flight for you," she replied. "Shall I buy it for you now?"

Dan hesitated and looked at Dastan, hoping he had another idea. Dastan looked back and replied, indicating that there was no negotiating this.

"If it is only one flight, then we must book it. I take you to the airport tonight and you stay there before flight home tomorrow. I think we must take this one."

Dan hesitated, desperately wracking his brains for an alternative solution. Reluctantly he heaved a sigh of resignation, anxious to be airborne at the earliest opportunity. Sensing that offering any other suggestions or being difficult was going to be futile, he agreed unenthusiastically to the 07:55 flight tomorrow morning.

The woman needed no further instruction and returned to her computer screen. She took Dan's passport and entered his details into the booking before passing it back to him without making eye contact. He had given her the fake Mason Hunter passport. His heart raced as she created the flight booking for him in that name. Tomorrow morning he would run the gauntlet of getting through Bishkek Airport on a fake British passport, the thought of which made him feel sick as he stood there in front of the kiosk.

The young woman worked fast and diligently, clearly very adept at her job. A few moments later she asked him for payment.

"You pay cash, yes? American dollars is all I can take from the tourist."

Convenient, Dan thought cynically to himself.

"Yes," he replied. "I have cash."

Reaching into his pocket, he withdrew the pale-blue envelope that Dastan had given him at Tash Rabat and took out the fifteen hundred dollar notes. Dastan and the girl watched him in silence. Despite this being a considerable sum of money in Kyrgyzstan, neither of them batted an eyelid as he thumbed through it to count out six hundred dollars. After all, Dan wasn't the first tourist to pay cash for a flight like this.

He passed the woman the notes, which she took and counted out on the ledge of the kiosk before folding it in half. Producing a metal cash box from under the counter, she took out an elastic band, secured the small wad of cash and gave Dan his change in the form of a tatty fifty-dollar note that was so well used as to have almost turned to fabric.

"Thank you."

She continued working without looking at either of her two customers. A minute or two later and an old printer at the back of the kiosk whirred into life. It clicked and groaned for thirty seconds or so before ejecting a piece of paper. The woman spun round in her seat and caught the paper just before it slipped off the printer and on to the floor. She scanned it briefly and passed it to Dan.

"This is your ticket. Please check your spelling of name is correct. You fly tomorrow morning to Istanbul and you connect to flight to London, same day. This is your reservation number," she said, pointing to a six-digit number in the top right of the booking. "You need that number and your passport when you go to airport. That is everything you need." She turned to Dastan. "I booked him seat 6D. It is aisle seat."

"Thank you," Dan replied, slightly confused as to why Dastan would need his seat number. He shrugged it off, assuming it was just her way of ensuring Dastan remained engaged in the conversation. It would be tomorrow morning before he learned that truth.

As Dan folded the piece of paper in thirds on the countertop, Dastan continued talking to the girl. "*Spasiba*. Thank you," he said, before continuing in Russian.

"Do you have any question before we go, my friend?" Dastan said, turning to Dan.

Dan shook his head. "No, I don't think so. Thank you for your help," he replied, looking at the woman. She had been ruthlessly efficient, and, realising that this could be a pivotal moment in the course of the events of the last two weeks, he thanked her again.

"OK, let's go. Thank you. See you again soon," Dastan said, retaking control of the situation.

Dan opened the car door and got in. The driver who had been dozing in the front seat, woke with a start and sat up, adjusted his sunglasses and made himself comfortable in his seat. Dastan got in and pulled out his mobile phone. He sent a short message to a friend and laid his phone on the dashboard.

It was almost ten o'clock. Dastan looked over his shoulder at Dan.

"OK, we have quite lot of time to kill today. I think we go to café, where you can relax before your flight. I have job tomorrow, so I must take you to airport tonight. You can sleep there. It is no problem. Kyrgyz people are always sleeping at airport! It is like free hotel!"

"Ha!" Dan laughed. He liked Dastan, but the thought of being under the gaze of security guards and CCTV for what he expected to be around twelve hours did not fill him with much joy. He thought back to the border guard with the fat fingers at the Torugart Pass. He pictured himself sitting in a small room again being interrogated by airport officials and being handed over to Chinese police, who would deport him back to where this all began. Fate would catch up with him and he would find himself in custody in Beijing once again, fighting for his freedom. His palms began to bead with sweat as he stared out of the window at the city that surrounded him.

He zoned out for the next few minutes, running through a few worst-case scenarios in his head and their possible solutions, his back-up story in case he was questioned, his reasons for "always having wanted to come to Kyrgyzstan" and the names of the places he had been since crossing the border.

Thirty minutes or so after leaving the kiosk they turned into a large, dusty car park that was made of rubble similar to that on the Torugart road. They were on the very edge of the city now, just beyond the suburbs. To one side of the car park was a long, single-storey building with dusty, dark windows. It had been painted dark green once, but now stood fading and peeling much like the rest of the country that Dan had seen. There didn't appear to be anyone else here. Dan wondered if there had been a single point in Kyrgyzstan's history where all the buildings had been vibrantly painted, and what those halcyon days had been like. Or whether this was just an ongoing cycle of paint-and-fade that had always existed in Kyrgyzstan for as long as there had been paint.

The driver parked the car facing a low wooden fence that ran around the almost perfectly square car park. Dastan turned to Dan again.

"Let's go in. We can get a Coke and maybe some lunch soon. You can leave your bag in the car. Our driver take you to airport later. But I think should take your passport and money with you. Keep safe with you."

Dan agreed and they got out of the car. Walking up to the door, he still could not see anyone inside the building. He felt strangely exposed walking through that car park. If ever a sniper were to take him out, he thought, it would be in a place like this.

Two wide wooden steps led up to a decked area at the front of the building. They creaked and bowed as Dan and Dastan walked on them. Dastan pushed the front door open, the glass of which was cracked in the bottom right-hand corner, where Dan guessed someone had kicked it, perhaps drunkenly. It swung open into a darkened room.

"Ah, they have power cut!" laughed Dastan, as a young woman emerged from swinging saloon-style doors between the café and the kitchen at the back. She was visible thanks only to the white of her apron as she made her way towards her two visitors.

She greeted Dastan by name. They gave each other a friendly hug as they spoke excitedly in Russian. Dastan was clearly very well connected in Bishkek. Either that or he had only taken Dan to places where he knew people, perhaps to give him the impression that he was well connected! The woman explained the power cut to Dastan as he nodded and looked around the room.

Dan did the same, noting the ubiquitous square tables and the same plastic tablecloths again.

The woman pointed to a table by one of the front windows – one of the only ones visible in the darkness. Dastan appeared to agree that it was a good idea and, following the young woman's outstretched hand, the two made their way towards the window.

The metal chair legs scraped on the dusty wooden floor as they pulled them out.

"You drink Coke?" Dastan asked, sitting down. "They have no food now because of power cut, but the drinks are cold. My friend said that to me she think it won't be long before the power come back. This is common event in Kyrgyzstan."

"I'll have a lemonade, if they have one," Dan replied.

Dastan got up and walked back towards the kitchen. He was gone for several minutes before emerging with a drink in either hand. Sitting down again he produced an opener from his pocket and flipped the metal caps off both bottles. The drinks were only just cold.

The two sat in silence for a good five minutes before the electric fan on the ceiling above them began to creak back into action. It moved slowly to start with and Dan watched a small shower of dust fall from it, illuminated in the shaft of light that streamed in through the window. A moment later the dozen or so lamps dotted around the café began to glow weakly on the walls. The fluorescent strip lights on the ceilings were the last to come on as they slowly flickered back into life, once again filling the room with a dim yellow-white light. From behind the saloon doors Dan heard what sounded like an extractor fan whirring into motion. The restaurant was back in business.

"Ah, good," Dastan commented as they both watched the three ceiling fans gather speed.

As the light spread throughout the room Dan noticed that the walls were adorned with framed old black-and-white photos that appeared to depict groups of mountain climbers either at the base of mountains or at their summits.

"You like the pictures?" Dastan asked him. "They are very famous Russian and European mountain climbers who come to Kyrgyzstan long time ago to make history. They are very brave men. Look, they have no special equipment, just, how you say, fur coats."

Dan continued to scan the pictures as Dastan went on.

"Many people die on Kyrgyz mountains in that day. But if they survive, they go back to their countries as heroes! Kyrgyz mountains are very difficult climbing. We have lots of snow and wind. There are many bodies lying in deep snow in Kyrgyz mountains. Look at this picture."

Dastan motioned to one of the photos and stood up, scraping his chair again in the process. He walked over to a set of images to the left of the front door.

"How many people you count in this picture?" he asked, pointing to the left-most of three fading black-and-white photos. Dan looked at the photo for a moment. It showed a group of people in thick fur coats with nothing but stout wooden poles and a few ropes to aid their ascent.

"Eleven," Dan replied.

"*Da*. And this one?" Dastan asked, pointing to the middle of the three photos. It showed a group of people stood proudly atop a mountain summit, with further mountaintops disappearing into the background. They were smiling for the camera, despite their beards being almost entirely encased in ice that hung in long shards.

"Um, seven," Dan replied before moving his eyes onto the last image. There were only three people in it, but he recognised them from the other two photos. The last photo was out of focus compared to the others.

"This was very bad accident trip," Dastan explained. "Twelve people started the trip and four died going to the top. On the way down, they lost five people in big avalanche. The photographer also died, so this last photo is taken by Kyrgyz horseman. You see, it is not good focus? This also tells story."

Dan looked again at the photo, this time more intently. The men appeared to be back in a similar place to the first photo, yet their faces were sunken and their expressions solemn. He lost himself in these images for a good few minutes. The men had been smiling at the summit, despite apparently losing four companions on the way up. At the bottom, they had lost a further five fellow climbers. The four on the way up seemed to have been an acceptable rate of loss, whereas the five on the way down had been a disaster that was written into the faces of those that had survived.

"They are German climbers. They had very bad luck, but also they had no preparation for big mountain like this. The bodies of those men are still here in Kyrgyz mountains somewhere. One day, they will come to surface again and people carry them down. Every year, we are finding body or two like this."

Dan gazed at the photo for another few minutes, noting the date on the corner of the last one: 1926. The photo appeared to be original.

The two returned to the table, where Dastan regaled Dan with several more stories about other famous alpinists who had made their names in Kyrgyzstan and how some of the highest peaks had been conquered. Mountaineering had been a fashionable pursuit of the elite classes of Russia and Europe, and Kyrgyzstan had for many years been at the centre of it.

Before long, a couple of hours had passed and Dastan decided it was time for lunch.

"They do good burger here. You happy with burger?" Dastan asked.

Dan was, and they ordered two of them from an older woman who had appeared from the kitchen. Again, they sat in silence, although they had now been joined by several other people whose lunchtime chatter filled the restaurant.

To Dan, the burger was divine. Large and meaty, with bacon, cheese, tomato and lettuce, it was the best food he had had for several days. This was going to be one of the last meals on a trip that had started out with such promise but which had taken a truly unforeseeable series of cataclysmic and existential events. He devoured the burger as if it were the last meal request of a man on Death Row. If this evening and tomorrow didn't go to plan, this thought might be prophetic, he realised. It was precisely the fear of that that had led him to run from Beijing in the first place. And here he was, several thousand kilometres later, still confronted by that possibility.

As they finished, Dastan's phone rang. He looked wide-eyed as the name of the caller appeared on the screen. He swallowed hard, looked at Dan, excused himself, stood up and walked outside. Dan heard him answer the phone in English as he reached the door. He paced around the car park, nodding to himself, alternating between kicking stones in the dust to looking up at the clear blue sky. He was clearly rattled by the phone call, or by the person who had called him.

He was outside for at least ten minutes, during which time the older woman had cleared their empty plates from the table, leaving Dan with a glass of tap water that he didn't touch for fear of getting sick.

Eventually Dastan came back into the restaurant. He sat down with Dan and inhaled deeply. He looked at him gravely.

"That was your friend Lisa," Dastan said. "She tells me police, they heard you go to Kashgar and they looking for you there. Lisa told me that they checked border details books, but your name not there, so they still look for you in Kashgar. Lisa said it 'too close for comfort' and she asked me if you book flight to London yet. I said you go to the airport tonight. She said we must be careful. I have friends at the airport, so we be OK, but we should be careful."

Dan listened intently, not wanting to interrupt Dastan as he told him about the Chinese police going from house to house in the Old Town of Kashgar. It was headline news – they believed they were closing in on him and that he would be caught in the next few days. Atash and Karim had abandoned their workshop, sealing and disguising the entrance in the hope that it wouldn't be found. Lisa had decided to return to Urumqi and was flying there this afternoon. They hadn't, as far as they knew, made the connection between Dan and her, and she thought she would be safer back in the bigger city. Things were starting to kick off in China and he was lucky to have made it out when he did.

Dan's heart was racing as Dastan relayed Lisa's story to him. He pictured the chaos unfolding in the narrow streets of the Old Town, wondering what consequences there might be for him if Atash's counterfeiting operation was discovered and dismantled, having been responsible for bringing the police to their door. Dan hoped Atash's reach didn't extend to England.

They sat in silence, Dastan clearly on edge before he excused himself and went outside again to make another phone call. Through the dusty windowpane Dan watched him take out his mobile phone and make two or three more calls. After almost fifteen minutes, Dan decided to join him in the afternoon air. He wanted to know what was going on. Dastan saw Dan coming and looked at him as he approached. He was speaking Russian, fast but calm. He smiled as Dan perched himself on the wooden fence, allowing Dastan to finish his conversation. The sun was warm on his face although the breeze was cool. Tall poplar trees surrounded the car park and Dan watched a large squirrel scamper along the ground between them.

Dastan finished his phone call.

"I have few friends who work at airport. I try to find which friend is working today. They can take good care of you. One friend is working there soon. He says we can go to there and he help. Once you are in airport, people not looking for you. You can stay there safe. We should go to the airport now."

Dan looked at his watch. Somehow it was now four o'clock in the afternoon. His flight wasn't until 07:55 the following morning but getting safely through the security checks, particularly if Dastan had a contact, seemed more important than worrying about how to spend sixteen hours at the airport.

"OK. Let's go," Dan said nervously.

This was it.

Dastan tapped on the driver's window, waking him up again. The driver wound down the window and the two of them exchanged a few words. The driver got out of the car, straightened himself out and got back in again.

In a cloud of dust the driver reversed the car into a U-turn and they left the car park. Skirting the northern edge of the city, they headed out towards the airport, close to the border with Kazakhstan. Dan was calm for much of the journey but his pulse began to quicken as they picked up the signs for the airport. All too soon the airport building itself was visible ahead, a large concrete construction no higher than a four-storey building. Blue neon lights spelled out the name: "Manas International Airport". They drove into the concourse and pulled up at the departures entrance.

All three got out. The driver opened the boot and for the first time since he'd met Dan lifted his bag out of the car for him. Dan got the hint, fished in his pocket for the fifty-dollar note he had received earlier and gave it to the driver, shaking his hand in the process. The driver nodded gratefully, slipped the money in his pocket and passed Dan his backpack.

He smiled and waved a friendly "Goodbye" before muttering a couple of words to Dastan and getting back in the car. Driving off, he left the two men outside the entrance doors.

Inside the terminal building Dan's heart was pounding. There seemed to be more security guards here than any other airport he had ever been to. His mind raced as his legs, weak with nerves once again, carried him to the check-in counter.

Was the security here just more visible than elsewhere? Were there always that many personnel or had they put on extra staff today for some reason?

Dastan seemed unfazed and made his way to the Turkish Airlines check-in counter. Flight number TK349 was not yet on the departures board but Dastan spoke to the man behind the desk and explained in English that he wanted to check in now for the flight tomorrow morning. The man looked at Dan and agreed. Was this Dastan's contact? Something about the undertone of frostiness in his voice as he asked Dan for his ticket and passport suggested not.

Dan passed his fake passport and the piece of paper the young woman had printed off for him earlier this morning. His real passport was in the inside pocket of his smaller backpack. He'd need it when he got back to the UK, after all. The man scanned the passport into the machine. It didn't work. He tried it again.

Dan began to sweat. The electronic chip on the passport wasn't working. He hadn't needed it at the Torugart and he hadn't thought about this. Had Atash truly screwed him over this time? The man looked at him enquiringly and wiped the passport on the sleeve of his jacket. He tried it one more time and much to Dan's relief his details appeared on his screen. The man asked how much luggage Dan was checking in. Hands shaking, Dan placed his big backpack on the scales beside the desk. The man noted the weight and Dan watched as his bag, now tagged, disappeared along the conveyor belt and into the luggage system behind the check-in desks. His final escape was now under way.

A few moments later the man issued Dan his boarding

pass. TK349, departing at 07:55 tomorrow morning. Seat 6D. Everything was in order. Dan thanked the man and turned to Dastan, who stood behind him. He pointed Dan towards the departures security gate.

As they reached the barriers, the man in charge of this part of the process turned to Dastan, looked at Dan and then nodded back to Dastan. This was the contact.

Dastan turned to Dan. "This is it, my friend. I leave you here now. I hope you good journey back to England."

Dastan extended a hand and Dan shook it firmly. "Thank you, Dastan. Thank you for all your help these last couple of days. I don't know what he would have done without you."

He took out the envelope with the remaining money but Dastan stopped him.

"No, no tip. No need. You are friend of Lisa's. This is business, you will see. I am paid already."

Confused, Dan put the envelope back in his bag.

The man on security, sensing the moment, asked Dan for his backpack. He opened it and looked inside. While Dan was still with Dastan the man took the bag around the X-ray machine and placed it on the inspection table on the other side. He took an orange "Security Checked" sticker and wrapped it around one of the straps. Neither of the two other men on the desk even raised a glance to him. Dan felt an odd wave of unease come over him at the simplicity with which one could circumvent the security here, and the deliberate obliviousness of this group of men. For those with the right connections, just about anything was possible.

Dastan put his hand on Dan's shoulder and urged him forwards. They shook hands one last time before Dan walked through the body scanner. As expected, there was no alarm and nobody asked him to remove his belt or shoes as had happened routinely at other airports he had been to.

He turned around and Dastan waved a final goodbye. Dan picked up his bag and returned the wave before disappearing down the hallway towards the flight gates. He took a deep breath and exhaled slowly. He was through what should have been the most difficult part of the process. All he had to do now was watch the clock tick down through the night and board his morning flight.

The airport was small and Dan could see much of the departure lounge from one central atrium as he sat in in one of the quieter corners where he also had a view of the runway. There were the normal comings and goings of an airport: the endlessly repeating security messages, the occasional page for a missing passenger, the ebb and flow of gates filling and emptying as flights came and went.

In the centre of the waiting area was a vodka bar that served the spirit by the glass or by the bottle. At midnight, the tired-looking woman who had been working there since Dan had arrived pulled the noisy metal shutters down on it for the night and turned the lights out. The airport was largely deserted at this time of night and the only real activity was the quiet "peep, peep, peep" of electric vehicles making their way from one side of the terminal to the other. Outside, people worked under floodlight to move containers from warehouses to a handful of cargo planes that took off over the hours that Dan sat and watched.

Around two o'clock the following morning Dan drifted to sleep, only to be woken by the metal shutters on the vodka bar being raised again. It was six in the morning and the airport was starting to get busy. There were less than two hours before take-off and he was still a free man.

13

THE SECOND ENVELOPE

As the plane climbed into the air over Bishkek, bound for Istanbul, Dan felt the stresses of the last two weeks drain from his body. He sank deeper and deeper into seat number 6D, pressed his head firmly against the headrest and closed his eyes. He breathed slowly and deeply, exhaling the pains and worries of the most unbelievable two weeks on the run in China.

After several minutes he opened his eyes slowly and immediately caught sight of a female cabin attendant sitting in the jump-seat diagonally opposite him. She had dark shoulder-length hair with a slight wave to it. Dan guessed her to be in her late twenties. She was looking directly at him and smiling with the kind of caring warmth he hadn't felt since he had left the UK. He returned the smile out of politeness and was about to close his eyes again when she nodded at him and mouthed the words "well done".

Dan was instantly confused, and it took him several seconds to compute what she had just whispered across the aisle. He frowned as he searched for what she could possibly have meant. The woman was still looking at him and could sense his confusion. She winked quickly and looked away. The pilot turned the seatbelt sign off and she stood up and walked away down the aisle behind him. Dan was still confused and begin to ask himself what else she could have meant. He replayed it over and over in his head, but nothing else made sense; it had unquestionably been a "well done". It was unambiguous but how could she know who he was. He felt uneasy, on edge and conspicuous.

Tired from his night in the airport, he closed his eyes and drifted off to sleep again. The next thing he knew he was being woken by a woman's voice speaking softly into his ear.

"Sir, tea or coffee? Would you like a drink?"

It was the female cabin attendant again, standing over him. She was so close that Dan could smell the alpine fresh detergent on her uniform. She was bent over him so as not to raise her voice over those sleeping in the seats around him. To begin with he was somewhat disgruntled with having been woken. She didn't appear to have disturbed anyone else, but he was too tired to complain.

"Um, I'll just have an apple juice, please," Dan replied feebly.

The woman poured him a plastic cupful of apple juice and placed it on the tray table in front of him. She then passed him an envelope that had Chinese writing down the right-hand side. Dan held it in front of him, clasping it with both hands. It was unmistakable. It was the second of the two envelopes

Lisa had given him as he had left her behind in China. Again he was plunged into swirling confusion. Nervously, he turned the envelope over. It was sealed.

Dan turned to the cabin attendant only to find that she was no longer standing beside him. He turned around to look down the aisle only to see her disappear behind a curtain halfway down the plane. It was the last time he saw her.

Cautiously, Dan opened the envelope, unsure of what he was about to find inside. Enclosed was a letter. Three pages of thin blue writing paper with a message handwritten in black biro. The paper was so thin that the pressure from the pen tip had given the letter an embossed, braille-like feel. The pages had been stapled together in the top left-hand corner. His heart began to race as he took the letter in his hands. He checked that there was nothing else in the envelope and placed it carefully on the tray table. His hands were shaking.

The letter was dated four days earlier – the day before he had crossed the Torugart into Kyrgyzstan. It started "Dear Sam". By now his palms were clammy and he felt his brow begin to dampen. He swallowed hard, his throat beginning to tighten as it had done so many other times over the last two weeks. He turned to the back page to see who the letter was from. At the bottom, just below the last paragraph, it read "I love you. Lisa x".

His heart skipped several beats and he shook his head slowly in disbelief. This couldn't possibly be happening. If it was true, it meant the flight attendant was in contact with Lisa. How on earth were they connected? And how did the flight attendant know who he was? Dan's mind was working overtime again as the questions began to deluge him. He had to read the letter.

He moved over to the empty seat next to the window and propped himself up against it, shielding the letter from anyone behind him. He began to read.

Dear Sam,

By now, if everything has gone to plan, you are on your flight to Istanbul. My contact has just given you this letter and you are alone, reading it, confused. I cannot imagine the questions that must be racing through your mind as you digest this.

I am writing this from a friend's house in Kashgar. I have just left you at Ali's, having just got back from our first run at the border. I had my bag packed and would have gone into Kyrgyzstan with you, but I have changed my mind. I belong here in China with Ali, Atash, Karim and the rest of our group. I owe you an explanation, however, for there is much to tell.

The first thing you need to know is that those are not our real names. Like Sam is not yours. The second thing you need to know is that we have been following you since Beijing. Since you first met Nancy in the Forbidden City, to be precise. She is not really a guide; she works for us. The other student you met – the young man who sold you the scroll – is not who you thought he was either. He works for us too. You have been part of an experiment. A test.

In the bottom of the scroll painting you bought from Nancy is a small device that emits a GPS signal. It's a small black disc hidden inside the false bottom of the cardboard tube you've been carrying with you this whole time. You were supposed to carry it through China for us so we could track where you were going. If you look now, you'll find it. Be careful, though. The other package in there is ice. You wouldn't want to be seen with that at Heathrow...

Don't worry – there was never any chance of you being stopped at Bishkek Airport, for the same reason you are reading this letter now. You need to pull the bottom compartment off the cardboard tube and remove the package and device. Leave both in the bin in the toilet on the plane.

Nervously, Dan stood up and reached for his backpack in the overhead compartment. He unzipped his bag and rummaged around for the scroll painting. Pulling it out, he immediately saw what Lisa was referring to. At the top of the tube was a cap that was around eight inches in length that slid over the body of the tube. At the other end was a separate small section of cardboard around three inches long. It was an integral part of the tube. He gave the bottom part a sharp twist and it began to come free. He pulled and twisted it until the end came off in his hand with a quiet "pop". As Lisa had said, inside was a small transparent plastic bag containing the unmistakably brilliant white shards of crystal meth.

Dan tipped the package into his hand. Below it, stuck to the bottom of the tube, was a small black disc about the diameter of a two-pound coin covered in black plastic shrink-wrap. Everything Lisa had written was, so far, true. With his hands shaking uncontrollably, Dan put the package back inside the compartment and reassembled the tube. He placed it between his right leg and the side of the plane so that it was hidden from view and carried on reading Lisa's letter.

Several of our packages have gone missing en route recently, so we are testing the tracking device. The package was supposed to be retrieved by someone who was going to meet you in Hong Kong but things went wrong when the two girls took that photograph of you. They are nothing to do with us. The first we knew you were in trouble was when Nancy contacted us that night after seeing you on the news. They were not part of the plan.

We expected you to be caught that evening and we had people in positions at police stations all over Beijing waiting for you to be brought in. The next thing we knew, you were on a train to Xi'an, heading west.

That is where I came in. I was doing a one-off guiding job in Jiayuguan and was called to pick you up. You think we met at that restaurant by chance? None of this was chance, Sam. Once you left Beijing, you were pretty safe. You came close to being caught in Xi'an but we made sure the police thought you were in a carriage at the back of the train. We really do have people everywhere: Mr Feng works for us. Mr Feng's brother works for us. Dastan works for us and the flight attendant who gave you this letter works for us. She was scheduled to be on this flight today, which worked out perfectly, hence your two-night stop in Tash Rabat. I hope you didn't just think you were there to enjoy the scenery!

You'll understand now that a lot of effort went into making sure you stayed safe, Sam. You're probably wondering why we didn't just take the GPS from you and turn you over to the police. Once we knew you were safely under our watch we wanted to carry on testing the device. To see how far we could push it. To see if we could get it all the way to Bishkek, which you have done.

And how about the border crossing? Surely we don't control that as well? Well, not quite. Have a look at your new passport. Look at the number we gave you. The last four digits – 9413. In Chinese that can also be read "Nine Deaths, One Life". It means a 90% chance of death, a 10% chance of survival – a narrow escape. The border guards at the Torugart know what this means and that they had to let you through. You've probably heard what happened to the last person who tried to stop one of us getting through. The guys on the Kyrgyz side work for us entirely. A little cash goes a long way in Kyrgyzstan. I hope they didn't give you too much grief up there! You carried this letter across the border yourself – you gave it to Dastan.

Atash funded your journey to Kyrgyzstan, but wanted you killed the other side of the border once your job was complete. I have stayed in China in exchange for your life, Sam. The money for the flight was my own.

So here you are. A free man again. I admire you for running, I really do. You did pretty well. Almost as if you had done it before! But you were never really in any danger once we picked you up. I hope you are not angry with me. In reality, I saved you. Even without us, those girls would have taken the photo and you would have been on the run. I wonder how far you would have got…

All you have to do now is put the package, the GPS and this letter in the bin in the toilet behind you. She'll see you go in – don't worry. After that, you're free of all of this and you'll never hear from us again.

You'll believe me, though, when I say that if you don't, you won't be reboarding the plane at Istanbul…

Take care, Sam.

I love you. Lisa x

Dan was stunned. Incredulous. His head was well and truly spinning, struggling to take in what Lisa had written. The accuracy with which she had described the events since leaving him at the border was chilling. He had been played. For the best part of two weeks he had been a pawn for an organised crime gang. At this very moment in time he was en route to Istanbul with a consignment of illegal drugs. He had been nothing more than a mule.

But Lisa was right. If the girls who had taken his photo really were nothing to do with it then he *would* still have run. How far *would* he have got, if Lisa hadn't picked him up? He felt sick to the pit of his stomach. This whole thing had been a game to everyone he had thought was genuinely there to help him. They had few cares as to whether he really got out of China or not. He was nothing more than a guinea pig.

On top of that, many of the survival decisions he thought he had made himself had turned out to have been orchestrated. He wondered just how many people had been watching his progress, little more than the beeping of a GPS signal on a screen somewhere as he crossed the wild Taklamakan desert and mountain passes of Central Asia. Where on earth was this group based? Would they still be watching him when he got to Heathrow? He took out his fake passport and sure enough the last four digits were 9-4-1-3. He shuddered. It was at that point he noticed a spelling mistake on the opposite page: a paragraph titled "Expry date". It was the only error in what was an otherwise fraudulent masterpiece.

Dan took a moment to consider his options. He could arrive in Istanbul and declare everything. He could give them names, locations, connections and help the authorities there disrupt an apparently highly organised international criminal operation. But how would he know who to trust? Everything in Lisa's letter had been true to a fault and she had warned him about the risks of not following her instructions; he would not be reboarding the plane in Istanbul. He also ran the risk of the Turkish authorities simply not believing his story and ending up being arrested for drug trafficking. With two passports in his possession – one of which would probably be shared with the Chinese authorities.

If he disposed of the package as instructed, he would be free of everything. He would enter the UK under his real name and slip back into society undetected. But he would be unable to prove or do anything about what had happened to him over the last two weeks. If he even wanted to, of course.

Dan read Lisa's letter one more time. It was overwhelming, and his whole body trembled as he recalled some of the details of the last few days. He felt like crying. Where he thought his life had been in mortal danger he was in fact being played. Where he thought Lisa, or whatever her name really was, was a well-meaning tour guide, she was in fact a key player in a drug trafficking cartel. His eyes were stinging as he gazed out of the window upon the vast expanse of Central Asia spread out below him. Despite what Lisa had written, underpinning every decision he had made over the last two weeks was a desperate fight for his freedom. Freedom that had been threatened the second that fateful photo had been taken.

He looked through the letter one more time, lingering momentarily on the last line of Lisa's handwriting before folding it out of view once and for all. Putting it back in its envelope, he wrapped it around the cardboard tube and gripped the two together.

He stood up, the flight attendant nowhere in sight, and made his way down the plane. In just thirty more seconds or so, if Lisa was true to every word of her letter, he would be a free man again.

And China would carry on looking for him.